On
its
Own

On its Own

Swa Raj

PARTRIDGE
A Penguin Random House Company

To order additional copies of this book, contact
Partridge India
000 800 10062 62
orders.india@partridgepublishing.com

www.partridgepublishing.com/india

Contents

Dedicated to
The mighty minds of the old,
the unnameable genes
they have bequeathed

Prologue

Lacene

Happiness is all around me.

I am certainly on a high. I have been on a high since George called me two days ago from base camp and assured me that he would be on the summit the next evening.

I couldn't help reciting to him once again, along with Emily, my favourite Tamil lyric meaning 'All towering peaks are beneath us'.

For quite some time now, I have been at the height of excitement with the firm knowledge that George would make it at last, fulfilling one of his lifelong dreams.

Though not the partying kind, I throw an elaborate party at Emerson Hall in Auckland for my friends and office staff. I dance, party and even get a little drunk that evening.

I kept telling my friends about *how George had dreamt of achieving this feat all his life; how I have lived to see this day; how I could have also climbed K2 with George but had to stay behind for my beloved daughter Emily.*

My friends must have heard that a million times that evening!

Earlier that morning, I woke up from my usual horrifying nightmare.

I am drowning in a large pool of water, being pulled down by a rope tied to my ankle. Struggling to rise up, I cannot get my head above water. Then I feel a palm lifting me from my bottom. I am being pulled down by the rope and pushed up by the palm alternatively for eternity. Finally, I get a thrust from the palm, which causes the rope to snap, and I manage to pull myself up onto the concrete floor around the pool. That last thrust is one hell of a moment in my life!

I jumped out of my bed as though out of deep waters, breathing heavily and cursing myself as to why I could not get free from this nightmare. That palm is still behind my bottom with its fingers between my buttocks and its thumb on my groin.

From evening till that late night, I have been expecting the great news of George's conquest. Messages from K2 can only come through the support staff that have stayed at the base camp. I deliberately extend the party late into the night to hear the ultimate news. Auckland being almost eight hours ahead of the K2 zone, I have to stay awake till past midnight.

While most of the guests are gone by midnight, a few close friends remain until one.

The message I have anxiously been expecting does finally arrive.

It is just a blunt message: 'atop now', sent from the base camp by the support staff. And that was the moment I was waiting for to burst into joy and celebration!

Handshakes, hugs, and kisses abound. I do not get tired; I wonder how.

Soon after that, all my friends decide to 'call it a day' and retire to their homes. All along, Emily has been at home thanks to my maid who agreed to stay there overnight.

Reaching home in such high spirits, I peep into Emily's room. Happy to see her fast asleep, I jump into my bed.

I must have fallen asleep soon and must have slept till late; so late that I only see the text on my iPhone in the afternoon.

It is almost past noon when I get up from bed, and I immediately reach for my mobile. The message in it rocks me out of my jubilant mood.

'G lost in avalanche; hope to get him. Mark.'

With anxiety and fear slowly gripping me, I look at the time of the message - 03:15. It must have come from his team at the base camp.

I try to figure what could have happened. 'G lost in avalanche' spelt very bad news. Could George have been swept away in the snow? Unsure about his condition, I send a text message asking for details.

The message cannot be sent. I try to call that number, but it does not go through. The number is not reachable!

My anxiety grows as minutes tick by. My only option is to wait for any incoming message or call. None comes by until dusk.

George

Darkness is all around me. It is extremely cold.

Cogito ergo sum. I can think, so I must be alive.

I can't move my body or do anything to confirm that I still exist. The cosmic hum drones in my ear. The cosmic darkness surrounds me.

Where am I now? Is this hell or heaven or just the passage to one of them? Are the dead bound so tight while being carried to either? I can't tell if I'm completely paralysed or just feeling the effects of being carried at great speed.

Is the body also taken? That's not how I've understood it – from any religion!

I try to recall my last cogent memories.

I remember being on top of the world. Literally.

It had been a dream-come-true moment. My team and I had just conquered K2, the second highest peak in the world. If this wasn't a moment of triumph, of achievement, then what is?

Hours later, I recall plummeting down its treacherous slopes.

We'd arrived at Camp 3 on the K2 shoulder without an incident. We wanted to reach Camp 2 before dark, so we left in haste.

We should have stayed.

It must have been an avalanche. What else could it have been?

I remember slipping off my rope, careening downwards, as a great white wave swept me away from the rest of my team.

I remember hearing their voices in the distance, through the white dunes, shouting out to each other, and perhaps to me, but as I plunged into a crevasse, they faded into silence; just the eerie ululation of the wind blowing against the mighty Godwin Austen.

And then, darkness.

What is that smell? Something is on my face, some sort of skin. I know that smell. Yak! Am I wrapped in yak leather? Maybe this is what they do to the dead in the Himalayas.

Images of the boy called Luke Skywalker and a llama-like animal flash through my mind, and I decide maybe I'm not dead after all.

I can feel the warmth of my own exhaled air. It takes a while for that air to get out of the yak-hide sack. When I inhale, I get a mixture of this warm air with the cool, fresh air from outside.

I try to roll. It is a bit hard, but I am able to move my whole body. I try to turn to my right side. I succeed, but I realise that it is far colder on my right where my arm touched the – what does it touch?

I reckon I am lying on some kind of platform that is very cold. I feel that my whole body is tied to this bedding but loose enough to allow me to turn on to my sides.

Does Lacene know of my predicament? Emily must be missing me very much. I have never been away from her for this long – more than two months at a stretch.

Right now, I want to sing our favourite line in Tamil to her - *Uyarndhú nirkúm sikaram ellám enakkúk keezhey* meaning *all towering peaks are below me* which she would immediately correct to *namakkúk keezhey* meaning 'below us'.

She had picked it up from Lacene who loved the language with all her heart. She must have recited this Tamil lyric umpteen times before I left

Auckland, and lastly when I spoke to her a week ago; was it yesterday? What day is it anyway? What time is it now?

Am I ever going to see them again? Where the hell am I? What happened to my teammates?

I'm losing consciousness now, I reckon.

Suddenly I get a jolt. I feel that I am lifted up with my bedding. I can feel my head, neck, and back resting on something, my legs hanging lifeless being dragged across the floor.

Where am I? Am I being carried by my saviour or by Yama's messenger, my executioner?

While my mind gets bogged down with questions, my senses are numbing down again. I'm losing consciousness for sure.

———◆———

1. Elephant God

Just as A is to the alphabet, the original creator is the first of everything in this universe.

'Why don't we spend our travel with some discussions? You say it will take more than four hours to reach Dharamshala. Tell me something about your various gods and goddesses,' the rabbi, Jonathan Bernard Levite, asked Ganesh Viswanáthan, their guide.

The various framed pictures of different Hindu deities fixed on the inside walls of the van would have prompted him to ask so. Besides, the rabbi had taken a liking to this young man.

'What is the greatness of your Elephant God? I believe you call him by several names and do not start any venture without paying obeisance to him. We couldn't ask such questions at the conference. What does your name signify, Ganesh?'

Ganesh appeared to have been waiting for such an opportunity! The eight clergies were from the just concluded Religious Conference in Shimla and were heading towards Dharamshala to meet his Holiness the Dalai Lama. The Dalai Lama was to have participated briefly in the conference too, but last minute obligations had kept him in his abode.

The tourists had learned the names of the three men escorting them. Omar Sherfuddin was driving the van. Jitender Siddhu was the spare driver seated in the front with Omar. They were expected to reach Dharamshala before midnight.

Ganesh wanted to show the religious scholars that he had adequate knowledge about his religion. As their travel agent, he had convinced the tourists that it would be a pleasant drive from Shimla to Dharamshala in the evening. Taking a flight, with security formalities and early check-in time requirements, would not have saved much time besides being very expensive. The clerics appreciated that proposal.

Ganesh started with a warning that his answers might be very long. He wanted his listeners to interrupt him with questions.

Evidently, they were eager to pose questions and thus started a discussion between the nine people in that van. Ganesh partially opened the glass window that separated the driver's cabin from the passengers, so that his words would be audible to Omar and Siddhu.

'Most of our religious leaders wouldn't give this answer that I give you now, but I believe this is the true reason for that importance. You are all men of god, and I wouldn't tell anything that is untrue.

'The Hindu religious scriptures say that when Lord Siva returned home after a long sojourn, he was stopped at his doorsteps by a child who claimed to be the son of his consort Sakthi. Though the details vary between regions and sects, the crux of the matter is that Lord Siva got infuriated both at being stopped at his own doorstep and by the boy's claim. After some arguments – and even battles, as some say– Siva beheaded the child in a fit of fury for which he is famous. Some people claim that the child was beheaded by Siva's men.'

'I think I have learnt that much. Also that Shiva gave him an elephant head instead after Shakthi spoke with him. But how does that give him so much importance? What does the name Ganpath signify? Why should you begin everything after paying obeisance to him?' Imam Yahya Syed Bhukari intervened. He had heard the names only as 'Shiva' and 'Shakthi, not as 'Siva' and 'Sakthi', the way Ganesh pronounced.

'I shall come to that. After prolonged arguments with Sakthi, Siva regretted his act and found the nearest available head, that of a baby elephant, to resurrect the child. May I claim that it was the first ever and the only "head transplant"?

'The child gained his importance from the fact that he confronted Siva himself and for the fact that he was a product directly of Sakthi, without involving Siva. He was made the "protector" of the entire universe since he so capably protected his mother's abode.

'While Siva and Sakthi are divine representations of matter and energy that pervade the whole universe, their more commonly known names are Siva, Easwar Mahadev or Rudra, and Sakthi, Kàli, Uma or Pàrvathi, which are the earthly representations. Together, Lord Siva and Goddess Sakthi are the origins of the universe.

'While matter in the universe is locked in the countless celestial bodies, Sakthi, the embodiment of all forces in the universe, is present everywhere. Interstellar space is filled by a force that literally controls the formation, existence and eventually, the extinction of all celestial bodies. These celestial bodies are known in Hindu scriptures as "ganas", and the force that sustains them came to be known as Ganapathy, Ganpath, Ganeswar. You may equate "gana" to what we know in English as a "galaxy". "Pathy" means "husband, protector, lord".

'Since such a force could only be a product of Sakthi, the energy or force, it is quite appropriate to claim that the celestial Ganeswar is a product of Sakthi only. Perhaps the story you heard now of how Siva and Sakthi gave the child an elephant head is just a "humanisation" of the celestial creation of the "force", the "galaxy protector" or "Ganpath". Science calls it the "dark energy" or "dark matter".

'Vignas are hurdles or deeds. Eswar, as you all would have now come to know, is Siva's other name. So Vigneswar is the remover of all hurdles and the one who resurrects us from all evil. From our Earth, to reach the ultimate God who is believed to be at the centre of this universe, one has to pass through all these galaxies and celestial bodies. One can't do that without the approval and blessings of Lord Ganesha, the protector of all galaxies and interstellar space.

'So it is no wonder that Ganesha is worshipped first, even ahead of his parents! Every new venture begins with an invocation of Lord Ganesh for his blessings.

'He is known by several names but the popular one is Vináyak. Náyak means "hero", "Vi" means "greatest, most powerful", so Vináyak means the greatest hero. His brave encounter with Lord Siva gave him that title.

'Perhaps to give an imaginable size of this "greatest hero" to a commoner, and to explain the enormity of the dark energy controlling all galaxies, the huge and dark-skinned elephant was brought into this story to represent that force. For a Tamilian like me, he is known by the name "pillai yár" meaning "whose child" or "who is this child"?'

'You have such names for your most revered deity?' asked the rabbi.

'Tell me about what you said of the Tamils – you said he is known as "pillai yár" to them. Does this have anything to do with the arguments between his parents?'

This came from an unexpected quarter. Bishop Juan Ferdinand Guillermo seemed really interested in these stories. 'Are you a supporter of the Tamil Tigers who were recently vanquished?' he asked Ganesh.

The Sri Lanka Buddhist monk in the group, Bikku Gunasekhara Ariyaratne looked at Ganesh curiously.

'Well, I do not want to talk about the Tigers, that's politics. We are now on religion. Let me finish with that. I haven't completed my explanations of the other names. But this query comes from his Reverend, and I have to prove him my mettle! Just imagine the scene after Siva beheaded the child. It goes thus.'

All eyes were on Ganesh as he began a monologue:

Sakthi: How dare you kill my child?

Siva: Your child? Whose child is it anyway, dear? You know and the whole world knows I have been away for a very long time. How can you claim that you had a child in my absence? Whose child is he?

Sakthi: Are you out of your mind, my dear Siva? What on earth made you believe that I can't have a child without you? I do not want to believe that you are assuming – rather suspecting – that I had this child from someone else. No, I conceived him on my own!

Siva: What nonsense are you talking? Well yes, I don't, even in my dream, imagine that you would have betrayed me. But to tell me that you have got a child without my contribution, that's ridiculous! Impossible! No one is going to believe us! There is going to be chaos and anarchy. Siva's wife ought to be beyond suspicion!

Sakthi: How do you think I bore this child then? Hán?

Siva: Maybe you found this child as an orphan and took pity on him. Maybe you took your maid's child as your own!

Sakthi: Then I would say so, Sivaji. I do not have to hide it from you!

Siva: So you stick to the same story – you got this child on your own?

Sakthi: Certainly. I do not need any man's input to bear my own child!

Siva: Sakthi, do not infuriate me with such a nonsensical claim. It is such an inconceivable notion that a woman could conceive without the contribution from a man. Perhaps the unenlightened common folks may believe that a child is a gift from God and may not probe into scientific reasons for a birth. But the learned people and sages know for sure that a child is the product of a man and a woman.

Sakthi: She can, my Lord, sure she can! Is that not how we were bearing our offspring before you men came into being?

Ganesh paused to look at his audience and was extremely proud that they were so attentive and anxious to see what followed next!

Siva: So you claim that we men came into being after you women? Don't you know that people in most parts of this world believe that the Almighty God first created the man in his own image and then the woman from the man's rib?

Ganesh winked at his audience to indicate that those words were his own concoctions.

Sakthi: Those are stories made up by you men after you had become more powerful than women in physique and grew in numbers to equal us. The truth is that we, the women, created the men. And until we did that and started to depend on the men for producing our offspring, we were procreating our offspring on our own, from our own selves. Mind you, we haven't forgotten that art as yet!'

The audience was perplexed but was eager to hear more.

Pundit Girilal Prasád Gobindha Ánandhá, a scholar from the Hare Krishna cult, intervened here. 'This is quite interesting, and I will have some points for my debates with my Shaivite friends. Go on.'

Ganesh continued.

Siva went into meditation, calmed down in dhyáná. Deep in meditation, he recollected the truth.

Life originated as a single cell that could reproduce another life within itself. This capability for reproduction marked the single distinction between lifeless matter and a living organism. Single cells befriended neighbouring single cells and formed bodies of multiple cells to improve survival and longevity.

Multiple cells cooperated to organise themselves, forming organs and external structures for different functions, to facilitate the search for and absorption of food. At each stage, the creature was in a position to beget an offspring that resembled the parent in every aspect – a clone – bringing with it all new features the parent had developed.

But the life span of each generation was quite short. There always was shortage of food, danger from predators, loss of habitat, and natural calamities that threatened the continuation of life.

Creatures found their own ways of extending their limbs, varying their capabilities as they deemed fit and evolved themselves into multi-organ species. Organs such as the liver, lungs, and kidneys and superficial body parts like the limbs, hip, head, and neck, and facial parts evolved over a very long period in time. But the last one to evolve was the male organ – the penis!

The unisexual creatures among various species soon realised the need to make exclusive, the job of procreation, from the other important job of finding food. It was at this stage that fellow creatures communicated among themselves to 'pass on and store' the offspring one had developed within oneself on to another fellow creature so that one could roam around freely fetching food both for oneself and for the fellow creature who agreed to 'store the offspring within its womb'.

The structure that evolved to perform this 'transfer of offspring' into the friend's body was the penis. Soon after that evolutionary stage, all the creatures that happened to be born with 'penises' at their birth, as opposed to the usual genitalia, later came to be known as the 'male' offspring. Gender had just started to become a permanent feature among these beings. Unisexual creatures gave rise to the two sexes.

Cooling down, balancing himself and opening his eyes, Siva said, 'I do not want to disagree with you, Sakthi. But I do have a question.'

Sakthi: 'I know what you want to ask, Sivaji! How is it that I got a male child when all along, until men evolved, we only gave birth to female or unisex offspring from our own selves. Right?'

Siva: 'Very much, dear! How does that come about? You should be capable of making female children only.'

Sakthi: 'There are two possibilities. Firstly, since the time we gave birth to the first male being and until we started making both female and male children, our reproductive systems must have retained the necessary adoptive skills to produce a male child of our own. It must have been passed on from generations of women to generations, missing out here and there in the genetic pool but not completely eradicated. That, I believe has a lot to do with genetic mutation combining with our basic evolutionary adaptation.'

Siva: 'I assume so, although the likelihood of this being successful – like in your case now – is rare. What is the second possibility?'

Sakthi: 'The 'sperm sac'! Like many other species, the human female also may have developed a sac to store her male partner's sperms and to choose the most appropriate time to fertilise her egg by injecting a mature sperm into her ovary. Maybe not all females have developed this sac, I may say. I myself could not feel anything from my inside; but when I was longing for you after so many weeks of your departure, I experienced a wonderful feeling in me and sensed that I might have conceived! I simply cannot explain my feelings during those wonderful moments!'

Siva: 'That appears more probable. Let us then go and proclaim to all in this world that this is *our* child.'

'And thus,' Ganesh said, 'the child also came to be known as 'whose child'–'yár pillai', or 'who is this child' –'pillai yár'.

'The Tamils have not forgotten the original happenings that led to these arguments following the birth of Ganesh and so they call him Pillaiyár.'

'Does this story have anything to do with the "phallus" symbol for Lord Shiva?' Pastor Richard Joseph Biden showed the extent of knowledge he possessed on this topic. For him also, it was 'Shiva', and not 'Siva'.

'Does this story have anything to do with the "half-man, half-woman" posture of Shiva?' the pundit chimed in, not wanting to be left out.

'Quite correct, Mr. Pastor, my guru believes that, following that incident, Siva proclaimed, "Procreation is only possible with the union of a male and a female." Incidentally, "yoni" – most probably the origin of "union"– is the word for female genitalia in Sanskrit.

'Perhaps Siva felt outwitted by Sakthi's demonstration of a feat that defied his knowledge and logic. The fact that an old imprint in the DNA could resurface after a long period in evolution took him by surprise. It also meant that there would be chaos in societies if women started bearing offspring on their own.

'Siva symbolically disapproved the belief so far held by almost all humans that a child was a gift from god. A child would be born, rather creation would take place, only by the union of the two genders and not by the female alone, nor just by the will of god. His insistence on that point famously came to be represented by the "phallus in a yoni" symbol, famously known as the "lingam".

'This symbol actually marked one of the most important stages in the evolution of life – the splitting of genders or rather "the emergence of the male gender from the female".'

Arthur Kingsley clapped his palms mildly. He represented 'nones', the atheist genre of people as known in the USA, believing in no religion and in no god. This Shimla conference was the first to have a 'non-theist' delegate in it.

Ganesh continued.

'We can even claim that Rudrá of the Himalayas declared that the "penis" was the last of the body parts in the evolutionary process to improve "life" itself. His devout followers not only made Rudra the embodiment of Lord Siva but also made the "bull" as his wagon and the "phallus-inside-yoni" as his logo! Most probably, the Tamil word for penis – "pool" – could be the basic word for "bull" and "phallus" while "lingam" could be the source of "link".

'And to answer our pundit here, I am in full agreement with him. He hit the bull's eye! The "Ardha-nári-eswara" posture of Siva, half each of himself and Sakthi, was to proclaim to all humans that every child is a product from an equal share of the man and his woman – precisely what science discovered later on the 23:23 chromosome divide. Perhaps Siva wanted issues to be settled clearly. Man and woman. Not woman alone!'

The pundit was not in agreement with this view that women could reproduce without men. 'Our laws differ from those of the Gods,' he said. 'Gods and goddesses can produce off-springs at will, but human beings have to follow the path set for them.'

Most of the other clerics agreed with him.

Moulana Zhulfiqar Ali Ansari was surprised. 'Do Hindus believe that a woman can produce a child without a man?'

The rabbi interrupted, 'How do you believe that God made the female first and then the male? This is utter ignorance!'

Arthur intervened. 'This is parthenogenesis. But so far no one has proved that it had occurred among humans.'

'Partheno-genesis! What is that?' asked the bikku.

'Well, science has found evidence of such asexual procreation among quite a few other creatures, but no evidence so far that it could happen among humans. I am hearing this for the first time – that too from Hindu mythology, truly amazing!' answered Arthur.

The bikku intervened, 'Buddhism fortunately does not believe in such deities and controversial incidents. Even Buddha himself was neither a God's avatar nor a deity. Only some followers elevated him to such a status and built statues for him.'

The bishop was not far behind them. 'All Abrahamic religions believe that God created Eve from Adam's rib to give him company.'

The pastor said, 'Although I may differ from him on other issues, I second the reverend!'

Ganesh answered them, 'Well, you form the majority in the world, almost sixty per cent – all the followers of Abraham's faith – the Jews, the Christians, and the Muslims. I beg to differ with you all in at least this aspect. The majority need not always be right!

'Whether it is creation or evolution, or even creation followed by evolution, it was the woman who came first. I say this not because my guru has taught us so. It sounds more logical and scientific to me too. Even Hinduism is explicit in its admission of this fact. Well, stories the other way around also abound in the Hindu faith.'

The imam was obviously not amused. 'Majority or minority, what the scriptures say are the final words. We are people of the "book". Our faith will not let us believe any other way. God made the first man and woman together. Period!'

The bishop agreed. 'Whatever stories science or other religions or some guru may come up with, there are some basic tenets we cannot question. Man first, then woman.'

Arthur, intently listening to everyone, smiled for every comment.

'I beg to differ, dear Father,' quipped Ganesh. 'My guru's theory is quite supportive of your Christian belief!'

'Come on, Ganesh, what are you talking about?' the pastor said, with a tone of annoyance.

'Well, this theory goes well with the belief of Virgin Mary. Mary was one of the last of women who managed to beget a child on her own. Christians were made to believe that it was God's will, but my guru and our team believe that Mary just repeated what Sakthi did.'

Arthur clapped his hands soundly in appreciation of the idea!

Ganesh continued, 'Faithful followers of Christianity firmly believe that Jesus, the only Son of God, came into this earth through the immaculate womb of Mary. Others need not necessarily believe that. There are people who accept Jesus as a messiah but do not subscribe to the virgin birth theory. But many such virgin births must have taken place until a certain time in the journey of mankind.

'My guru firmly believes that the virgin birth of Jesus was one of the last of such feats. But it was propounded in a completely different way. There could have been many similar but sporadic incidents all over the world that might have gone unnoticed. Our great epic, the *Mahábháratha*, written by Sage Vyásá, has examples of such births. Karna and the five Pándavas were all born that way.'

'Are you trying to say that we can equate Lord Ganesh with Lord Jesus at least in as far as the way they were born?' When the pundit opened his voice to say something further, the buzzer from the front reminded Ganesh of his next job.

'Khaane ka time,' the navigator Siddhu said animatedly.

Ganesh responded, 'Sorry, I forgot! It is time we all enjoy our meals now, it will be too late otherwise. Omar will drive slowly to make you feel comfortable.'

Though the clerics did not prefer eating in a moving van, they realised that it would save time.

Meal packets, clearly labelled with their names, reached their hands. Each one found to his delight his favourite dish in the pack. Wraps,

shwarmas, noodles, rice mixed with yoghurt, fruit salads, and kheer. Fixated
with his appealing food, each of them began to dig in.

Looking at the driver, Arthur asked, 'When will Omar eat? We can stop
the vehicle somewhere, and he can also join us.'

Ganesh said 'Don't worry, sir, Omar will eat after Siddhu finishes and
takes over driving. We do not want to delay.'

The pundit did not forget what he wanted to ask. 'You can't paint all
these with the same brush, Ganesh. Kúnti conceived her four sons with the
grace of the famous demigods, starting from the Sun, and then the Lord
of Death, Yamá, and so on. She taught that skill to Mádhri, her husband
Pándu's second wife, who begot two sons in that manner. If we are to believe
the Bible, Mother Mary conceived the Lord's only Son by the grace of the
Holy Father. These are faiths you can't dare question!'

'Although Islam does not recognise the claim of virgin birth, we do
revere Jesus as one of the important messiahs of Allah! At the same time, we
do not recognise the various gods worshipped in the epics, be they Indian,
Greek, Roman, Persian or Egyptian or for that matter from any part of the
world.' Quiet listener until now, the moulana Ansari Zhulfiqar Ali must
have felt that it was time he opened his mouth too.

The rabbi despised being left behind!

'And assuming you are right, you have not come up with a convincing
answer to Shiva's point on the male child from a woman all by herself! And
I believe, all the examples you have given are male offspring, including Jesus
of Nazareth. How come?'

'We are told about the Y chromosome factor that biologists claim is
only applicable to and passed on only amongst males. How can we believe
or accept that, whether it is Shakthi, Kunti, or Mary, a female could give
birth to a male child on her own? At the very least that needs a surrogate
father! Otherwise heavenly intervention is the only possibility.' This came
from the pastor.

Ganesh answered them all. 'There are many species that beget a male
offspring without male input. Recently, a female Komodo dragon in

captivity and in isolation for a couple of years gave birth to two male and one female offspring to the great astonishment of its curator and caretakers. Scientists were thrilled by this incident and are studying the case more intently. To witness parthenogenesis taking place in a large reptile was an event of great importance to the scientific world.

'There are many such events in the animal kingdom that prove my theory. But to answer you all with solid proof from authentic records, I must go to the origin of this universe. The big bang!'

'So be it, begin!' said the pastor, clearly on edge. 'We do not want to equate what happens in the animal kingdom with our human world, Ganesh. You'd better start from the big bang. Although most of us do not subscribe to theories of the big bang and evolution, I am willing to listen to your concoctions. They are interesting and help us pass our time on this tedious journey. So go ahead.'

'Well, the learned pundit rejects my examples. For him, the examples from epics and scriptures are divine interventions. What can I say?' Ganesh mumbled.

Ganesh then deliberately started on a dull note and dragged his story along. But none of the clerics were in a position to keep their eyes and minds open to listen to him. Knowing that perfectly well, Ganesh went about doing what he was assigned to do.

———◆·◆·◆———

In less than fifteen minutes, the eight visitors dozed off into a deep slumber. The van veered off the highway and travelled on a gravel road towards a no man's land.

Having approached an airstrip where a *Pilatus Turbo Porter PC6* was waiting, the van stopped near the aircraft. From a small building there, two people came to receive them. Along with those two men, the trio bundled the clerics neatly into sleeping bags and swiftly moved them aboard the aircraft.

'Ismail is not returning with us, Abdul?' asked Omar in a hushed voice. Ismail chided him. 'Jádhu! Do not call us with our real names! Some of them may not be fully unconscious!'

Abdul smiled and said, 'Fikar mat karo, Ismail! The diazepam that I have added in their food has a good effect on them. They are fast asleep now and won't wake up for almost a whole day!'

As if to prove him wrong, Arthur turned around in his bag making a mumbling sound. Abdul patted him on his shoulders. 'Time to sleep, Mr None, time to sleep.'

They all made their last Salat – Isha for the day in the small office building in that airstrip. Ismail got into the aircraft while Omar and Abdul returned to the van. They had other assignments in Shimla.

Abdul told the ever-inquisitive Omar that Ismail, returning with that aircraft the next day, would bring instructions from their high command with details of their next assignments.

He and Omar did not even wait to see the plane take off. As Abdul jumped into the navigator's seat, Omar started the van and within seconds had shifted to fifth gear. They knew very well that the eight hostages were in the custody of people more competent than them.

Omar was curious to know more about their group's plans from Abdul as he was aware that among his group mates in Shimla, only Abdul was privy to those plans.

'Are we going to execute all of them, Abdul? I believe and sincerely hope we spare our Muslim brothers! What are our plans on those holy sites Ismail told me about? When are we planning to set them off? Are you sure that there are no masjids in that list? Ismail said that it's a possibility, how come?'

Omar could not withhold anything; he had to blurt out all that was in his little mind.

Abdul smiled and then cautioned, 'Do not talk too much, Omar! I do not tell you much because I know you like to brag about such things with your friends and neighbours, not realising that there are ears everywhere around us. Discretion is an important virtue for people like us. You may land all of us in trouble.

'And you know the price we will all pay for that. The coveted reward of everlasting happiness in heaven will be showered on you only if you sacrifice your life for our noble cause. Not if you, with your loose tongue, cause trouble to all of us. Remember.'

Omar kept quiet, clearly expressing his disappointment in his silence. He also felt that he had to learn to behave better. He looked at Abdul with admiration and envy. This Madrási is a clever guy!

'How did you learn so much, Abdul? You talk so impressively with those Angrezis in English.'

'Well, I can only say that where I grew up I was free to learn anything. There was no discrimination at all. Despite being in a small minority, I had all the opportunities to learn many things and to get a good job.'

Omar sincerely wished he were as learned as Abdul was. Where he came from, he was allowed to learn only about Islam. And as if he remembered just then, he muttered, 'Amma wanted you to come home for supper tomorrow. She's planning to grill trout. But remember: I chose the name Ganesh for you!'

Saying this, he pressed on the accelerator. That was the only way he could express his feelings. Abdul did not mind that as he knew Omar would drive much better in such a mood.

'Sure, I'll come; of course, you chose that name and it worked well with the foreigners. Shukria!'

'Ismail said you must read the news that he has highlighted, Abdul; I forgot to tell you earlier,' said Omar, showing his satisfaction on Abdul's recognition of his contribution.

Abdul took the newspaper on the dashboard; a column highlighted in a page attracted his attention. It read:

Bengaluru: A compound wall of the ISKCON temple in the outskirts of Bengalaru city collapsed in the early hours of yesterday killing two women, an old man, and a child who were sleeping near the wall. Three more were injured and are being treated at the nearby primary health centre.

Police did not suspect any foul play and blamed poor construction on loose sand for the collapse of this newly built wall. But the temple authorities alleged that some miscreants might have committed sabotage to undermine the foundation of the wall and bring disrepute to their sect.

———◆•◆———

2. Hand of God

Pray to God but row away from the rocks.

---◆◆◆---

'I am so happy for your miracle, G.'

Lacene started with those words when George called her from Skardu, Pakistan. He had spoken to her from the same place before setting off for K2 three weeks ago. From base camp C1 he had conveyed his survival message to her the previous day.

'Indeed it's a miracle that I am alive and talking to you now, darling. How is Emy?'

'Restless, eager to talk to you, here she is.'

While listening to the conversation between George and Emily, Lacene could not help recalling her own miraculous escape from certain death twelve years ago in a pool near her Kansas home. She had a rerun of that nightmarish incident in her mind. She felt as though that palm was permanently supporting her bottom.

'Mummy, talk to your G.' Emily gave her the receiver sheepishly. 'Am so happy we will see dad soon, wants us to meet him in India!'

'G, what is it?' was Lacene's reaction. She also longed to see him but was wondering why George was in a hurry to meet them. It was not his nature to make a fuss out of such incidents.

Lacene was handling their business alone in New Zealand while he was away. She knew that he wasn't keen on leaving it in her charge for too long.

With loads of work pending for him to personally attend to, why would he want them to travel to India now?

'And he knows that I have to go to DC for a conference next week!' Lacene thought to herself.

'I've got a lot to share with you urgently, personally,' George spoke in broken Tamil and Lacene understood that he wanted to be a bit discreet about what he had to say. 'You have to read that list and the diary. I'm pretty sure that the person who saved me left them with me. What's strange is that it's marked for your attention!'

'My attention?' She could not believe her ears! 'How could someone in the Karakoram know me? What's happening, G?'

'That's exactly what we must find out. You must be here with me for that, more so because the list seems to be very important. My concern is about Emy. We can't afford to take her with us when we go on such a mission.'

Not knowing what the mission would be and where it would take them, Lacene told George, 'I'll find a way for her, G. Don't worry.'

She called him back within minutes.

'My dad has been longing to have her with him and would be pleased to grab this chance. I had earlier told him that I would be coming to the US with her next week. Remember I have to put up my posters at the NWO (National Women's Organisation) conference at the Smithsonian? I've spoken to him now. He would take her with him and display the posters on my behalf. Emy loves him and would be happy to go to Kansas. I don't mind missing the conference. Emy can miss school too, but what about office?'

'I've already asked Jerome to handle all the office work. I can guide him over Skype. All I need is Wi-Fi access wherever we go. You may leave enough signed bank documents for him to run the show for, let's say a fortnight, at the max?'

They decided to meet in New Delhi the next day. Her father, David Levite would reach New Delhi within the next two days from Kansas. Lacene knew that David had a visa for India. He had planned earlier to join his twin brother Rabbi Jonathan Levite for a tour there, but had dropped it due to some other assignments that had cropped up.

————◆•◆•◆————

Waiting with Felix, another wounded member of his team at Skardu airport, George recalled the moments from the accident till the time he realised that the diary was in his bag. Mark had arranged a helicopter from the base camp for George and Felix for treatment at Skardu.

Mark could not believe his eyes when he saw George greeting them as he and his team arrived safely, but worn out, at Camp 1.

From the moment George went missing after Camp 3, and until they left Camp 2 earlier that morning, Mark was tormented by the thought that George could possibly have succumbed to the treacherous and savage conditions of K2 after his slide and fall. The situation had never been conducive for his team to even consider going back in search of George. They were unanimous in the decision that they would strengthen their team after reaching Camp 1, wait for the weather to improve and begin the search then.

Even if not alive, they hoped to find him at least in one piece.

At 20,000 feet above sea level and another 8,000 feet to the peak, the base camp (Camp 1) along the K2 trail in the Abruzzi spur route on the Pakistan side was already higher than the highest point in Africa, the summit of Mount Kilimanjaro – which Lacene and George had climbed together ten years ago.

Camp 1 was a secure place with no danger of avalanches or snowstorms at that time of the year as compared with the rest of the route from there to the K2 summit including Camps 2, 3, and 4.

K2 is statistically five times more dangerous than Mt. Everest and the most fatal of the 8000 m giants in the Karakoram Range of the Himalayas. Falling off the shoulder between Camp 3 and Camp 2 while descending K2 would mean that there could only be a slide or a freefall for almost a kilometre, resulting in sure death.

Not without reason did they name it the 'Savage Mountain' as it had taken more lives of the bravest climbers than any other mountain. The problem on K2 is that if you reach the top, your chances of returning are quite significantly reduced.

Perhaps there is no one who has lived to tell the tale of tumbling down the slopes of K2.

Seeing George sitting outside the camp chatting with the Baltistani porters was therefore an unbelievable sight for all of them. And a very pleasant one at that! Whatever they heard from George as he narrated his remembrance of the past sixteen hours were like episodes from epics with divine interventions.

The climb to Camp 2 from Camp 1 includes a fifty-meter wide crack called the 'House's Chimney' and is full of ropes left by past climbers, most of which are not greatly relied upon by current climbers. Camp 2 is sheltered by a large rock but still experiences high winds and gets extremely cold. The stretch from Camp 2 to Camp 3 is called the 'Black Pyramid', with approximately 400 meters of vertical and near-vertical climbing on a mix of rock and ice. And that is exactly where George met his fateful fall.

All George could remember was the sudden slide and fall and the drift of snow that rained over him and carried him off the ground, even as he lost consciousness. After an incalculable time, he regained consciousness and had a feeling that he was being carried by someone on something that felt like a sledge.

As he was trying to fathom how long it had been since he was dragged away, he felt he was blacking out again. When he woke up, he found himself on the snow-laden scaffolding near Camp 1 without realising where he was. He heard human voices.

It took a few desperate croaks from him to gain the attention of the Baltis who took him to a shelter and revived him. Talking to them, he learned from them that he could only have been saved by the man known to them as 'Dada'.

'Who is this Dada?' George asked. 'If he really saved me, not only would I like to thank him in person but would like to know how the hell he managed to rescue me from such a treacherous zone and situation? What was he doing up there at that time?'

'*Dada never gets too close to visitors.*'

'*He is a very private and quiet man.*'

'*He can be anywhere and everywhere all the time*'.

'*He has direct links with the most powerful men of this region.*'

'*Nothing escapes his eyes; there is no one here he does not know.*'

'*He can surprise you with your life's story much better than you yourself may know!*'

'*He climbs K2 mostly to clean it up of all the debris that you guys litter it with.*'

'*He always says, "Where man sets foot, nothing thrives".*'

In turns, each of the five Baltis replied George.

'*He was here a couple of hours ago,*' *said one of the porters.* '*He came into this tent and took something to eat or drink and moved on.*'

'*In which direction did he go?*' *asked Mark.*

'*That is difficult to say, he may have headed south, not sure.*'

George thought, 'That means he hasn't gone far, but no one can go after him. All are worked out. Will I ever get to see him?'

Camp 1 offered space enough to have a number of tents on its sprawling, snow-filled platform with several peaks surrounding it. Minutes after his entry into his tent, George forced himself into his sleeping bag, although sleep eluded him. A number of questions were bothering him, but the most pressing one was how he could convey his survival message to Lacene and Emily.

He was worried that they might be under great duress if the message sent from the base camp last night had reached them.

Communication facilities were available from Camp 1 in the Abruzzi spur route on the South East Ridge of K2, but were rarely efficient. Communication equipment is often supported with a satellite telephone and email facilities on extended expeditions at the base camp from where George tried his luck. With an oft-interrupted line, George did briefly manage to convey the tale of his survival to Lacene, but could not elaborate on how he escaped certain death.

It was just before being escorted to the helicopter Mark had summoned that George noticed an extra item in his baggage. It looked like an old book. He did not have time to take a look at it then, so he just slipped it back into his bag, wondering how it got to be there.

'The book! Why didn't I think about it?'

George took it out and started flipping pages – which were more like loosely bound sheets – of the book. It had two hardboards as front and back covers and a bunch of sheets between them joined by a canvas cloth serving as the binder, glued to both the hard covers. Inside were about 200 sheets of paper not uniformly sized, sewn together at one margin with the canvas. As he was holding the book, George could not help fearing that some of the sheets might fall off at any moment.

There were entries in English, Tamil, and two other languages he recognised as Arabic and Pashto. Reading a few pages in English, he was both fascinated and baffled by its contents and was increasingly curious to know what else would be in the other pages.

The name 'LACENE' etched on the piece of cloth tied around the book was what made George jump out of his seat. His immediate reaction was to call her and ask her to travel out to meet him as soon as possible.

There were several mentions of Osama Bin Laden, Mullah Omar, al-Qaeda, and Taleban. Some pages in the middle had detailed notes on the 9/11 attack. Names that seemed faintly familiar, events that seemed globally significant were strewn across the pages of the book.

Most of the pages were handwritten barring a few which were either printed or were newspaper cuttings. What made him get more anxious were the two loose sheets inside the book, literally hanging by a thread. One of them was a list of ten names; the other had numerous names of religious sites across the globe. One name in the first list seemed familiar to him. He looked at that list again.

Bishop Juan Ferdinand Guillermo – Catholic – Brazil
Pandit Girilal Prasad Gobindhanandha – Hindu – India
Moulana Ansari Zhulfiqar Ali – Shia Islam – Iran
Bikku Gunasekhara Ariyaratne – Buddhism – Sri Lanka

Rabbi Bernard Jonathan Levite – Judaism – Israel
Imam Yahya Syed Bhukari – Sunni Islam – Algeria
Arthur George Kingsley – None – UK/USA
Pastor Richard Gregory Biden – Pastor – USA
Bishop Desmond Tutu – Catholic –South Africa
Daishi Ippen Ingen –Buddhism – Japan.

Bernard Jonathan Levite, twin brother of Lacene's father David Jonathan Levite and a prominent rabbi from Israel was at George's wedding and was instrumental in convincing his brother to accept Lacene's choice, George, as opposed to David's preference and Lacene's other suitor, Jeremy Perez Zadok, an American Jew.

George vaguely remembered Lacene mentioning before his departure for K2 that her uncle would be visiting Shimla for a religious conference. After he told Lacene about the list over phone, she came back to him within minutes saying that it was a conference of people belonging to various religious faiths from around the globe. She wondered why only ten names would find their way onto the list.

She had also checked with her father, David, who confirmed that his brother was in Shimla and that he had plans to travel to Dharamshala along with some other delegates to meet the Dalai Lama. The rabbi had no one else closer to his heart than his brother and was regularly in touch with David. Lacene told George that David hadn't heard from the rabbi for the past thirty-six hours, though.

The eyes of all the eight men of god were fixed on the setting sun. After a horrifying day in the middle of nowhere, they were weary, hungry, and terrified. The sun, fast descending behind the hill, was only adding despair to their clueless situation. The last rays of light reflected off the snow-capped mountains, extending the day by an hour. They couldn't imagine their fates beyond dusk and shuddered at the thought of having to sleep on stones in that desolate cave.

Earlier that morning the bishop had woken up from an unusually deep slumber at the howl of what sounded like a wolf. He was startled by the strange condition of his surroundings and the biting cold air in the small room. Was that even a room?

No furniture, no door, nor windows. Even the walls and ceiling appeared strange. He found himself in a sleeping bag and managed to get out of it. Wondering how he got into that, he looked around and saw two other sleeping bags on the floor laid on a thick carpet – what the locals called a 'kambli' – similar to the one he was lying on. Before waking them up, he wanted to find out where he was and moved towards what seemed to be the brightest corner of the room. The ceiling was low and he had to stoop to avoid hitting his head.

The short, narrow passage emanating light at the end was more like an underground tunnel. As he reached what looked like an exit, it opened into an unbelievable sight! The bishop came out to see a beautiful mountain slope, a silent stream taking a steep curve beneath him and three mountains on the other side of the stream. There was a flat bed of rock below his feet and a stone canopy above his head. The sun was well into its zenith; a misty sky and the canopy hid direct sunlight from his eyes. Looking closer, he realised that the canopy was a natural feature outside where he had slept the night before, a place he would liken to a cave.

A sudden bark from a mastiff, staring at him from a lower deck a couple of meters from him, startled but didn't scare him as the dog seemed friendly. Two more clergymen – the rabbi and the pundit – emerged behind him simultaneously from the cave asking, 'Where are we, Father, doesn't seem like Dharamshala? How did we get here?'

Others followed suit, coming out from the cave one after the other. They all raised the same set of questions even as everyone explored their surroundings. The mastiff had long stopped barking and was intently staring at them.

They were standing at about fifty meters from the bottom of a hill whose height they estimated to be 400 meters. It was surrounded by larger mountains, with peaks varying in height and had a crystal clear stream running beneath. The stream took a bend around the mountain on its other side, which had a broader base and fewer slopes at its bottom. As always, the other side of the stream was greener at its base, a clear evidence of the water level having risen over time. The side of the bank that the men stood was steeper and rockier, not leaving much room for vegetation to grow.

Arthur's watch showed Friday; just a night has passed. With the position of the sun, they deciphered that their cave faced south-east.

Another noticeable element causing concern and even fear in all of them was the absence of any sign of human activity in the visible proximity. Each one looked at the other with the same look in his eyes. 'Where on earth are we? Are we safe? Is this anywhere near Dharamshala? Where are Ganesh and his mates? What happened to us since we last ate in the van and slept?'

The food. They had all been unconscious whilst being brought to their current destination. They were convinced that something in the food must have put them in that state. But surely Ganesh wasn't involved in that? Could it have been the driver Omar and the other guy – Siddhu?

They attempted to recall the events leading up to their getting into the van with Ganesh and their contact with the travel agency. The pundit and Arthur were the ones who arranged that trip.

Just as their minds cast back to the last forty-eight hours of their lives in Shimla, they set their eyes on their present abode and its surroundings. Dividing themselves into three groups, they set about exploring the area. The bishop stayed near the cave.

The sunlight was adequate enough to give them a clear view of everything around them for several miles, but the landscape was filled with mountain peaks and nothing else.

The climb down to the stream flowing at the bottom of that hill wasn't easy. One had to be very careful in choosing his path on the slopes. A single error would send one tumbling down into the cold waters. The moulana and the bikku did not venture to go too far from the cave.

There were patches of snow scattered across the eastern side of the cave. The imam, who accompanied the pundit, stood paralyzed when he heard the latter holler. The pundit spotted something that rustled amongst the bushes, half expecting a bear to appear. They relaxed when it turned out to be a yak – a calf, at that. The mastiff did not fail to notice it and barked to its heart's content, perhaps happy at the sight of another life there.

The rabbi and Arthur set out towards the west and tried climbing above the canopy. They had a good view from atop the canopy, an extension of a rock resting on two other rock pillars. There was at least a 10 cm layer of snow on the canopy.

The whole afternoon was spent in clueless wandering and discussion. Their baggage was found ransacked; only some clothing, toiletries, and medicines were mercifully left. They had nothing to eat or drink. Their phones and cameras were gone.

As they gathered again at the bottom of the canopy, resigned to the idea of another night's sleep in the cave, they heard a shout. A human voice beckoned the mastiff, which started running uphill at a brisk pace. All eyes turned up, but the canopy blocked their view causing them to move out to discern where the sound came from.

With mixed feelings of relief, horror, and anxiety, they saw a tall, bearded man draped in a long robe, carrying a cloth bundle in one hand and a rifle on his shoulder. 'Looks like a Pashtún', the imam murmured. Others seemed to nod their heads.

Not expecting a gun-wielding person anywhere near Dharamshala, all of them stood frozen as the man descended the hill rapidly, deftly placing his feet on safe spots on the rocky, partly grassy and snowy surface. Approaching them, he half covered his face with a cloth.

'Are all the eight of you here?' were his first words on approaching them. His eyes rolled over to view them. 'Do not dare to go far from here. I cannot guarantee you your life if you venture out.'

'Where are we, and how did we reach here?' Arthur had the courage to ask him loudly as the Pathan was far away.

'Allah is great! He has brought you here to serve him and his true worshippers. You will sacrifice your lives for jihad! Heaven is your reward on judgement day. Allah Ho Akbar!'

Shivers ran down the spines of the eight men!

David Levite was expecting a call from his daughter but not with such a strange request. Not a favourite of the Facebook and Twitter culture, his mode of communication was mostly using e-mail, Magic Jack, and Skype. Whether he managed to talk to Lacene or not, seeing and talking to Emily on Skype at least once a week was a must for him. He was anxious to know if George succeeded on his K2 mission.

So when Emily called him early that morning, his first words were, 'Did your father reach the top? And is he back to the base?' He was obviously concerned about George's safe return.

Hearing the whole story from Lacene, he instantly agreed to visit India and to take Emily with him. When he heard about the list with his brother's name on it, and remembered that the rabbi had not contacted him for the past two days, he started worrying about the safety of his brother. He immediately made bookings for travel to New Delhi.

More importantly he wanted to call someone for advice about getting federal help to trace his brother. Concerned about the safety and security of Israel citizens visiting countries like India, especially after the 11/26 Mumbai attacks, he wished his brother to be out of trouble.

'You're sure you'll be fine, Irene?'

'Yea dad, how many times do I've to tell you?'

'Uma's mom will also be around for the next three weeks?' Morgan wanted to be sure. He couldn't leave this teenage monster alone whilst going away on vacation to Hawaii and hope to enjoy his time there, unconcerned about her well-being.

'You're a bore, dad!' was the only way Irene could reply.

Irene was happy to stay back for the next three weeks in Newark due to the load of her study material and her long-deferred visit to her Mother in Florida. She knew that her father wouldn't mind leaving her alone when her friend Uma and her parents were around.

Morgan Stanford, in the past decade, had been instrumental in the capture, trial, and execution of more than a dozen terrorists connected with the 9/11 disaster. He thoroughly enjoyed his job. He had been busy with tough assignments over the past couple of years and was happy that he would be going to Hawaii on a long holiday. Life at the NSA (National Security Agency) certainly wasn't a bed of roses. Full of excitement, thrill, anxiety, and near-death moments, there was never room for entertainment. For him, his job provided adequate entertainment, though.

He had a few other assignments waiting for him, but he needed that long-awaited break. Having obtained leave for three weeks, he had planned to go to Hawaii where an exciting time awaited him. He hoped to make merry there with his newfound interest – a divorcee he came in touch with through the digital word, who had an inclination to marrying him. He was anxious to meet her in person. For the past year, she had been rekindling his romantic flames, virtually!

But he was not that lucky.

Little did he realise that a mere phone call from one of his old friends would upset his plans. Irene reminded him of that call.

'I told you. David Levite from Lawrence called an hour ago. I'm going to Uma's for a sleep over'.

Irene knew that Morgan wouldn't refuse a night out with Uma.

Morgan had given his landline number to only a few trustworthy friends. David Levite, a good old friend from Kansas where he began his career as a swimming coach and then as a CSS (Central Security Services) agent, was one.

David told Morgan briefly about the happenings that led to the probable disappearance of his brother in India. He was desperate to know his brother's whereabouts after leaving Shimla two days ago.

'I know you won't be able to do anything about it since my brother is an Israeli. You can do something about the probable disappearance of Richard Gregory Biden, an American, who went with the rabbi.'

'I will take it up with the relevant authorities, David.'

'The interesting part of this story is that George has a diary, probably written by his rescuer that contains valuable information about the Taleban and al-Qaeda. He has also left two lists that seem to be of great significance to our national intelligentsia.'

Morgan did show some interest when he heard of al-Qaeda and the Taleban but said that he would check about the clergymen and reply as soon as possible. But his mind was on the Hawaiian trip that included a cruise in the Pacific.

As part of a winding up routine, he was scanning through all the pictures and videos of 9/11 in his possession. He was in the process of packing all of them up and sending them off to headquarters for good. That was when Irene popped into his room to tell him she was going for a sleepover at her friend Uma's home and reminded him about the call from David. He switched the screen off as she entered.

Irene had her own plans for those three weeks and would spend a week in Florida with her Mom. Florence, waiting for court orders for her divorce from Morgan, was living in Miami for the past three years with her mother. Florence's mother had always maintained that her daughter married below her status.

David couldn't help comparing George's rescue to Lacene's miraculous escape from death on her wedding reception a decade ago. Only divine intervention could have saved her on that dreadful day.

It was dinnertime on the evening of their reception at the community hall in Lawrence, Kansas. Lacene had suddenly disappeared from the party. David had not noticed it. When he saw her fully drenched, half hidden behind the back door of the reception hall, signalling to him to come over to the backyard – without others noticing, he was shocked.

Sobbing and stammering in between, Lacene briefed to a shocked David, how she was lured to the pool by Jeremy for one last talk; how he suddenly jumped into the pool as she turned to go back to the hall; then, how the rope that inexplicably noosed around her right ankle, pulled her into deep waters and did not let her rise to keep her nose above water; and how a palm lifted her, supporting from her bottom struggling to keep her afloat while the rope was drawing her down; and how she was eventually pushed up by the hand so forcefully that the rope snapped, letting her seek the surface alive.

David could not believe the story although he never doubted Lacene. He thought that perhaps Lacene was mildly under the influence of alcohol – something she wasn't used to. Looking around and seeing no sign of Jeremy or anyone else, it was only the sight of the scratch marks around Lacene's ankle that made David believe what she had said, at least partially. Such was the trust he had on Jeremy – Lacene's other suitor whom he favoured as against George Swenson.

David ensured safe passage for Lacene to Auckland with George the next afternoon. He managed this by not immediately revealing the sad news of Jeremy's floating body in the waters of the stream behind the community hall. He told them about it only after they landed in Auckland. He believed that Jeremy must have committed suicide, as he had so dearly loved Lacene and could not stand the grief of losing her hand to someone.

He convinced the police to accept that theory through his trusted friend Morgan Stanford. Morgan, working then for the State Department, was

Lacene's swimming coach years ago. He was not fully convinced that it was a suicide, though.

His belief in Yahweh's miraculous ways and his sincere prayers left David firmly convinced that it was the 'hand of God' that saved Lacene from imminent death that night. Twelve years later, it was the same hand of God that saved George from the snowstorm on K2.

David went into a deep, long session of prayer and recitation of the Talmud. He prayed and thanked Yahweh. He had another reason to pray for. He was desperate to know about the welfare of his brother.

'Abdul, did Ismail speak to you? He couldn't get you on your mobile. He wants you to read this newspaper; he says you know what to look for.' Omar's tone was quite low. He knew that Abdul wouldn't like him to talk of such things loudly. Both of them were enjoying the trout served by Omar's mother. She looked at Omar angrily. 'Why don't you let him enjoy the food?' was her obvious shout.

Abdul scrolled down his iPad, immediately searching for that article.

> A small column in *The Colombo Times* reported the collapse of a Hindu temple in Nyanimadam, a suburb of Killinochchi, in the northern Sri Lanka. The Siva-Vishnu temple crumbled during the wee hours of Monday. The cause of the collapse was not immediately known although the paper suspected that it could be due to earlier periods of heavy artillery shelling in that region that could have weakened the structure. No casualties were reported.

Omar saw a slender smile across Abdul's otherwise serious face.

3. No God but God

Every country is my own; all the people are my kinsmen

———◆———

The next morning changed everything for Morgan. All his holiday plans had to be dumped. He decided to take up a new assignment in a completely different part of the globe.

All because of that one page email from David.

David's email had interesting information about the diary in George's possession. The writer of that diary seemed to have had a long sojourn with the likes of Osama and Mullah Omar, besides others. The very mention of Omar got him interested in the contents of the diary.

'A diary by someone in close association with Omar – whose fate has been a mystery – is valuable. Osama is history, information about him may be useful, but any information about Omar is most welcome.'

CBN (Christian Broadcasting Network) flashed breaking news about eight clergymen who had allegedly been abducted in India. Further details would be relayed as they became available to the channel. Morgan mulled over the circumstances in which the diary came into the possession of George. The fact that the diary had a list of those who may have been abducted made Morgan decide that he had to get a hold of the diary's contents as soon as he could.

More importantly and intriguingly, David's mention of a second list with more than 200 religious sites spread across the world triggered nervous excitement. What could that mean? Are they just places this rescuer of George had visited or intend visiting? Are they linked to the alleged abduction? What was the significance of those 200 or so sites?

He instantly dropped his plans and decided to go to India with David. Turning all his attention and energy towards getting approval from his office for this newfound project, he first wanted to ascertain that the clergymen had indeed been abducted. He fervently wished that it were true, so he could justify his need to go there and get his hands on the diary. The media couldn't be wrong.

His office replied soon with the good news of the abducted eight clergymen and its approval of Morgan's project. Two of them were US citizens – Pastor Biden and Arthur Kingsley, full details of whom would soon be sent to him. The NSA was looking for someone who would take up such a mission, in fact!

Waving from his window seat to Irene, Morgan could feel his train departing from Newark station. He should be able to catch the flight to New Delhi although he only had two hours from the New York station to JFK (John F Kennedy) International airport. His eyes were focused on Irene and her companion Uma, who came to drop him off. With a dot on her forehead, Uma's face had a distinct charm, he felt. His mind rewound to the past three years of his troubled family life.

Florence had separated from him three years ago and they were preparing for a mutually agreed divorce. His secret services job was one of the reasons for the split between them, but Morgan would always blame his mother-in-law, who had despised him right from the day of their marriage. Irene was a very difficult girl to handle after the split and he had to be very careful in handling her amidst his busy schedule. The friendship that had blossomed between Irene and the slightly older Uma was a blessing in disguise for Morgan.

Uma Saravanan, a research student in Urban Health Systems at the same university in New Jersey, was helping Irene in her undergrad studies in Nursing.

Irene simply adored Uma. Morgan had occasional doubts if the two girls had a physical relationship. Such was the closeness she had with Uma that he never heard Irene mentioning any other friend's name to him.

Members of Uma's family were quite trustworthy although the combination of an Indian father and Japanese mother was a bit strange for Morgan. Uma had some kind of an aura around her that made even Morgan trust the young woman from the first instance of meeting her. Since then, Irene had been less of a worry for him.

Both families lived in Edison, just three streets away in that quiet neighbourhood. That should have enabled frequent meetings between the two families, but Morgan was always a busy person. His only consolation was that, after his wife left him, Uma's family provided Irene the much needed love and security whenever he was away on his assignments. He had visited Uma's family twice in the past two years for dinner and had taken their family out for lunch twice. Uma's father Saravanan, a NASA (National Aeronautics and Space Administration) scientist, had briefed Morgan on how his family came to settle in the US.

At the Indira Gandhi International Airport, New Delhi, George was patiently waiting for Lacene and Emily to clear immigration and customs. The new airport building looked fantastic and deserved its 2011 ranking as the second best airport in the world in the twenty-five to forty million passengers category. But the formalities were still as cumbersome as in the past, and nobody could be blamed for that.

'Terrorism's major victory is this frustrating delay at every imaginable security checkpoint to the commoner, more so in countries like India, vulnerable to such attacks,' he thought.

'Daddy, I'm here!' Emily left Lacene and rushed to George who lifted her above his head. Lacene came with her trolley; George hugged her, landing kisses on her cheeks.

'First things first, here is your diary. Keep it safe and read it after you have had sufficient sleep. You need to rest to fight jetlag.'

'Are you not interested in knowing who might have sent it to my attention?' asked Lacene, as she looked at it with wonder and then put it in her stroller.

'I am, but get some rest first. Your dad arrives only in the morning.'

As they waited by the platform for their cab to pick them up, Lacene screamed when she realised that someone had snatched her stroller and her handbag. George noticed a young man running towards the other end of the platform, clutching both items in his arms. There was another guy running towards him, presumably to take over part of the burden. George pursued the snatcher swiftly and managed to fling the small gift pack he had bought for Emily. It hit the snatcher on his shoulder, and he dropped Lacene's handbag. Picking it up as he chased him, George decided to use his pistol and put his arm into his holster in his vest. Even before he could do anything, another passer-by caused the snatcher to stumble and fall.

Without even turning back to look at him, the snatcher ran away while his accomplice also took to his heels when he saw George taking out his pistol. Lacene shouted to George, 'No, G!'

Profusely thanking the passerby who helped, George picked up Lacene's belongings and walked back. Scanning the contents of her handbag, Lacene was satisfied that nothing was missing.

The drive to their hotel was long thanks to the Delhi traffic. Emily kept George busy with her talks and queries on K2 while the diary engrossed Lacene. Within a few pages, she recognised the writer and was excited.

She couldn't help interfering in the conversation between Emily and George. 'I am really surprised, G! I just can't believe that the person who so impressed me and almost transformed my life a decade ago would come into my life again by saving my husband from sure death. And that he had chosen me to compile his memoirs to be published for the good of society, I feel honoured! Really elated! He is the priest you once met at Kansas City Hindu temple!'

George couldn't hide his surprise too. 'Is he the one? Sadhà? You never fail to mention him when you get the chance, La!' But he had to continue with Emily who did not want to lose his attention.

'This man has travelled a lot it seems, G!' she screamed. 'And, you're right! He has met the most feared groups of people on earth.' As her thoughts started journeying to the past, she dozed off into a dream world, recollecting the day she first met this man.

———————•◆•———————

Fresh tulsi leaves, the aroma of which she was so attracted to, brought Lacene to the Hindu temple in Kansas City. The priest in that temple, a certain Achàrya, had introduced it to her. Impressed both with its effects on her and with his talks about his religion, she went to him whenever possible to hear about Hinduism. She felt that the hour-long drive from Lawrence to that temple was worth it.

Those holy basil leaves did have a good effect on her health. The flu that seized her that winter gradually vanished without any medical treatment. The regular intake of tulsi water for a fortnight cured her completely. Regular gargling with warm ginger water was a good complement. She was thrilled at the power of such herbs – with no side effects – and at the inexpensive, simple practice. She treated herself to a regular dose of tulsi water.

All one had to do was to soak a few tulsi leaves for an hour in lukewarm water and then drink the water. Once a day would be sufficient, but twice a day would have a healing effect, especially when one was sick. The Hindu priest's soothing and positive words had their own comforting effects too. She had also learnt the 'Gayathri mantra' from the priest - a prayer for everyone's welfare, considered to be the Supreme prayer of sorts among the Hindus.

But when she visited the temple again in June the year after on her return from her exchange program at Wellington, New Zealand, she found a new priest there. This man sported a thick moustache and a huge red dot in his forehead. Achàrya was fully shaven and sported a long vertical red mark within a white 'U' mark in his forehead. The differences could not be left unquestioned.

'Achàrya ji has gone to India. His father passed away a week ago. He will only return after three months. How may I help you?' were the first words this new priest spoke with her. 'My name is Sadhà Sivam. I am not a professional Hindu priest, have just come to fill a short-term vacancy. I can see that you have been here before.'

'Yes, I was helped by Achàrya with tulsi leaves; they were very useful to me. I was interested in Hinduism and Achàrya was informative. In between my busy study schedule, I spent some time learning about Hinduism from him,' said Lacene. 'But you are pronouncing Achàrya's name differently, A-chàr-ya-G is that correct?'

'"Ji" is just a term used in North India when one addresses elders or people held in esteem. You can't assign a meaning to it, but it is a practice that we use "ji" in our conversations. It closely equates to the use of "Sir or Madam"', said Sadhà Sivam, the new priest. 'It's quite interesting to hear that you have learnt about Hinduism from Achàrya ji. Have you been to India?'

'Not yet, but would like to. How different is your name from Achàrya-ji? What does it mean?'

*Sadhà took Lacene to the garden beside the temple. **V**rindhà**b**an or **B**rindhàvan as it was called – the former by Achàrya, the latter by Sadhà – this garden contained a small number of aromatic and flowering plants. Herbs like tulsi, pudinah (mint) and flowers like hibiscus, Artemisia pallens, rose and jasmine were regularly reaped to decorate the deities in the temple and to offer to the patrons of the temple. Tulsi-soaked water was offered almost in the same way as wine was offered in churches.*

Lacene did not fail to notice the marked differences in the pronunciations between Sadhà and Achàrya. What was Shiva to Achàrya was just Siva to Sadhà.

'Siva, as you may know, is the name of the Supreme Hindu God – Mahadev. Sadhà can be equated with many words – 100 per cent, always, forever, etc. You may take that I am supposed to 'always chant Siva's name and sing his praise'. Have you been to the other Hindu temples in the US? The one in central Texas or in Pittsburg?'

'Have heard of them but not been there, need to allot some time for that, I'm certainly very keen. If you don't mind, may I ask what Achàrya –ji means? I never asked him, but after getting your name's meaning, I feel like asking.'

'Well, most Hindu names carry a meaning. Achàrya can be pronounced in two ways. Achàrya means "discipline or regulated good habits" and with a slightly different accent -'àscharyà'means "rare, surprise – a pleasant surprise rather". To be a priest, one should be a disciplined person. And to find a disciplined person is also a rarity!'

'Wow!'

'A bachelor is called a "brahma- Aschàrya". He is expected to be a celibate And if he is, he is a surprise to Brahma, the creator god.'

'How does he surprise the creator god?'

'Brahma wonders how this young man, supposed to perform his command of "go ye and multiply" (winks) has still not started doing that by practicing abstinence and not straying around. There is marked difference between a bachelor and an unmarried man, you see!'

'Wonderful! While most of us in the west have known Hinduism as a pagan religion, Achàrya ...ji has told me a lot about the greatness of your faith. Fifteen per cent of the world's population is a great number to ignore. In fact, I am planning to take the '"Bakthi" – devotion – movement in India for my doctorate research thesis.'

'That's great! Then you should start learning Tamil.'

'Tamil? I know I'd be covering Tamil as part of my study but . . .'

'I can explain that to you, if only you have the time for it. "Victory" is from "vetri", "powder" from "podi", and "pearl" from "paral". The wheel was most probably invented by South Indians because the Tamil word for "axle", the rod that holds two wheels, is "atchu" that has been in use from times immemorial.'

'Is that so? In German – which is the source for English "axle" – it is "aksche"! Sounds almost like what you said.'

'To add to that, 'chakra' gave 'circle' and 'úrúl' is the source for 'roll'. 'Úrúndai' means 'round' – just to support my statement!'

'Even Achàrya -ji surprised me with some such points, with etymology of so many European words that have sources in Sanskrit. I couldn't believe it when he told me that the English word "widow" had its source from Sanskrit "vitaw", I was impressed because in German it is "witwe"'.

'True, did you get the meaning of "witaw"'?

'I didn't ask him; maybe that is why he didn't tell. So there is a meaning for that word?'

'Tamil and Sanskrit have most words coined with some reason. The prefix "vi" means great or something superlative, "tav" or "tap" means "penance" although it is not the exact translation. For a woman to live alone after her husband's demise in the Indian society was the severest of challenges. She has to have great self-control to thrive. Great penance, vi-tav.'

'Understandable and meaningful. But the European equivalents do not seem to have carried that meaning!'

'True. For that matter, "word" has its roots in Tamil, too. The Bakthi movement in India, historians believe, started from the South. Let me know when you have some time to sit and talk.'

'I am keen to learn anything that will be of use to my research. Perhaps I will see you tomorrow afternoon, will that be okay for you? Between two and five in the afternoon?'

'Fine.'

It didn't take long for Lacene to get hooked onto Tamil. She was amazed at the antiquity and literary wealth of the language. While she had wanted to verify most of what Achàryaji told her about Hinduism and India, she somehow believed everything Sadhà told her. Was it because of how he presented them to her or because he substantiated everything with some kind of scientific reasoning? She could not tell.

But she was drawn into a quest for learning Tamil at the earliest possibility. One of the first Tamil verses Sadhà detailed was the famous 'Yàdhum Oorey, Yàvarum Kelir' line which translated to: 'Every country is my own and all the people are my kinsmen'.

Any place is our place; all men are our kinsmen;
Good and evil emanate not from others;
Ailment and good health are also similar.
Even death is not new to us.
Neither do we claim life to be pleasant
Nor would call it, in despair or spite, unpleasant.

Like how, when lightning strikes
Clouds burst, pour, and drum on rocks
And on the roaring abounding floods
Hay is tossed in the dancing waves,
So are our lives tossed in the abundance of destiny.

With the enlightenment of this truth
And with the eyes of the wise,
We would not –
Marvel at the glory of the mighty,
And, more so, we would **never**
Despise the meek for their timidity.

For someone to have written with so much equanimity one-and-a-half millennia ago was something astounding to her! Such a society must have reached the pinnacle of civilization to have such ideas blossom in its fold. Lacene was looking at that period –a couple of centuries after the birth of Jesus Christ. The entire Mediterranean belt was awash with warfare. Equanimity was not a word anywhere in the minds of those people whose history built the foundations of the so-called first world.

For the next three months or so, Lacene made regular visits to the Hindu temple and learnt a lot from Sadhà about Hinduism, Buddhism, Jainism, and Sikhism – faiths that had their origin in India. She learnt Tamil quite rapidly and was in a position to read and write reasonably well besides managing simple conversations.

The rapid advancements in information technology and the faculties for Tamil in some of the US universities also aided her. From Sadhà, she came to learn more about the Tamil poets 'Avvaiyàr', 'Thiruvalluvar', 'Thirumólar', 'Nàladiyàr', and 'Bhàrathiàr' all of whom she immediately took a liking to.

On one occasion, she took Sadhà to her house to introduce him to her father. David Levite, who until that meeting wasn't too happy about her deep involvement with a Hindu priest, came to terms with the reality that this man was too wise to be ignored.

Sadhà gave a completely new interpretation to the name of the Jewish God 'Yahweh'(YHWH). He made David repeat the equivalent of Yahweh in English. David kept saying 'I am' until he got tired!

Then Sadhà told him that it only meant that the Lord simply wanted everyone to realise that each of us is a god. 'Prophet Moses, an enlightened one like the Buddha, explained this phenomenon to his people who did not understand it properly. You know how frustrated he was with them when he gave them the Ten Commandments.'

For David, that was preposterous! 'It was God who said, "I am" – to emphasise that "no one else is God but I am", and he did not mean that we must each claim "I am God"', he contended.

To Sadhà, Judaism was not a monotheist religion. 'It is the perfect embodiment of pantheism, where every living being is a God or God's avatar here! Moses was essentially preaching "Pantheism"!'

*Then Sadhà explained to both that the advaita philosophy – a key pillar of Hinduism – actually propagated the theory that 'everyone is what s/he is looking for'– the '**that thou art**' phrase meaning 'you are that God' philosophy. 'The Sanskrit term for that is 'tat tvam asi' - popularly briefed into 'tatwam'– meaning 'philosophy'.*

Judaism is another proponent of the 'advaita' philosophy and pantheism, claimed Sadhà, although it was unfortunately misconstrued as a proponent of monotheism.

Lacene had noticed that David spent many days discussing that view with his friends and his twin brother with great interest. Although many appreciated that view, they preferred to stick to the Torah as taught to them as per traditions. To Lacene it was an identity crisis. She appreciated Sadhà's view.

Lacene got a call from her dad just after he got his boarding pass. The call confirmed David's arrival in New Delhi the next morning.

After spending a day with him and seeing off Emily, George and Lacene were to take a flight to Shimla in search of her uncle.

Little did she know that her father would bring with him her former swimming coach Morgan, and make her life more complicated!

When they woke up the next morning from the same cave beds, the eight clergymen realised that they had slept well. Was it because they were all really tired or, perhaps, the power of Ganesh's food still had an effect on them, they could not tell.

They did not see any person until late in the afternoon, not even the Pathan who was with them the previous evening. They were a bit worried. The mastiff also was missing.

The Pathan had kept on shouting slogans repeatedly praising Allah and the Prophet Mohammed the previous evening. And each time he mentioned the prophet, he didn't fail to say 'Peace be unto him'. It was quite irksome for the non-Muslims present to hear him repeat those words so many times.

They wondered if the Prophet would not be at peace if those words were not recited like that. Rather, they felt that the Prophet's peace was disturbed each time his name was thus recited – more so by people who really did not live up to his expectations!

The Pathan had also exalted jihad and the great benefits of being a jihadist. He claimed that killing infidels like them was not a sin at all and that his team would be rewarded suitably on Judgment Day.

He branded the Muslim clergies in that group as traitors as they were teaming with those infidels and compromising their sacred faith, talking in conciliatory languages during international gatherings just to please the infidels.

After the Pathan had left, the eight men debated among themselves about their abductors. All names of jihadist groups known to be operating in that region – like al-Qaeda, Taleban, and fringe groups like Jaish-e-Mohammed, Lashkar-e-Taiba, Hezbul Mujahedeen, Hezb-i-Islami, Hekmatyar, Indian Mujahedeen groups – were mentioned.

What was not clear to them was whether they would end up being released after the ransom demands were met, or whether they would perish in the hands of those jihadists. They talked of how they got into this mess in the first place, the blame mostly falling on Arthur and the pundit for booking Ganesh's travel agency.

They had nothing to eat that evening. Hunger slowly draining them, they wondered how the remaining days of their lives would pass. Only the diabetic rabbi was spared. From the Pathan, he got back his pack of snacks that he had brought with him in his bag.

The Pathan had pointed out a shelter in the lower level of the hill saying that they would find a facility for ablutions. To their surprise, a portable toilet was hidden beneath that rocky shelter, with a built-in water tank. A signboard clearly read: 'Poo. No pee'. They wondered who would replenish the facility.

The Pathan had taken some pictures of all of them, some in groups of two and three, and some with all eight. He took the pictures very casually without preparing them for those shots.

It was quite late when each of them began to sleep – thanks to the inclement conditions there – despite going to their beds early.

The second day was eventless until the afternoon for the hostages. Their wanderings in the approachable areas around the cave did not give them any clue as to where they were and whether there was any other living soul in the vicinity.

———————◆———————

The Pathan came to meet them late in the afternoon with the mastiff. He was carrying a bundle wrapped in clothes. He threw a part of the bundle to the imam and asked him to share that with all. He then bid the imam to sit closer to him so that he could address all his hostages. Then he started a preaching session that lasted more than two hours until sunset.

He was relatively kinder in his behaviour that evening, extolling his captives to follow the wise words of the Prophet (PbuH).

'The Jewish people are inhuman as they deny the rightful place of the Palestinians in their own homeland.

'Does not the Zionist regime believe in their scripture's definition of Philistines as uncouth people? How can we consider the Jews as decent people on earth when they define a whole tribe of people in their midst as *ignorant, ill-behaved and uncouth persons hostile to art, culture, and intellect, who prefer the life of materialism, and conspicuous consumption as the paramount human activity?*

'For that matter, is there any Jew who is not materialistic? In fact, the Jewish community was the first one to make the most out of the humanity's inclination to materialism. If they can inculcate in the minds of every new born through their scriptures that a 'philistine' is a despicable person, how can we expect them to be citizens of this world? They cannot become global citizens, at any rate!

'The Americans created and funded Israel for their own national interest of controlling oil in the Middle East. They continue to support Israel to maintain permanent conflict in the Middle East. Did not their President

Nixon openly admit 'it was cheaper to fund the Israeli government than maintain a seventh fleet in the gulf'?

'The Americans are the worst enemies of humanity. They strategically entertained conflicts in other regions so that they could have complete control of all regions of the world

'The Indians are denying Kashmiri Muslims their right to rule themselves as a free and independent nation. When Pakistan was created for Muslims, the natural choice of the Kashmir citizens should have been considered rather than the ruler's. India is stifling the voice of the freedom-seeking Kashmiris, denying them their basic right to rule their nation. Indians are also ill-treating the Muslim population within their country, denying them their rights.

'If these three nations changed their behaviour then there would be no reason why the justice-seeking Muslims would have to declare jihad against them.

'Then there is this most un-Islamic regime ruling in the name of Islam. The nation that happens to have within its boundaries the most sacred of Islamic sites, yet has submitted itself to the dominance of western powers – Arabia, the Saudi's Arabia.'

'How can we tolerate the holiest of Islamic sites to be under the control of such cowardly rulers who have pledged their entire national security in the dirty hands of the Americans – the worst among infidels? No way! We have to redeem our most sacred sites soon from this unjust regime.'

'There are a few other pockets in the globe where the Muslims are denied their rights that need to be corrected too.'

'Once we redeem the Holy Land that our Prophet (PbuH) had walked on, we shall liberate the whole world of its woes. The caliphate will be reinstated, and we shall rule the world justly under the guidance of our Holy Quran and Sharia law.'

At sunset, as he rose to leave, the Pathan told them that they were not prevented from fishing in the river, as long as they did not try to venture too far. They should not stay too long in the open nor should they go in groups larger than two. Not that he was afraid they might run away or escape – which was impossible – but that he was sure they might end up being killed in the most horrific of ways. Staying indoors within the cave would benefit them. Aircrafts or helicopters – even US drones – might mistake them for jihadists!

He parried all questions put forward by his hostages save one. The imam asked, 'How long are we going to be here?'

'It all depends on how soon all the demands of our group are met by the UN and member nations, I can't elaborate on our demands, can't reveal their responses. But I can assure you one thing. All religions are facing their toughest ever challenge. Their most revered religious sites across various parts of the world will be razed to the ground in the next couple of weeks! All praise to Almighty Allah. There is no God but Allah.'

In the comfort of their suite in Hotel Meridian, Lacene preferred to hit the sack early. George and Emily were engrossed in their incessant discussions that continued during and after supper. Emily imitated Lacene's mannerism of making sounds with the use of her tongue touching her upper palate at different places. George looked at Lacene meaningfully and giggled. Lacene laid her head on the pillow and reminisced about the incident.

George wondered why Lacene made sounds by moving her tongue touching different spots on her upper palate in the middle of conversations. Lacene said, 'Sadhà once wrote for me the transliteration of a Tamil poem in English with words like 'Thirùkkùral'. Finding too many variations in the letters as against the normal 'Thirùkkùral' I asked him to explain.

'If you notice the different spots on your upper palate that your tongue touches when it pronounces the English letters 't' and 'd', you will recognize that

the strong or grave accent for 'd' stems from the tongue touching the upper palate at a slightly higher location above the gums of the incisor teeth as compared to 't' for which it touches the gums of the incisors.

'Apply that procedure to letters like 'l', 'n' and 'r' as you do for 'd'. You will get sounds as used in 'shoulder' for 'l', patron for 'r' and 'sound' for 'n'. Most European alphabets do not have a letter for such grave accented l, n and r. Almost all Indian languages have separate letters for these. So, when I transliterate them, I use a bold letter wherever applicable.

'To express vowels with such grave accent, I use the grave accent symbol to differentiate. Hence the 'ù' in Thirùkkùral. Otherwise, a reader may pronounce the 'u' as in 'cut' and read it as 'Thirakaral'.'

Sleep eluded her as always, and the memories of Sadhà returned to haunt her as she tried to close her eyes.

Lacene was very impressed by some of the poems of the great-grand Tamil poetess Avvaiyàr wherein she supposedly answered queries from Lord Muruga, son of Siva. Sadhà explained,

'Lord Muruga, known in North India as 'Kumàr' meaning 'son', is almost the 'patron' god of the Tamils. He is believed to have literally created the Tamil language using the scholarship of a certain Sage Agasthiar. Lord Muruga is said to have indulged in childish pranks with this poetess Avvaiyàr posing difficult questions to her as though he was asking them out of ignorance.

Answers the poetess gave to two such questions impressed Lacene very much. In terse verses, about fifteen centuries ago, she had clarified life's mysterious questions and ultimate goals.

'What is the "rarest" of all, Granny Avvai?' Muruga quizzes.

'It is rare to be born a human, my boy;
Rarer though to be born without any mental or
Physical handicaps and illnesses;
Having thus born,
Rarer still to be able to acquire knowledge and wisdom;
Having obtained all these, the rarest of all is to

Acquire through disciplined penance, the gift of *giving*;
And for those who attained this discipline and benevolence,
The abode of the gods will open its doors on its own!'

The Talmud's famous saying 'The highest form of wisdom is kindness' ran through Lacene's mind.
'Well, Granny, then what is the 'most pleasing' in the world?'

'Solitude is very pleasing, my dear son,
As that enables contemplation;
Better still, is seeking the '*Ádhi*',
The origin of everything.
Further pleasing is the quest for,
And acquisition of, knowledge.
And the most pleasing of all is being,
both while awake and in dreams,
In the company of wise persons!'

Lacene could not help recollecting Robert Southey's nineteenth century poem she had read years ago at school that began with,

'My days among the dead are past;
Around me I behold,
Wherever these casual eyes are cast
The mighty minds of old:
My never failing friends are they,
With whom I converse day by day'.

Tears had bedewed her cheeks with gratitude when she understood that poem. When she heard this Tamil poem wonderfully recited by Sadhà, she could feel her cheeks getting wet.

A similar emotion engulfed her when Sadhà recited a devotional poem from Bhárathiyàr's collections, which went thus: (addressing Lord Ganesh, the other son of Lord Siva):

'I dare speak (to you) on what none have spoken before;
I dare ask (you) for what no one has ever asked so far;
All the creatures on earth – grass, plants, trees, worms,
Insects, reptiles, birds, animals, humans – all of them
Shall live in peace and happiness without any trouble
Whatsoever, thanks to my deeds.
From the centre of the knowledge-space I shall say:
'May there be peace on earth; may all beings live in
Harmony, happiness, and prosperity.'
And then thou, my Lord, shall just say: 'Amen.'

This is my prayer to thee, my Lord, and may you grant me
My wishes this day, this moment, right now, O Lord!'

All that this poet demands from God is just an 'Amen'! The poet places himself in a convenient location in the cosmos and declares that peace and prosperity should prevail among all creatures in the world; and all that the Creator has to do is to just say, 'So be it'!

What a demanding prayer! Only a mind that has crossed all barriers set by human divisions could think of such a wish or prayer! Lacene was thrilled. That single poem led her to read all works of Bhárathiàr, turning her into an ardent fan of his writings.

Several other excerpts from Tamil literature narrated by Sadhà further fuelled her desire to learn the language. She desired to visit Tamil Nadu and spend time with the people there under one pretext or the other.

Her dreams, as though by default, drifted to the events on the eve of her wedding with George that inevitably ended in a nightmare. That evening was when she last met Sadhà.

Jeremy was a more familiar person to Sadhà. Jeremy had accompanied Lacene quite a few times to the temple. But George happened to meet Sadhà only once in Sadhà's short sojourn at that Kansas City Hindu temple. That was when George and Lacene announced their decision to get married and David tried to dissuade her from doing so, as he preferred Jeremy.

David's twin brother Bernard, the rabbi, came to Lacene's rescue by having long discussions with both David and Lacene. He was from the orthodox block and personally favoured Jeremy Zadok. But he noticed Lacene's strong will to marry George and did not want to go against her wishes. Finally, his persuasions with David helped the marriage between Lacene and George to materialise.

Sadhà had subtly conveyed his appreciation of her choice of George as opposed to Jeremy. Although he had met George only once with her at the temple, he told her that she could trust George with her entire life.

She vividly remembered seeing him at her wedding reception night although he was in a hurry to return to the temple early. He had given her a lovely gift of a metal carving of the 'dancing Siva' and a portrait of poet Bhárathiàr — with his familiar 'fireball eyes' — before he left. She had kept the statuette in the drawing room in her Auckland home. Not a single visitor had failed to admire it.

A sudden thought sprang in her. She sat upright in her bed.

'I never saw this man since then, did I? I didn't even check if he had dinner that night, didn't contact him for a while after reaching New Zealand. Long after that, when I continued my pursuit of learning Tamil by visiting India frequently, my attempts to contact him were in vain. His cell phone was not reachable, my emails to him bounced. I gradually lost hope of contacting him.'

Emily was cuddling George in her sleep next to her. The long separation must have made her cling to George, Lacene felt.

'Sadhà is the one person who left indelible marks on me and partly transformed me. I then ventured into the study of Indo-European languages besides Tamil. It took my life to very exciting horizons. I have every reason to remain grateful to Sadhà for guiding me towards a passionate career for myself.

'How could this man have moved from Kansas to Karakoram in a decade? And have familiarised himself so well with the Himalayan conditions that he could rescue someone from such a perilous situation? What could have brought him there? Perhaps, he was assigned to some Hindu temple in Afghanistan or Pakistan? Poring over the diary further might help.'

But she did not know which pages of the diary contained information about his life in the past decade. She felt that she might have to read the diary in its entirety. But she also needed to catch up on lost sleep. The next time she would be able to lay her hands on the diary would be when they both landed in Shimla a day later after handing over Emily to her father. No hurry.

She decided to get back to sleep but the drowning episode opened up in her awakened dream, as usual.

The palm beneath her bottom. Her perennial nightmare.

David picked up the *New York Times* from the pouch in front of his seat. The page on the front as left by the previous passenger had a column highlighted with red ink. With curiosity, he quickly read it before moving to the next column.

> *The Algiers Post* reported the collapse of a mosque in Algiers Bay in the outskirts of Algiers. The mosque structure crumbled at the tomb in the wee hours of Monday, and the reporter alleged that one of the four pillars might have given way due to corrosion at its base. He warned all such buildings near the seaside to take note of this danger. No casualty was reported. The *Fajr* prayer was hardly ten minutes away when it occurred. No one was injured in

the incident as fortunately none had arrived at the mosque when it collapsed, the newspaper reported.

'Mahàkavi' Bhàrathiàr

4. The one and only God

Any place filled with love is filled with happiness;
Love and happiness are inseparable twins.

———◆·●·◆———

'We shouldn't have given that book to Morgan, Lacene. We are being unfair to the person who trusted it with us. I don't mind the lists but not the book.'

George didn't hide his displeasure from Lacene, while they were returning from the airport to the US embassy in New Delhi.

'You saw what little chance I had keeping it out of his hands, G. I can't blame my dad for bringing him into this. He has his concern about the safety of his brother. He must have mentioned this diary to Morgan, obviously to drag him into this operation. He has no other reliable person in the federal enclave. We must appreciate him for taking Emily. He would have gone in search of his brother otherwise.'

George was only partially convinced.

'Am glad Emily waved goodbye to us happily, hope she'll be fine with dad,' Lacene tried to change whatever was on George's mind.

'Believe so, she was looking pretty excited,' George responded.

While on the road, they discussed the possibilities of their success in tracing the whereabouts of her uncle. Any clue to the path they may have to take would only be obtained from Shimla. They made a booking at the same hotel where Lacene's uncle had stayed and decided to start their mission from there.

'Did they take you for a terrorist, Grandpa? Did you tell them about your brother?' Emily asked an exhausted David on the flight.

'Well, not a terrorist really, but a suspicious businessman, perhaps! I will explain it to you later, Emy. Need some rest for now, shall talk to you after a nap, okay?' David tried to smile but he could not come out of the trauma at the transit lounge before boarding.

Emily pulled his jacket and sought his attention to the PAS (public address system), which disturbed his conversation with Morgan on his mobile while in the departure lounge. 'They are calling you, Grandpa,' she said as she tugged gently.

'I'll talk to you a bit later, Morgan.' Disconnecting the call, David went to the security desk with Emily. An airport security official asked 'Are you Mr David Levite? May I see your papers and all your baggage?' He demanded that Emily's baggage also be shown. Protesting that all their belongings had already passed through the scanner, David demanded an explanation.

'What's the purpose of your visit here, Sir? We notice that you arrived here yesterday and you're returning within thirty-six hours. What kind of business did you have here? Who are your contacts? Who did you meet on this visit?' The official shot his questions at one go.

Bringing all their checked-in baggage, they opened even Lacene's posters – David protesting all through. Obviously finding nothing suspicious, the official let him go with a 'Sorry for the inconvenience, we are just doing our duty'.

When David looked at the official with some contempt and tried to say something in protest, 'This is no worse than the way your airport security treated our celebrities, including our ex-President, Mr Abdul Kalàm, sir!' said that officer with a wry smile.

The final call for boarding was blaring out of the PAS when David called Morgan to continue his talk.

'I can see many events in his life wherein he had had close association with Osama bin Laden, Mullah Omar, Al Zawaidi, Khayyami, and many Taleban leaders. He had spent time in Yemen, Sudan, and Libya, and most of the last decade in the Afghan-Pak belt. His life had been intrinsically entwined with the most wanted terrorists. And you are saying that he could not be an enemy of the civilised world?' Morgan wondered, looking at Lacene.

Morgan spoke these words in front of Christopher T. Lee, the US embassy official representing the US Central Intelligence Agency (CIA) in Asia. Lacene was pretty sure that everything was being relayed live to CIA headquarters.

'You are an US citizen, and it's your duty to hand this over to the federal authorities, Lacene! This indeed is classified data and isn't for everyone to read.' Chris tried to project himself a kinder person.

'Maybe classified data for you, but all these should go to the public because they have to know what transpired between those terrible minds in their private discussions. These minds need to be laid bare!'

Lacene wondered how they could have read so much from the book in that short time, and then said,

'You can see that the writer of this book has won their confidence and had worked with them for so long. He had also been instrumental in preventing quite a few horrendous attacks on other nations and in forewarning or passing information to the western world about quite a number of their important plans – most of which were later subverted thanks to the hints he had provided. You can't brand him a terrorist!

'And, perhaps, if I read more of this diary, I may be able to prove that he isn't guilty. Knowing him personally, I can't imagine him causing or being part of anything causing the death of innocent civilians!'

Morgan said, 'But unfortunately, that is what he has done for most of the past decade, Lacene! Look at the way they had planned and executed the 26/11 attacks in Mumbai, killing hundreds of people. He had known about it. He participated in discussions and had contributed to the meticulous planning and execution of that inhuman attack. How can you give him a clean chit?'

'He had been associated with the al-Qaeda team operating in Yemen that has conducted several attacks on civilians, US installations, and the government's military camps, killing hundreds,' said Chris.

'He had been advising them on the strategies they should adopt and how they can keep themselves hale and healthy in the most challenging environments and circumstances. He was like a family physician for the most dangerous men in the world! What kind of a contribution is that if not for evil designs?' asked Morgan.

Lacene felt that they were grilling her as though she had abetted terrorism.

Lacene could realise that within hardly twenty hours of being in the possession of the diary, Morgan and his team had copied its entire contents and had read – rather rushed through – many pages from it. They must have assigned a few persons with that task and shared the findings. She wondered if she should protest their behaviour.

'You can't make copies of my book without my consent, Morgan! I can't believe that you would do so!'

'I only did what you should have done, Lacene! Can't you see how important these pages in that book will be for tracing your uncle? Because I respect you and Mr Levite I return it to you now! We could have taken possession of it instead, citing federal laws.'

Chris said, 'There are several pages my team has not read because of other languages and the horrible handwriting.'

Lacene said, 'Well, unless one reads that book in its entirety, it would be too imprudent to brand him and his actions as evil.'

Morgan said to himself, 'I have enough evidence to consider Saddam – who you say was a Hindu priest – an enemy of the USA. I'm sure to get the nod for the capture of and if necessary the elimination of this man'

But he told Lacene, 'I believe so. We shall wait for you to read the book fully before coming to any conclusion. Help us by constantly updating me on your progressive understanding of this "Saddà-m".'

The list of more than 200 locations all around the world was not legible. The US embassy had taken a copy of it but had not discussed it with any other country, including India. Lacene sat silently with a hurt look as she collected the diary and the lists from Chris.

Morgan did not tell Lacene about the attempt by someone at the patio in the pool bar at his hotel to rob him of the diary or the list.

Sipping espresso at that pool bar and turning the pages of that difficult-to-read diary of Saddam, Morgan left his table for a while to answer a call from Chris, as the bar was noisy. Chris asked him to read a particular page, which his staff found interesting and informative. Three staff members at the embassy were deployed to pore through that diary's copied pages.

That was when another patron at the bar shouted, 'Hey, what are you doing?' so loudly that Morgan turned around and saw a young Indian man running away from his table. He had to choose between going after him and picking up the book he found lying by his table on the floor.

The person who shouted – an elderly Indian wearing shorts and a sports T shirt- told Morgan, 'I saw that guy flipping through pages of your diary as though you had kept some cash between the pages! And obviously, when I shouted, he ran away, dropping the book in panic!'

'Thank you, sir. Thanks a lot for saving my book. I didn't keep any money in it, though!'

'Good that you didn't!' signed off the man with a proud face.

'But I know I had a more valuable list in it which is with my colleague now, fortunately' mused Morgan. 'If that guy was flipping pages, he must have knowledge about the diary, the list. We are being watched.'

Chris promised Lacene that the copies of the diary they made would be treated as classified documents accessible only to very highly placed officials in the CIA and the White House. 'No information would leak to the media. Your mission of writing a book on this strange person will not be compromised nor jeopardised at any stage, although we do not appreciate that idea. Your rights will be fully honoured, but . . .'

Lacene could sense that Chris had the clearance from the higher-ups to let her do so. 'Perhaps the diary wasn't so damaging after all'.

Chris had engaged Jacques Ortega, an expert decoder to find out what those religious sites had in common and whether the names and addresses shown on the list were for genuine sites. The metadata with NSA - records collected by snooping, came in handy for that task.

Jacques, running his own business providing digital security, was a regular at the US Embassy, conducting such operations. The process of tracing online correspondence and links to so many sites would take a long time. He made it clear to Chris and Morgan that any feedback from him on the matter would be after a few days, if not a week.

Waiting for Lacene in the embassy reception lounge, George utilised the time to perform his business tasks. He expected Lacene to come out with a red face from that meeting, to which he was not invited. After learning from George the circumstances in which the diary came to his possession, they did not have anything else to ask him.

As Morgan escorted her to the reception from that grilling session, the TV in the lounge telecast a spokesperson for the Indian government, briefing the public on the abduction of eight religious men by a jihadist group near Shimla. The Home Ministry official assured that the government would leave no stone unturned to rescue the tourists.

The trio concurred that this would soon become a hot topic everywhere. Various debates, discussions, and expert analyses would soon fill the pages of newspapers. Globally, TV channels would allot more airtime to this issue. 'Good fodder for the media,' they felt.

Morgan had a lot of things to do at the US embassy. He needed to establish wireless communication links with them from Shimla and wherever else he may have to move about in that region. He would have to get a few more passports for his use. He would require help from the local Himachal Pradesh state authorities in his hunt for the abducted clerics and their abductors. He got himself bedecked with a tracking device on his person for the NSA to monitor his movements.

Reaching their hotel room in Delhi, Lacene read out a few pages that were in Tamil to George. Sadhà had indeed discussed potential safe hideouts in Pakistan for Osama. Way back in 2005, he had advised Osama to move out of the Afghan border region which could any day be hit by US drones.

'I see a number of notes clearly highlighting Sadhà's contributions to the activities of the Taleban and al-Qaeda groups. His close interactions with such leaders speak volumes about the clout he had held with them, G! If he gets to read those pages, Morgan will certainly go to any lengths to prosecute his favourite 'Indian Saddam'.' Lacene sighed.

Showing no reaction, George just passed a 'is that so?' look at her.

———◆———

The Israeli government provided full details of the rabbi, Bernard Jonathan Levite. Considered mildly secular among the ultraorthodox clerics of Jerusalem, he had a track record of being the peacemaker between the various factions within the orthodoxy. He had tacitly backed the 'women of the wall' movement and had stalled extreme measures of repudiation on them by the synagogue. He had attended two international religious conferences in the past, and this was his third and purportedly the last.

He was an admirer of the Dalai Lama and had expressed his eagerness to meet with him during this conference. It was quite understandable that he could have joined a group of interested delegates to meet with the Buddhist monk, the popular Tibetan leader in self-exile.

Born in Britain but raised in the Texas-Arkansas belt, Arthur Kingsley started his career as a pastor of the United Methodist Church and gradually turned agnostic. After a short stint with the Scientology sect and getting disillusioned with it, he became an atheist, supporting the likes of Richard Dawkins and Sam Harris. He had dual citizenship – a British passport too.

This was the first time an atheist was admitted as a delegate in a religious conference. Developed nations supported such participation.

Pastor Biden had started the other way around. He grew up as a non-believer in a poor carpenter's family on the banks of the Mississippi but changed course when he was adopted by a church in Flowood in the Rankin county. He never turned his face against God since then. He had moved between the south central states in the USA and had settled in Southaven.

Details of the other five clerics were awaited from the respective countries. Once obtained, Jacques Ortega would analyse all data to present the probabilities of links between the names on the list and the delegates and any other suspicious online activity. He had an ocean load of electronic communication material, provided by the secret surveillance organ of the US intelligence, from which to decipher or decode anything useful for Morgan in his investigations. He fit the stereotypical description of a 'nerd' to the Embassy staff.

When they woke up on the third morning since their abduction, the eight men realised that they had had a decent night's sleep. The previous evening's simple food was adequate for their bodies' needs. The only person who went to bed starving without minding it was the pundit. Fasting wasn't new to him. He did not want to eat the roti brought to him by a Muslim. 'May be it was cooked along with meat!'

The day's first words were spoken by the bishop. 'How do we get out of this wretched place?'

'Don't you like this place, Father? I love the scenery, the weather, the serenity and seclusion. How do you feel, Pastor?' Arthur was the only person living the moment, unmindful of the next.

'Well, I do wish I had such a place near my hometown. I would visit here as often as possible! Giving sermons in such a location will have amazing effects on the listeners! I do like this place, Arthur, but one cannot stay here for long. We have to find a means of escape. I am not a hardliner, but I do have reservations about these Islamic terrorists.

'Islamic fundamentalists are a real threat to world peace. I am pretty sure that Ganesh must be a Muslim. Did you see the way he was concocting stories about Hinduism?

'I blame the Indian Government for its laxity in providing adequate security for foreign nationals. And they must do something to rescue us from this place. We should also do our best to escape from here. We are totally cut off from the civilised world!'

The pundit stepped in. 'India's leniency and soft handling of such terrorists has resulted in strengthening the confidence of the jihadist groups. It was their fault in 1999 when they bowed to their demands for releasing the aircraft and passengers at Kándahar.

'Again, it was the weak Indian stand after the 26/11 attacks in Mumbai that emboldened such elements. Now, they have gone to the extent of holding religious leaders from other countries for ransom in Indian soil! We have to do something to get out of this place.'

The pastor did not seem to have finished talking. 'Look at the unbelievable stories Ganesh told us about Hinduism! I'm pretty certain that he is an Islamic terrorist in the guise of a Hindu travel agent. He was trying to indirectly deride Hinduism by mocking its beliefs. The UN, the West, and India must do something quickly.'

The imam and the moulana could not hide their displeasure at the way others linked Islam to terrorism. Though he expressed confidence that the terrorists – whoever they might be – would not execute the hostages, the moulana was concerned at what fate awaited a Shia Muslim like him. Deep inside his heart he felt that the Pathan's gaze on him wasn't too kind.

The Buddhist monk from Sri Lanka lamented, 'I wonder why I opted to join this group to meet the Dalai Lama. Indeed, I should have stayed back. The Japanese monk, Ippen Ingen, changed his mind at the last minute and went to Bodhgaya instead. I also had a seat booked on the flight to Bodhgaya to visit the Mahabodhi temple.

'I was quite eager to visit the Mahabodhi temple built by the famous emperor Asoka circa 3 BCE to honour the 'Enlightenment' achieved by Buddha. Will I ever make it to my Sangha?'

Arthur Kingsley, an American of Scottish descent, the only non-believer in the group, was trying to make everyone remain optimistic about their fates. He encouraged the others to take it as a different experience. He was expressing confidence that the CIA would do everything in their power to save all of them from any calamity.

'Don't you realise that it would be futile looking for means of escape? In such an open landscape like this, being spotted from a long distance would be easy. We could get killed or captured,' he contended.

Most in the group concurred with him.

Deciding not to go too far and dividing themselves into four groups, they strolled around the hill and the nearby riverside. Arthur and the imam managed to catch some fish from the river. Taking the guard's caution seriously, they made sure that the small fire they started for roasting the fish did not produce much smoke nor lasted long.

The pundit ran away from the scene, unable to bear the smell of fish.

The Pathan was kind enough to leave a pint of milk for the pundit the previous day. He did not drink it though, unsure what milk it might be. It was only after some hard persuasion from Arthur and the rabbi, that he drank some of it. The Pathan had signalled *three days,* as he threw the Tetra Pak at the pundit. Nobody could tell which animal's milk it was, but since he liked its taste, the pundit consumed it over the next three days.

Arthur prodded the pundit. 'You say you are a Brahmin from Kolkata. But I have noticed many Brahmins from Bengal consuming fish! Are you not from that class of Brahmins?'

'Well, those are 'macha Brahmins', meaning 'fish eating Brahmins'. With the confluence of the perennial Ganga and Brahmaputra rivers forming a large delta, fish is always abundant in the region, so it's no wonder the topography influenced that culture. I'm a pure vegan.'

'Lacto-vegetarian, you mean?' asked the pastor. The pundit nodded.

They sat below the canopy and spent their time discussing the various civilizations that developed languages, arts, and sciences in their wake, besides various faiths.

And various food habits, of course!

'Do you agree with Ganesh's version about the birth of Ganesha? That was an interesting view point indeed!' Arthur asked others.

'This view is not one held by any of the scriptures as far as I know. May be some modern scientists hold such a view, not the old wise sages of the Hindu religion,' said the pundit.

The rabbi seemed inclined to accept Ganesh's version but looked hesitantly at his Christian mates. Neither the bishop nor the pastor would accept it. The two Muslims would also not accept it. He remained quiet.

'Accepting this view of parthenogenesis among humans would mean that we question the 'Son of God' theory of our religion. This will not get acceptance at any level in Christianity,' the bishop quipped.

Arthur was quite affirmative when he said, 'Scriptures could possibly be wrong. After all, they were written by human beings, that too, predominantly by men. Although they were projected to have been written by divine influence or interference, we can't prove that effectively. Without concrete evidence, the younger generation will not accept any divine link to scriptures as claimed by religions.'

The other six men did not argue much against Arthur's theory. But each one expressed the same 'divine interventions' view as though supporting each other.

'The divinity of the Holy Scriptures should never be questioned. Such an act would only amount to blasphemy.'

None of them gave any importance whatsoever to Arthur, whom they all considered a person devoid of god-fearing values. The imam explicitly wondered how an atheist was a delegate in a religious conference.

'All of you seem to be convinced beyond doubt that we are held hostage by a jihadist Islamic group. I have my doubts. No sincere Muslim, reciting our Prophet's name (PbuH) and Allah's glory can ever do such a thing. This is certainly the work of some dubious elements. Ganesh does not seem to me to be what he posed himself to us as.

'This must the work of groups fighting for the liberation of Kashmir from Indian control. I expect us all to be released soon once India releases some Kashmiri freedom fighters from Indian prisons!'

While most others appreciated the imam's view on Arthur, they did not agree that their abductors could be a group other than jihadists.

'If they are Kashmiris, the Pathan need not have derided countries like the US, Israel, and Saudi Arabia!' said the pastor.

They did not look out for the Pathan that day. They were resigned to the fact that he would make an appearance very late in the afternoon, like the previous day. They wondered where the Pathan could possibly be spending the rest of his time and where he was coming from.

But the Pathan did turn up that day a little earlier than the previous day. The mastiff was not with him. He instructed the moulana to stay closer to him when he addressed them for that afternoon.

'We are great admirers of Ali for his sacrifice! We want the two sects of Islam to bury their differences and amalgamate into one Islam with one Prophet (PbuH). We have many Shiites in our fold.'

That was the first admission by him as to his group's leanings – although he did not reveal the name of his group.

And for the first time, his behaviour made some of them wonder if he was from Baltistan, where a great majority of the population were Shia Muslims. Yahya openly commented, 'Maybe he is a member of Iran's Islamic Revolutionary Guard Corps.'

The moulana's pulse rate increased manifold; He was really excited at such a possibility. 'I'd be spared then,' he thought.

'Our group encourages Iran's nuclear project,' the Pathan said.

'Two Islamic Nuclear powers in the region would be more welcome than one. Our group believes that the other Muslim nations in the Middle East are already puppets in the hands of the West. While Iran is openly defiant of the West, Pakistan handles the US and Europe in a very manipulative fashion. Many militant groups in the Hindu Kush belt admire Pakistan's army and ISI for their supportive role.'

'Empowering Islam to annihilate the infidels – when time ripens – is part of our group's strategy. Then, Pakistan and Iran will join hands to take on the enemies together. Afghanistan would be fully under Taleban control by then.' He was predictive and confident.

The moulana confronted him. 'Why then do most of the jihadist groups in the region hate the Shiites much more than they hate the infidels? Why do we see constant attacks on Shias, Ismailis and other sects in Pakistan and Afghanistan by jihadist groups? We see increasing incidents of conflicts between Sunnis and Shias in the Middle East! This is very un-Islamic and will lead to ruin!'

The Pathan replied with a firm tone: 'These are all the works of the Western masterminds, in collusion with Hindus and Zionists. I do agree that many other Taleban-affiliated groups do not like the Shiites at all. But our group is working ceaselessly to bring about a change of heart among the other groups who are against the Shias and other sects. We will unite them all under one umbrella, for sure!'

At the behest of the Pathan and with his Persian accent, the moulana gave a sermon on the history and faith of the Shiites. He reiterated the fact all Muslims so strongly believe in. 'The Omnipresent, omnipotent, and omniscient God is the one and only God.' No God, but Allah.

'Yes, Irene, I can hear you. You want to use the projector and screen for a day for your presentation? Okay, but take care, make sure you reconnect all appliances as before. Switch the power off.'

'Thanks, dad; shall take care. I'm not taking it out anywhere, just in my studio at home for a rehearsal. They provide me with everything for my presentation at the university.'

'Okay, good night.' Morgan was yawning as he switched off his bed lights and removed his iPad from its cover. As he scrolled for the latest news, he glanced upon a BBC headline from the Philippines.

> A column in the local city news page of *The Filipino Reporter* reported the collapse of a church building in Turumba, a suburb of Manila. The Church of 'Our Lady of Immaculate Conception' was wrecked in the wee hours of Monday. Cause of the collapse was not immediately known. A photo of the crumbling structure was not published in the issue for want of space.

—◆·◆·◆—

5. The Only Son of God

Thus the words and actions of the wise, regard;
Every little help, tenfold they reward.
But the truly wise know all men as one;
And, return with gladness, GOOD for EVIL done.

———◆———

The pundit came out of his cave that morning much earlier than anyone else. Or so he thought. The sun was well up in the sky, and he estimated the time to be around nine. No one was outside the cave, and a chilly wind was blowing from the river. He decided to get back into the cave and as he turned around, he noticed some movement across the edge of the southern side of the hill.

Intending to remain in safety, he got below the canopy, kept himself near the entrance to the cave and looked again. To his relief, he found Arthur walking towards the cave at a rapid pace. Emerging from the hiding, he shouted to Arthur, 'Are you all right?'

Arthur signalled to him to keep his voice low, and until he reached the cave, he kept turning back as if to see if he was being followed.

When he reached earshot, the pundit asked, 'Why go alone? Did you notice anything strange in the morning?'

Arthur gained his breath and briefed him. 'I heard the growl of some animal in the morning. When I came out of the cave, I thought I saw the tail of something disappearing at that edge of the hill. Curiosity took me there, and I soon realised that it was a cat – a tiger or leopard. When it turned around and looked at me, I took to my heels and came running.'

As if to support his story, a piercing pair of eyes of a leopard appeared at the ridge of the hill – a few meters below the point where the Pathan had been appearing all these days. Urging him to get inside, the pundit murmured, 'I wish this cave had a door or some form of a closure. I hope you have not invited trouble to us!'

They both went back to their beds, but sleep was elusive.

———•◦◆◦•———

While the trio were checking in at the Shimla Hotel, Chris sent Morgan a SMS, confirming that there was a message from one of the jihadist groups claiming that ten clergymen from various countries were in their custody. The group had contacted Indian defence officials at their Srinagar unit. The Jammu & Kashmir state government received confirmation too, through an insider.

Their demands for the release of the hostages would be revealed soon. Onus was on the shoulders of the Indian government to convey their demands to the UN and other countries and to get back to them.

The US embassy officials were confident that the Indian government was well equipped to handle this case. The US government was providing all possible help it could. Both the governments assumed that one of the LET's (Lashkar E Taiba) splinter groups was behind this abduction.

But so far, no further demands had been received from any group. And Morgan wasn't ready to jump to any conclusions.

The Pakistan government had stated that it vehemently condemned the abduction of the clerics and that there was no link to that incident with any organisation within its territories. Perhaps, it hinted, that it could be one of the jihadist groups fighting for Azad Kashmir operating within Indian borders – the Indian Mujahedeen. 'As always, the Indian government likes to blame Pakistan for every failure of its law enforcement agencies', its Foreign Affairs spokesperson said as cheekily as ever.

From Stuart Granger, the NSA chief at the US embassy, with whom he had worked in several operations in the Afghan-Pak belt, Morgan learned that the US embassy had already made links with Aziz Gulam Azmi, the Indian official handling the case of this abduction. The US embassy officials were quite comfortable working with him.

Stuart briefed Morgan on data gathered so far in the case.

Everybody in the Indian and US government circles took careful and discreet note of the fact that, while the jihadist group mentioned ten hostages, only eight were missing. All the other thirty-nine delegates to the recently concluded World Religious Conference in Shimla had reached their respective homes. Some of them had even provided valuable information on the circumstances in which those missing eight men had planned their trip to the Dalai Lama's abode.

Among the other two names on the list, Ippen Ingen, a Japanese Buddhist monk, was contacted at Bodhgaya. He narrated how he decided to go there instead of Dharamshala. He expressed sorrow on hearing about the abduction of the eight clerics.

Nobel laureate Reverend Desmond Tutu of South Africa did not attend the conference at all due to other preoccupations.

The US and Indian government officials wondered if the jihadists had abducted two other hostages from elsewhere in the region.

National governments of the eight abducted delegates were in constant touch with Aziz. They awaited further information on the hostages and about the demands of the abductors.

To the outside world, the Indian government's press release only said that an unknown jihadist group had abducted eight clergymen. More details would soon follow.

Morgan got another disturbing message from the embassy. Stuart told him that a threat had been released a few moments ago by an unnamed jihadist group. It had been sent to the UN through the Indian government, which said that, besides the abduction of the clerics, they had plans to destroy more than 200 religious buildings around the world, starting next week. There was no information about those holy structures, though.

Stuart concurred with Morgan that the sites on the list brought by Lacene and George were likely to be the sites targeted by these jihadists. It was obvious that George's saviour at K2 was directly linked to this group, having had the list of abducted clerics and of the locations now under threat of terrorist action.

Stuart also informed Morgan that Jacques was progressing with his snooping assignment. 'He is searching for clues from global digital communications of the past five years with connections to the names on both lists we gave him. He has come up with a term 'gadows', which he wanted to investigate further, and wants to know if we have ever heard such a word.'

'Sounds like 'gallows' doesn't it? Where the hell did he get this word from?' asked Morgan.

'That was my first reaction too. Where else would he get such words from, if not from the ocean of Internet traffic that he has dived into?'

'I have no clue whatsoever, but let me brood over it, will ask Lacene and George too.'

Morgan immediately got in touch with Lacene and passed on information about the new threat from the jihadists and his take on Sadhá's involvement in it.

Lacene retorted, 'Why are you always so suspicious, Morgan? Sadhá could probably have gained access to this list prepared by the jihadist group and must have passed it through George in order for the list to reach the authorities to forewarn them! Could it not be so? Why should we brandish him a traitor even before we gave him a fair chance to explain himself?'

Morgan could feel the angst in her tone.

'Well, I would have thought like that had I not read those pages of his biography! Did he not roam, eat, and sleep with them? Plan, and even scheme like them? Anyway, my intention is not to antagonise you but just to inform you of what I have come to know.'

Then he asked Lacene, 'Well, have you by any chance come across the term 'gadows'? And you, George?'

'Nope, will have to try and recollect. Strange word, gadows, is it two words or just one word? Where did you get it?'

'That may not be important for now. If you can recollect something from your memory, please share it with me. Let me set my room up before I go out to see the local police. Bye.'

'Sure, will do. Bye.'

Both George and Lacene wanted to free themselves from Morgan and his way of holding everyone guilty until proven innocent!

———————◆———————

Though he was not deeply religious, Morgan was a believing Christian. He compared the level of fundamentalism in other religions like Islam and Hinduism as against that in Christianity. He mused, 'Following the preaching of the ever forgiving and non-violent Jesus Christ, the Christians have predominantly been peace-loving people. How many terrorists has Christianity produced? Even the Crusade was for the redemption of its Holy Land and not an act of aggression. The efforts taken by the Christian West in containing terrorist forces in this world are fully justified.'

Christianity is the only religion with divine interventions, miracles and non-violence, he believed. Even the spread of Christianity throughout the world was through peaceful missionaries and not accompanied by any violent conquests, he convinced himself. He felt satisfied that he and his family members did not fall prey to the ever-growing anti-church activists in the USA.

———————◆———————

Lacene jumped from her bed when George suddenly shouted in a strange mix of joy and shock. It jolted her out of her deep slumber. Seeing her frightened reaction, he apologised to her and told her to get back to sleep.

'What is it, G? You can tell me.' Lacene leaned on his shoulder as he returned to the page in Sadhà's diary he had paused on.

'I was so thrilled at this background hand-sketch on this page, La. For some reason, Sadhà has folded a few A4 papers and has sewn the open ends with the binding such that one cannot read what's inside unless one slits open the bend on the free leaf side. Otherwise, for someone who flips through the pages, it would be like a normal sheet of paper written on both sides.'

'Clever of him!' Lacene exclaimed, her eyes scanning over the sketch.

'I found about four such sheets that I slit open now. I'm sure Morgan and his team could not have copied those pages. They will miss out some important information, I reckon. I will have to carefully check if there are more pages such as these that we failed to take notice of. Morgan will never get access to them.

'One of them was in Tamil. I first skipped that page, but as I was turning over to the next page, I glanced at this sketch and returned to it. Can you recognise the picture here? Decipher anything?'

It took a while for Lacene to get a clear picture; and once she did that, she shouted, 'Oh my God, G! How can that be?'

She leaned on his shoulder again and sobbed.

George also could not control himself; he realised that he was also sobbing at the revelation of a great truth in their lives.

Written in very small fonts in Tamil, the whole page detailed the events as they happened on that fateful evening of their wedding reception. Lacene read it aloud for George to hear. He understood her Tamil without needing a translation.

I told Lacene I wouldn't stay long that wedding evening as I had to reach the Hindu temple in Kansas City before 9 p.m. Achàryaji had just returned with his family after a long travel; they needed a good sleep. We stayed in the small house within the temple premises. Opening the gate for me late in the night would disturb them.

Lacene looked at George. 'He gave me that 'Nataraja' statuette in bronze. Remember how much I admire it and explain to every visitor to our home about its significance?' George nodded.

While leaving a few minutes later, I noticed Jeremy taking Lacene to the backyard, alone. I wasn't happy with Jeremy's body language and grew suspicious. I then discreetly followed them both and kept myself at a distance behind a shrub, watching their every move. I saw Jeremy jumping into the pool as Lacene turned towards the hall to leave. I was shocked to see her being pulled into the water.

Realising my suspicion coming true, I ran to the pool and jumped in.

The struggle under the water shouldn't have lasted so long but for the adamancy of Jeremy, who was intent upon drowning her. He would not have expected a third person's interference. After the initial shock at such interference, he must have believed that he could drown both of us. Unfortunately for him, however stubbornly unyielding he was, his underwater capabilities couldn't outsmart my tenacity. I managed to untie the rope from her ankle while pushing her up and pressing him down by locking him with my legs. I quietly slipped out of the pool after I saw Lacene going in with her dad using the stairs in the yard.

Lacene explained to George how that pool was designed to receive fresh water from the stream that broke away from the river and joined it again after feeding fresh water to the pool. The feeding pipe was filtered adequately, but the exit pipe had a closure disk that was usually left open fully for circulation when nobody used the pool.

They understood how Jeremy's body was seen floating downstream. That disk was open when they were all in the pool. Water current from the stream was pushing them towards the exit pipe during their battle. It should have assisted Jeremy in pulling Lacene down. Sadhà should have exerted extreme pressure both to battle the stream flow and Jeremy's pull as he pushed Lacene up to help her keep her nose above water.

As she continued to stare at the sketch of a palm lifting a female bottom, she felt the ever-attached palm beneath her bottom suddenly disappearing. She was sitting with her naked bums on the mattress for the first time in twelve years! A burden relieved!

So Jeremy didn't commit suicide in the river beyond the pool; he was literally drowned in the pool in an effort to save Lacene from being drowned by him. Sadhà had unintentionally killed Jeremy!

Lacene and George were lying on their bed wondering how much they owed this single person in their life – Sadhà Sivam. Is there a past life link between the three that created a 'karma' effect?

———•◆•◦•———

Lacene was still leaning on George's shoulder and kept looking at him time and again. George reciprocated that look. Lacene kissed him on his cheeks, and George kissed her on her forehead. Then they kissed each other passionately. As she thrust her face on his shoulder again, George could feel her tears on his body.

'What's it, La? You're okay?'

'Just remembering the shoulder discussion that we had when I first flung myself on to your shoulders, G.'

'Me too, what a lovely moment that was, Lacene! Besides realising our love for each other, was that not the moment it dawned on me that Tamil glued us together? Wasn't that the first time you addressed me as G? The first time you laid your head on my shoulder?'

'Although numbers were named in European languages mostly following Arabic or Sanskrit words, the very first number, 'numero uno' was from Tamil. Did you know that, George?'

'Is that so, how come?'

'In Tamil, it is 'onru', colloquially, 'onnu'. Fact being that Tamil is one of the most ancient of surviving languages, I do not have to establish that the number 'one' came from Tamil.'

'Interesting, so we learnt to start counting numbers from the Tamils, you want to say?' George was laughing mockingly.

'Not only that, even the word 'shoulder' was borrowed from Tamil, and it has such a sound meaning, unlike what we have in English.'

'I'm listening.'

'ThòL is the word in Tamil for shoulder. If you pronounce the words repeatedly you will know that they have a common origin. ThòL is also the origin of the Tamil word for friend – thòzhan, boyfriend, or thòzhi, girlfriend; thòzhamai means friendship.

'One who is of your shoulder height – equal in age or growth – naturally happens to become your friend; also, one who "lends his shoulder" is your friend! That's precisely why a friend and a shoulder go together in Tamil! A friend in need!'

'Marvellous! So thoughtfully created are the words in that language! This 'thòzhamai' you said now sounds close to the 'kizhamai' that you say for the days of the week in Tamil, doesn't it?'

'That's why I got so drawn to this language, G! That word 'kizhamai' for a day literally means 'the art or process of getting or becoming old'; 'ilamai', its antonym, is the art of remaining or becoming young. Every day we get older by a day, so a day is a kizhamai!'

'Fantastic! What a word for a "day"! But tell me what made you mention these two words – one and shoulder – today?'

The way Lacene looked at him caused him to feel as though he was levitating! Lacene leaned on his shoulders and said, 'You are the one, G, and you are the one whose shoulders I want forever.'

With Lacene on his shoulders for the first time, George was already on cloud nine; he never expected Lacene would fall in love with him, although he did so the moment he first met her. It was a 'dream come true' moment for him. And he felt greatly indebted to Tamil for that.

Morgan received a message that he must contact Stuart immediately. When he called, he was in for a shock.

Facebook and Twitter messages that were monitored and Emails intercepted by the NSA revealed a pattern among some users from various parts of the globe that had mentions of religious sites, some of which were found on the list Sadhà had sent through George. So far, five such holy sites had been demolished without any assignable reason or cause. Jacques had done a commendable job – and continued to do it – in sifting hundreds of thousands of Internet exchanges that carried the names of any of those 216 places listed.

But no one found any clue as to what 'gadows' meant.

In his analysis of the immeasurable amount of Internet traffic while searching for any possible usage of the names of the holy sites given to him, the one common term that Jacques chanced to come across, used by some of traffickers – bloggers and Internet commuters – was 'gadows'. For a brief period of only nine months, specifically between 11 December 2008 and 11 September 2009, a web site bearing the domain 'www.wasdog.com' had been in use. A Forum for discussions on religions was also in circulation during the same period. The forum and the web site were closed for good on 11 September 2009. But the terms 'wasdog' and 'gadows' had been used occasionally by thousands of Internet users all around the globe since then.

User data information, that he managed to obtain from service providers by using federal influence, revealed several names spread extensively over the globe. There was no pattern in the age, gender, race, or region of the traffickers. Stuart told Morgan that it was a mind-boggling exercise and experience for Jacques and himself. Though there was pressure from Stuart and Morgan, Jacques continued with the task as that was a good money-spinning job, however temporary. Those were the kinds of short-term assignments that fed him for the rest of the year to go on adventure travels that were so dear to his heart!

In his first report on the assignment given to him, Jacques simply said that 'gadows' had something to do with those sites. He would come up with more information soon.

Stuart could not find any commonality in the conversations or discussions between those Internet users. He was aware that with just one person assigned to the job, it would take a long time to read all the material thoroughly before tracking anything worthwhile. Morgan understood that but expected more people to be assigned to the job.

Stuart had to make Morgan understand that it wasn't so easy to get approval and funds allotted for such trivial cases!

'Trivial is it, Stuart, the abduction of eight clergymen and potential threat to hundreds of religious sites around the globe?'

'Yes, Morgan, in the eyes of the US federal authorities! Only six among those sites are purportedly in the US and only two hostages are Americans, with no serious threat to their lives so far. We can't expect taxpayers' money to be spent on each and every such case; they have other priorities. But I will keep pushing them. Jacques also demands more fees for his services and wants to be paid every week.'

Morgan wasn't too happy about all these setbacks.

Oblivious to the frenzied happenings in the outside world, the hostages were wondering, 'Are any efforts being made out there to rescue us? Do they have any clue where we are?'

'Why do we find ourselves in such an ordeal? May we answer that before we talk of anything else?' The rabbi was obviously the most disturbed person among the lot.

'What do you mean? It's all because we decided to meet the Dalai Lama! Who motivated us all into this trip? Ask straightforward questions, rabbi! Are you implicating one of us here?' The annoyance in the imam's tone was not hidden.

'Was it not pundit Girilal who first proposed that we visit Dharamshala?' This was from the pastor. 'And, of course, I seconded that idea. What's so wrong about it?'

'We must zero in on who decided to book Ganesh and his team as our travel guides; that's where it all started. What criteria were adopted in choosing them? Who did they contact first?' asked the moulana.

'Arthur proposed this travel agency, and he was the first one to contact them, he owes us an explanation,' said the bikku.

'Halleluyah!'

All eyes turned in the direction of the jubilant voice. To the pleasant surprise of at least some, the Pathan arrived earlier than usual, dressed in a new, white robe. As he descended and reached closer to them, they could see a completely different person. His beard was trimmed; between his right fingers a cross was dangling from a rosary.

Strangely enough, and true to his new costume, he talked of Jesus Christ. 'Who else did say, whosoever shall smite thee on thy right cheek, turn to him the other one also?

'Who else did pray to the Almighty for those who crucified him, "Father, forgive them, for they know not what they are doing"!

Can you show me any one in human history so benevolent, kind, and all embracing? No wonder that Muslims revere him as a messiah, and the Christians worship him as the Lord's only begotten Son!'

This was a pleasant surprise to the reverend and the pastor.

The two Muslims stepped forward to question how he could sport a religious symbol while being a Muslim. As if to explain it to them, the Pathan raised his voice, 'Tell me, fellow Muslims, does God really have a religion? You all know that Islam considers Isa as a revered messiah. Our group aims to engage the world's Christians to work with Muslims and to isolate the Zionists. We aim to take over the Holy Land of Jerusalem from the Jews. What do you say, Father?'

The bishop expressed no emotion as he heard those words. 'We are not on a crusade now, son. But, like you rightly pointed out, we want to follow the true advice of our Lord Jesus Christ – forgive and embrace. Embrace everyone.'

'Then you must speak to us about the glory of your Lord, the only Son of God, Father! And you too, Pastor!' As if to stress his demand, he pointed his rifle at them.

The two disciples of Jesus gave lengthy sermons on Christianity. There were noticeable differences in their presentations. The Catholic extolled the greatness of the Trinity, the moral upheaval in human civilization worldwide following the messages that the Catholics spread; many pagan sects thus came to believe in Lord Jesus.

The pastor talked about Mother Mary, Virgin Birth, and the Resurrection of Jesus. He advocated how one can directly communicate with the Lord. He did not fail to have a dig at the incidents of burning at the stakes of many innocents by the papacy branded as witches and devil's advocates.

As though in support of the rabbi, Arthur stepped forward. 'How can you deny Judaism its rightful place? It is the mother of two religions. Christianity and Islam have their roots in Judaism!' He sounded a bit sore with the way the talks were going on.

'I may have to agree with you here, Arthur. The birth of Islam had a lot to do with both Judaism and Christianity. The Torah was the basis for the old and new testaments. And most of the Torah's chapters were reproduced in the Holy Quran, with some variations, of course.' The Pathan's tone appeared conciliatory.

Arthur continued, 'The existence of polytheist and pagan faiths along with those two monotheist faiths in his region should have caused the Prophet (PbuH) to choose the best of them – monotheism. Those two books – Torah and Bible – had chronological narrations of creation and developments on this earth that appeared very authentic. Other faiths appeared quite illogical and unauthentic.

'Deeply involved and committed in the restructuring of the then flailing society, he must have decided to start off from religious faith before turning towards the social structure. As an atheist, I do not believe in God and angels. In order not to hurt the sentiments of some here, let me go by the belief. He must have prayed for divine guidance and the Almighty Allah chose him to be the next prophet. Through Angel Gabriel, Allah had guided the Prophet with the passage of the Torah and the two Testaments of the

Bible in his own format before continuing to offer him the rest of the Holy Quran.'

Both the Muslims present there differed with Arthur on his observation that the Prophet's choice of monotheism led him to be 'the chosen one' by Allah. 'He is distorting the truth here, Pathan,' the imam shouted.

The moulana tapped on the imam's shoulder. 'We know how Prophet (PbuH) was chosen by the Almighty and was given the verses of Holy Quran. Let this atheist blabber whatever he wants, you can't expect any better from him.'

Encouraged to some extent by the ease in the Pathan's tone and behaviour that evening, the clerics freely discussed the various preachings of the messiahs, prophets, and sages of all the religions.

Invariably, like all learned people, they enjoyed pointing out the similarities in the various scriptures and wise words of their messiahs and prophets who were all divinely ordained.

Arthur's was the only sour note. 'If all these messiahs and prophets were truly divinely ordained, the world should be a very peaceful place by now! But is it?' he questioned.

'Unfortunately, each of you believes in one kind of divine intervention or the other just to legitimise your scriptures. The truth is that there was no such divine intervention in any of these cases.'

'You always say so, Arthur! We won't listen to you,' said the pundit.

Arthur said, 'If God exists and if he really loves us and is 'all merciful' as we are always advised to believe, he would not be imparting hatred of other societies or communities! He will not be waiting for centuries and millenniums to send another deliverer. The sufferings of mankind have only multiplied to unbearable levels. Only mythology speaks of divine rescue. History doesn't show any record like that. Most of the prophets or avatars did not fulfil their missions. Most of them had miserable ends and did not depart this earth happily with their objectives fully accomplished.'

'That's a good point to ponder' said the Pathan. 'Someone can talk about the last days of those 'chosen ones'.'

No one had the courage to talk about the last days of the messiahs or avatars of 'other' faiths. Only Arthur came forward.

'They are plenty. I will speak of only a few popular messiahs.'

'Among the many prophets or messiahs of Judaism, their last days were a mixture of happy and sad experiences. Moses, the most enlightened one of all, who wrote the first version of the Torah, died a heartbroken person. His God did not permit him to cross the Jordan River because of his trespass at the Meribah waters. He died on its eastern shores, looking over the promised land of Israel, never setting foot on it until his death.

'The Hindu god Vishnu's two most recent and popular avatars, Rama and Krishna had quite unpleasant last days. While Rama repented his loneliness without Sita, Krishna died an inglorious death in a remote forest with none of his progenies around to take care of him or perform the last rites for him.

'Jesus Christ died on the cross, enduring horrible physical torture.

'Prophet Mohammed, who was highly revered but never considered either a demigod or an angel by his ardent followers, had relatively peaceful and satisfying last days except for a few ailments that were not unusual for an aged person.

'Buddha, the enlightened founder of Buddhism, was reported to have died of food poisoning, with controversial reports claiming that he ate pig's meat that caused his death. Some claim that he died of food poisoning, but the food did not contain any meat.' Arthur paused.

The rabbi could not understand how such a saintly and enlightened person of Buddha's stature could have died of food poisoning, that too, by eating non-kosher food. He admired the wisdom of his forefathers – and scriptures – in providing strict guidelines for safer living. He was anxious to express his feelings to those around but restrained himself, lest he offended the bikku.

He noticed the Muslim clerics tending to speak but refraining from hurting the bikku. He sensed that they were about to talk of Halal.

It was obvious to everyone that not many of them had peaceful ends.

They talked of other religions of the world. Taosim, Confucianism, Shintoism, Jainsim, and Sikhism and several other beliefs including those of Incas, Mayans, Red Indians, Egyptians, Greeks, Romans, Nordics, and a host of others. The Pathan was a silent observer.

Everyone felt a bit satisfied at the well-spent hours that evening discussing many aspects of religion.

Arthur wanted to speak about the need for banning all religions, but his proposal was shouted down by all others!

The pundit wanted to enlighten the audience on Hinduism, the third largest faith in the world. 'Tomorrow,' the Pathan replied.

They also agreed that the most painful and heart-wrenching scenario was that of the last moments of Christ, who died purportedly paying for all our sins. His was a unique life, preaching only love, peace, and forgiveness. With more than a third of the entire human race following him and a majority of the rest holding him in high esteem, Jesus Christ has had the most impact on the way we all live today.

'No wonder that he is considered as the 'Only Son of God'!' the pastor concluded.

———————◆:◆:◆———————

Stuart asked Morgan to read the *Dawn* from Pakistan. Finding no hard copy in Shimla, Morgan pored through the internet.

The *Dawn* reported the collapse of a Shiite mosque in the outskirts of Quetta, capital city of Quetta province in Pakistan. A series of bomb blasts in the city between eleven and noon yesterday had left more than eighty people dead and hundreds injured.

The mosque was completely shattered, and only some pillars remained at the site. No one was killed in that area, but three persons were injured. Messages of condolence and condemnation of such barbaric attacks on civilians and religious sites were pouring in from all parts of the country.

International leaders have also condemned the attacks.

---

6. I Am the Way

I was a stranger; you took me in!

———◆———

Lacene noticed the first missed call on her mobile phone a couple of hours after they checked in at Hotel Shimla. They were at the Indira Gandhi Square at city centre. The second one, from a different number, came about fifteen minutes later. On both the occasions, the caller disconnected the line after two rings. And, on both the occasions, the caller appeared as 'Private Number'. Lacene could not return those calls.

She wondered if the calls could be from her dad or Emily. It was well past midnight in Washington DC, ruling out that possibility. Emily was jubilant last night when she came on Skype because David had promised to take her to the Smithsonian Museum and spend the whole day there. She would be seeing all the models of flying machines and spacecrafts. Her excitement was obvious, and Lacene was happy. No chance of a call from them.

Her office colleagues from Auckland might have called, but George told her that he had spoken to Jerome at length from the hotel room on Skype, and there was no reason for anyone from office to call her.

When Morgan left the couple for a while for his private talks with Stuart, Lacene received another call. This time, she picked it up on the first ring. There was a stranger on the other end.

'Good morning, madam! I am Abdul from the Soaring Wings Travel Agency here. I got your number from the hotel receptionist who said that you wanted to visit Dharamshala. I can make all arrangements for your pleasant travel, madam! Is it for you and your husband Mr George Swenson only or do you have any one else with you? When would you like to travel? May I come to see you in a short while?'

'Thank you for tracking us and offering to book our travel, Mr Abdul. Yes, we do want to leave for Dharamshala as early as possible. Why don't you meet us at the hotel? We would rather check your credentials before we engage you, isn't that fair, Mr Abdul?'

'Hundred per cent, madam, hundred per cent! You can just call me Abdul, I am very young. I shall wait for you at the hotel at 4 p.m., is that okay? I shall bring our pamphlets, tour packages, and our best rates. You can also check with the hotel for our authenticity. May I bring a package offer for two?'

'It would be nice if you do so, but I have this pain in my neck,' thought Lacene. 'Well, we are three; we have with us Mr . . .'

'Mr Morgan Stanley from Canada?'

'You are smart, Abdul! You must have a close connection with the hotel receptionist, I am sure!' Lacene's tone did not hide the bitterness over the fact that the hotel staff could give out so much information so soon. But such an experience in India was not new to her. George smiled at her meaningfully.

Morgan had booked under a different surname at the hotel, indeed.

When Morgan joined them, Lacene excitedly told him about the coming tour to Dharamshala. 'How do you rate the chances of our mission's success?'

Morgan showed some excitement too. 'Fifty, fifty?'

Much to their disappointment, they did not notice anything unusual when they checked in at the hotel earlier that morning. No one seemed to even acknowledge the fact that there had been an abduction of alarming importance just a few days ago near the premises.

Any query about that incident was parried very smartly with a few words like, 'yaa, some priests were kidnapped', 'but it did not happen in our hotel', and 'they had already checked out'.

Morgan collected information from the local police on the incident but wasn't pleased with the level of seriousness they exhibited.

Sunderlal Nahata, the Deputy Director General of Police, Crime branch, Shimla region, was quite detached in his replies. It was clear to Morgan that as long as there was no gunfire or bomb blasts, nothing was worthy of concern to them! Morgan also sensed that the DDGP was not keen to give out much information to someone just because he was a white Westerner. Those days of 'trying to prove to be smart to a Westerner' seemed to have gone. Being smart meant giving the least importance to them nowadays! 'India is changing', Morgan murmured.

The van that had collected the eight clerics four days ago did not belong to any known travel agency. The hotel staff said that they would be able to identify the driver and the escort if they got to see them again or see their photos. None of the pictures of the known criminals of Himachal Pradesh shown by the police to the staff resembled those two. Unfortunately for the investigators, the clerics had made their own arrangements with some travel agents. The hotel staff had no clue as to who they could be.

The police couldn't even get the name of the travel agency the clerics had engaged. The registration plate of the van that transported the eight men had been recorded by the hotel security guard, who loaded their baggage into it. It was of a New Delhi registration. The police suspected that it could be a fake number plate as there was no such number in the Delhi transport department's records.

That was all the police could say to Morgan.

Quite frustrated by the snail-paced progress in the case, Morgan decided to move fast in his own way. He started making friends with the staff and waiters in the hotel. Providing 24–7 service, there were many among the staff he had to befriend as they were on shift rotation.

Sipping each one's favourite coffee at the bar, the trio had a chat with Abdul. Clad in a smart suit with a tie and shining shoes, well-kept hair, and a trimmed goatee, he was like a Bollywood star. He came with Omar Sherfuddin, whom he introduced as his colleague.

Morgan had arranged for one of his acquaintances among the staff at the hotel – Hritesh – to pay a visit to the coffee bar while they were sitting with the two travel agents. Hritesh was the supervisor for the third and fourth floors in the hotel. During the course of their discussions, Morgan noticed that Hritesh paid a second visit to the bar, bringing with him another hotel staff member to the lounge and discreetly showing Abdul and Omar to him. From the reaction of the other guy, Morgan could sense that either or both of those two travel agents were known to him. He would get more information from Hritesh soon after that meeting.

Morgan agreed that they could go to Dharmshala with Abdul and Omar. They would all leave by around 7 p.m. the next day as Morgan had some business to complete in Shimla, and Lacene needed rest.

Abdul made such a quick, good rapport with all three of them that he had no problem convincing them of their travel plans.

'Drive from the hotel is about five hours to Dharamshala. Check-in at Royal Palace hotel there, have a good night's sleep and then go about your business the next morning. I shall be with you all through your travels until you are back in Shimla Hotel after as many days as you may prefer. I shall, of course, arrange a chauffeur-driven-car at Dharamshala for you. This station wagon will return to Shimla and come again to Dharamshala when you need it.'

All three agreed to have dinner that night at a south Indian restaurant on Abdul's recommendation. Lacene and George were particularly excited about the prospect of enjoying south Indian cuisine in Shimla. They stayed back with Abdul and Omar at the coffee bar when Morgan excused himself to go out on his business.

Morgan learnt from Hritesh that his colleague had seen Omar at the car park outside the hotel that evening when the clerics checked out.

But he did not know that Omar was his name. He was the driver of the van which carried the clerics, Hritesh confirmed. Talking with Hritesh and walking casually by his side, Morgan reached his suite. After tipping him heftily, he called Stuart and spoke with him for a while. 'I have placed a transmitter in their suite, Stuart. I want to believe they are innocent but the way Lacene defends this Saddam, I can't take chances. And how is the signal from my transmitter? Am I on your radar?'

'Very much, you are now in coordinates N 31.053182078 and E 77.107855369 walking at 2.2 mph.'

'Perfect! Tomorrow we leave for Dharamshala, keep tracking.'

The moment Morgan went past the lounge to climb the stairs, Abdul abruptly changed the topic with Lacene and George.

'We know you have come here looking for Mr Levite, the rabbi, Mrs and Mr Swenson. We are the ones who escorted the clerics from the hotel to Dharamshala.'

Shocked, Lacene looked at George and turned towards Abdul. 'Really? And where are they now? Are they safe?' Lacene was so dumbstruck that it was George who reacted. Lacene's face clearly showed the level of shock and anxiety she was going through. Her hand reached for George's hand as if for support. Abdul continued: 'If you can be discreet about it – I hope you will – we can take just the two of you to meet the rabbi. He is fine wherever he is. We do not want Mr Morgan to know anything about us.'

'And may we have the list of the holy sites that you have?' Omar's tone had a blend of politeness and rudeness. Abdul looked at Omar with disapproval.

Lacene and George could not hide their shock when they heard these words from total strangers in Shimla. Lacene's mind was racing. 'Who are they and what do they know about the lists? Does it mean that Sadhá has links with these people and is party to the abductions and threats? Is Morgan correct in branding Sadhá a terrorist who needs to be nabbed and eliminated? Do we ask Abdul about Sadhá?'

George said, 'It is impossible for us to leave Morgan. He has accompanied us all the way to help trace Lacene's uncle. He is quite close to Lacene's family and can't be left alone here.'

Lacene was half-hearted in going with that but realising that there was little option, told Abdul firmly that all three should be together.

Omar said, 'Then you will not meet the rabbi. No way.'

George said, 'You can't say that. If you need the list, you will have to take all three of us together. We do not mind cancelling the trip to Dharmashala with you. We will make our own way.'

Omar showed his displeasure by getting up, saying, 'Well then, we know how to get the list from you. We do not need to beg you for that. Let's go, Abdul.' Abdul's angry stare at Omar signalling him to go gave them a cue.

'Can you give us a few minutes?' George asked Abdul. With a pleasant smile, Abdul rose. 'Sure, please decide wisely!'

It became obvious to Lacene and George that members of this group had tried to snatch her bags at Delhi airport. They were utterly confused as to how someone in Delhi and Shimla would know about their arrival and about them being in the possession of those lists – other than being informed by Sadhà? Lacene did not want Morgan to feel vindicated. More than that, she could not stand the thought of Sadhá's involvement in all these kinds of terrorist activities.

And how dare these two guys come and sit in a hotel and speak to us like this? What if, after they leave us, we inform the police? They have been seen by so many here, so identifying and capturing them wouldn't be difficult for the police! With what courage do they reveal themselves like this? There must be something – someone strong and powerful behind them, for sure. And, well . . . the danger to the lives of the abducted clerics looms large, if anything happens to these two guys.

'That list seems to be important to them. These guys are up to something very big – certainly not for good. We do not lose anything by giving them a copy of the list. But if we can meet the hostages – at least my uncle – we have achieved something.'

Abdul came back to their table alone, and they realised that he had sent Omar away. They also preferred to deal with Abdul alone.

'So what did you decide?'

'Well, we shall give you a copy of the list only if you take all three of us. And only when we meet my uncle will it be in your hands.'

'I agree to that. But let him not know anything about us. To him we are just travel agents. Would you mind if I meet you at your room tomorrow morning? Maybe we can talk more freely?' Abdul asked politely. Lacene looked at George for approval.

'That's fine with us,' said George.

'As long as you come alone,' said Lacene.

Abdul nodded with a smile – a captivating smile, Lacene felt.

Arthur did not fail to notice the enthusiasm when each cleric spoke about his sect within his religion. The indifference in their body language when others spoke was noticeable, more so when the person from the 'other sect' in their own religion spoke!

In each case, it was obvious that the indifference stemmed more out of historic facts on how 'my religion' was impacted upon or treated by the 'other' religion or sect. The real wealth of knowledge and guidelines in those religions or sects did not matter so much!

The rabbi seemed more lenient towards the polytheist eastern religions than towards the monotheist Christianity and Islam.

Very surprisingly, the Buddhist monk could not hide his displeasure towards Hinduism when he narrated how Buddhist followers were systematically driven out of their homelands and tortured or massacred. How a huge exodus from the north-eastern India took place to present day Sri Lanka, Myanmar, and Thailand preceding and during the Kalinga war of Emperor Asoka's times.

He also briefed them on how Buddhism spread far and wide in the entire Asian continent so rapidly but dwindled into a minority religion in the country of its birth, thanks to Hindu zealots of those times.

This was news to most of the clerics there. There was commotion in for a while with comments of all kinds freely flowing.

The pundit asked the bikku directly, 'Is that why the Buddhists in Sri Lanka are literally driving out the minority Hindu Tamils now?'

Denying this accusation vehemently, the bikku replied that Buddhists never would commit such non-dharma acts.

'Don't say so, monk! Our Muslim brothers in Myanmar are being executed and tortured by Buddhists mercilessly, being minorities there!' the imam intervened emotionally. 'Even in Sri Lanka.'

The Pathan, who was in the same costume as on day one, kept himself aloof from all of them for a while. He realised that each one was recollecting current events and events from history wherein his sect or religion was brought under extreme suppression in one way or the other by the other sects or religions.

Arthur wanted to brief them his observations of, and views on religions, before they could hear the pundit. The Pathan gave a 'go ahead' sign to him. The others weren't too happy about it, though.

'When Jesus Christ's words were disseminated by the four builders of Christianity, there was persecution of Christ's followers by Jews in their homeland, then by Romans who feared that the Christians might be a threat to their rule, and by every ruler in every region. But when Christianity slowly graduated to become the accepted faith of those Royals, the trend reversed. All those who were not Christians faced persecution. Jews were targeted as 'betrayers' in most of those Christianised nations.

'When Islam emerged and was not accepted by the Jews and Christians of that region as the extension of the Lord's authentic words through the Holy Quran, a permanent rivalry ensued between these three adherents of Abraham's faith. The bloodbath that resulted from that rivalry hasn't fully subsided yet.

'When it reached the shores of the river Indus, Islam was already five centuries old. Despite a millennium since its presence in India, and more than four centuries of total political control over it, Islam could not spread itself entirely in India. All the other Asian and North African countries where Islam was carried into, it gained acceptance – voluntarily or by coercion – by a majority of the population.

'At the time of Independence in the divided India, 10 per cent of its population were Muslims. Currently they are a little over 13 per cent, ranking India as the country with the third largest Muslim population. If Bangladesh and Pakistan had remained together with India as one country, it would be the single nation with a third of the world's Muslims. Besides that, the Muslims would be more than a third of India's population too.

'The very simple fact that Islam couldn't capture the minds of a majority of Indians was seen either as a failure by the preaching class in Islam's elite circle or as total indifference towards Islam by the Hindus besides Jains, Sikhs, and Buddhists. This view intensified their displeasure towards Indians and Hindus in particular. Following Jews and Christians, the Hindus ranked third in their hate-list. Most Hindus developed a dislike for Islam because they strongly believed that the Muslim rulers coerced their forefathers to convert to Islam.

The pundit intervened: 'you may be right here Arthur. We have a popular phrase 'topi pehana dhia' quoted by people of almost all regions of India with words meaning the same as 'so, you've been cheated to wear a cap!' This was a way of ridiculing those who converted to Islam. The phrase has come to be in normal usage now to denote anything that a person was cheated upon with.'

'Is that so?' the rabbi asked with a mix of admiration and surprise. The Muslim clergies did not like that intervention by the pundit. 'Conversions to Islam are always done with total acceptance of our faith by the converted in whichever part of the world it may have occurred.' The imam retorted.

Arthur continued: 'The Crusade wars had a background of religious hatred and rivalry, with battles that were fought for centuries. The formation of the League of Nations followed by the United Nations gradually brought an end to open wars. But they were succeeded by cold war and guerrilla wars culminating into terrorist attacks.

'India, the motherland for so many religious faiths, was no holy land either. Whichever faith a ruler embraced, irrespective of the size of his kingdom, its citizens who adhered to any other faith were subjected to some form of torture or persecution, forcing them to adopt the faith of the rulers. When a king embraced Jainism, he would force it upon his subjects – mostly Shaivites in those periods.

'A Shaivite ruler would in turn terrorise Vaishnavite missionaries within his borders. When Saivism and Vaishanvism joined hands eventually by forging relationships between their godheads, they ebbed out others. It took a very long time in history for sanity to prevail there.

'But it did eventually prevail there for more than a millennium. The insurgence of Muslim rulers only strengthened the resolve of the Hindu population to resist any pressure for change to other faiths. When Christianity found its way into India through traders and missionaries—it had existed in some pockets by then-, Indians were already a hardened lot. Only 2.3 percent of Indians are Christians now.'

'Similar atrocities over followers of 'other' religions or faiths abound in world history that can be attributed to every corner of this globe. Look at what Spanish invaders did to Incas and Mayans to 'establish' Christian faith! There was no mercy whatsoever in any of their acts although they were supposed to follow Jesus Christ!'

Arthur's speech was like a presentation of historical facts. His emphasis was on 'horrendous atrocities committed in the name of religion' by almost everyone. It gave the hostages an overall view of what religions have done to humanity. But views on the 'why and how' of what happened, differed widely between them.

Not one of them believed that religions should be blamed for those events. In their views, it was only fanatics and ill-directed souls who were to be blamed for such atrocities. Each one's religion was not responsible because all the scriptures had only preached love and compassion all along.

But no one answered Arthur when he asked them bluntly, 'Then why do your religions and their scriptures provide the 'scope' for such fanatical ideas or for such 'ill-directions'? Those fanatics and radicals quote the same scriptures only for their violent acts, killing innocents! Why can't you – erudite theologians that you all are – do something to rewrite your scriptures devoid of such ideas?'

No one answered.

'Hypocrites, all of you! You brood hatred deep in your hearts but talk with a sweet tongue as though you love all religions!' Arthur shouted.

He continued to remain the most unpopular person in the group for raising such unanswerable questions.

———❖———

'You mean what? What picture? Whose grandpa? Be clear, Irene!' Morgan went a bit louder. Irene had waited a whole day to call him. Obviously, she did not want to disturb him in his sleep.

Morgan was surprised to hear that he had left his projector system on in his studio. The last picture he was viewing when he left his studio had come up on the screen when Irene tested the system before disconnecting it to take to her studio. One of the two persons in that picture was Uma's grandfather!

'Which picture is it and who are on the screen?' Although Morgan clearly remembered that picture, taken by an amateur bystander at the scene of 9/11 attacks, wherein a man was photographed supporting another wounded man. The twin towers were crumbling behind them in a huge smoke of concrete dust.

Irene's description of the picture confirmed his memory.

'How do you know that he's Uma's grandpa?'

'Dad, I can't go wrong; I've seen his picture in her room. She's so fond of him and has spoken so much about him. And, I know I shouldn't have done that, but I brought her to your studio and showed her the picture just for reconfirmation.'

'You did that?' The anger in Morgan's voice did not last more than a second. That confirmation meant a lot to him. It would be easy to get information from Uma's family about that person. 'And who's the other guy supported by him?'

'She doesn't have a clue.'

'Send that picture to me immediately.'

Before Irene could say anything, he hung up. His mind was reeling.

It was the other tall man being supported by Uma's grandfather who had tormented Morgan in the past. He closely resembled Al Zawaidi, ranked ninth in the erstwhile al-Qaeda hierarchy. He was confirmed dead in the September 2007 drone attacks near the Waziristan border. To be able to know about a possible link with such a dangerous terrorist was at once a thrill and a cause for concern for Morgan. Concern because connections between an Islamic jihadist and an elderly Hindu was absolutely unimaginable and clearly indicated the extent of the terrorist network.

Irene sighed in relief. Seeing his reaction to Uma's visit to his studio, she felt she did the right thing by hiding the fact that she allowed Uma to take a snapshot of that picture on the screen before shutting down her dad's projector and system. Uma had to tell her family about it, obviously. They didn't have any news of her granddad since 9/11 and they had conceded to the theory of 'presumed dead' in the mishap.

Morgan tried to recollect whatever Saravanan, Uma's father, had told him about his family when he visited them for dinner last year.

'My Dad was a Maths lecturer in a college in the Southern Indian city of Madurai, where I was born. By then, my Dad already had a Post Graduate degree in Mathematics and was pursuing his Doctorate. We call that MPhil (Master of Philosophy) in our region. When my sister Saraswathi was born, he got an offer for teaching in a University in Addis Ababa, Ethiopia. He went there alone, leaving us in our mother's care. My mother was a housewife, devoted to her husband and to her children. After serving one contract of two years, he came back to India. He must have missed us so much and noticed how my mother had struggled to run the family alone, so he took all of us with him for his next contract.

'We spent all of our childhood and our youth in Africa – moving to Kenya, Uganda, Zimbabwe, and South Africa. I came to the States for my undergrad in Engineering and settled here. My sister followed me a few years later to do her doctorate in Sociology. Within two years after bringing my parents to the USA, my mother passed away. From then on, my father alternated between living with my family and my sister's family. He would go on 'pilgrimages' for months at a time to several places.

'He was much closer with my daughter Uma and nephew Innocent. Both were of almost the same age. My son Yuvan and my niece Lucky were too young to remember their days with granddad. They were very attached to him when he was with them.'

'Both Innocent and Yuvan want to be astronauts transporting people to a new planet – worlds that humans may find habitable!

'This is our family story.'

Shamino Nakura, Uma's mother, was teaching Dentistry at the same university where Uma and Irene studied. She spoke very few words and said that she owed her father-in-law a lot. Right from her marriage with Saravanan, the old man was supportive of their family's stability and prosperity, taking care of their children when both of them were busy advancing their careers.

Morgan remembered how he began to trust that family after learning about their history. He wanted someone to go and talk to Uma's family about her grandfather. He did not want to involve his office at that stage as that might alert the family.

He remembered David saying that he would have to visit New York and Washington DC to show Emily around and to attend a certain women's meet on Lacene's behalf. 'He must still be in the East Coast.'

'Yes, Morgan, I can meet the person you are talking about. You say she is the granddaughter of a victim in the 9/11 attacks? This place is a bit noisy. Let me get out.' David was at the Smithsonian.

Morgan briefly told David Levite about Irene, Uma, her grandfather, and the picture at the scene of the 9/11 attacks and the need to trace the background of this old man. David asked Morgan to send an email with all details. He would rather stay back in the east, complete all his work and tours, and then head back to Lawrence.

Lacene and George received further damaging evidence from Morgan that Stuart had sent him. It was about the diary. Sadhá had written more than five paragraphs across different pages, giving vivid details of his interactions with Mullah Omar Abdullah, the most wanted terrorist. When Lacene told Morgan that she had already read them and could not infer anything in them that could be construed as conspiracy against any nation, he countered by saying that they were clear evidence of collusion with enemies of the US.

Lacene blurted out to George, 'He is so incorrigible! How can he misinterpret such interactions?'

George pacified her. 'We must understand Lacene, that when the average American mind is beset with 'terror-phobia' you can't expect any better from its sleuths!'

David and Emily were picked up from DC by one of Morgan's contacts and dropped off at Morgan's Edison residence. Irene was accommodative and arranged for a meeting at her friend Uma's house. David read Morgan's email about Uma's grandfather, but the attachment picture he had sent did not open.

Emily was excited when Uma took her to their drawing room, which had a huge orrery. She almost fainted when Uma's brother Yuvan switched off the light and projected it onto the dome of the room! She had never experienced one in her life and had learnt about an orrery only the previous day at the Smithsonian.

Discussions with Saravanan went smoothly for David. He could see a typical Asian family keen to be in the race to experience the American dream. His Japanese wife, Shamino Nakura, was a very pleasing person and spoke a few words only.

At Morgan's behest and with permission from Saravanan, David recorded all conversations with Uma's family members.

Narrating briefly to the family the circumstance in which he was involved in this mission, David said that Morgan wanted him to meet Saravanan's sister Saraswathi as well. Since David was planning to spend a few days in DC, he wanted to meet her there.

'My daughter Lacene wanted me to attend the annual conference of the National Organisation for Women, due to take place the day after. I would like to meet your sister while in DC.' said David.

'Sure! You will see her at the conference. And I will arrange for a meeting with her soon after that.' Saravanan spoke to Saraswathi in Tamil in the presence of David and gave him her contact details.

That was when Shamino brought out their family photo album to show their family members to David.

———◆•◆•◆———

The pundit lectured at length about the beliefs and policies of ISKCON – the International Society for Krishna Consciousness. Founded in 1965 in New York City by Bhaktivedanta Swami Prabhupada, its core beliefs were based on millennia-old Vaishnavite holy scriptures like the *Sreemad Bhāgavatam* and the *Bhagavad-Geetha*. Following the Gaudiya Vaishnava tradition, this sect believed that Lord Krsna (Krishna) was the Supreme God and that he manifested himself as various avatars, as described in *Sreemad Bhágavatam*.

Arthur interrupted at that stage, with permission from the Pathan. All the clerics noticed that after Arthur's long talk from the previous day, the Pathan had become quite lenient towards him.

'The *Sreemad Bhágavatam* is a forerunner to the theory of evolution,' Arthur contended. Everyone looked at him with disbelief and disapproval. The pastor asked, 'When the theory of evolution totally contradicts the religious scriptures and questions creation, how can someone claim that the scripture was a prelude to this scientific theory of evolution? Let us hear from the pundit.'

The pundit set about explaining the concept of *Dasávatár*, the ten incarnations of Lord Vishnu, as narrated in *Sreemad Bhágavatam*. ISKCON believed that those incarnations were all of Lord Krsna.

Sreemad Bhágavatam talked of regular visits by the Lord (Vishnu or Krsna) as an avatar in every Yuga/era, to establish 'righteousness, peace, and order' – better put in one word as 'dharma'.

'Sambhavámi Yugey, Yugey' is a popular quote from the *Bhagavad-Geetha* meaning, 'Era after era, I will be present to establish righteousness'.

Arthur intervened again. The pundit rose to object to the intervention, but the Pathan signalled Arthur to go ahead.

'Will it not be interesting to hear from a non-believer rather than from a staunch believer like you, pundit?' The Pathan laughed aloud. Along with the pundit, Arthur narrated the ten incarnations of Lord Vishnu, underlining the similarities with the theory of evolution.

David jumped out of his seat as he saw the pictures. To his shock and disbelief, David recognised in an instant that Uma's grandfather was indeed the Kansas temple Hindu priest Sadhá!

David could not help repeating the words, 'Small world this, indeed!' He also realised that thus far in his discussions with the family, he had never asked for the name of Saravanan's father. They had only mentioned him as 'appa' whenever they spoke of him.

It was David's turn then to tell Saravanan's family the whole sequence of events from Lacene's first meeting with Sadhá, and the fact that he could well be alive.

David briefed Morgan about the meeting while returning with Irene and Emily. Irene was behind the wheel. When he called, Morgan was on his way to meet the police official to find out more about Omar Sherfuddin, the travel agent suspected of having been seen on the day the clerics were abducted.

'What? Is that so? Are you sure? He is the same . . . Saddam? Jesus! Oh, okay, you will also meet his daughter? Good. Please get as much information as you can. Good luck. Will talk to you later, bye.' The revelation about Saddam excited him so much that he wanted to share it with Lacene immediately. Lacene and George were not answering their phones though. Morgan was getting tensed at their silence.

———————————

When he ultimately told them about Saddam over the phone and his presence at Ground Zero with a terrorist, Lacene could not control herself. She simply kept saying, 'No, something is wrong somewhere.'

George could read her mind.

'Never mind, La. Like you always say, 'truth alone triumphs'. I strongly believe in that. Just don't worry. We must also not rule out the possibility that people do change over time – for better or for worse. Nobody can ever predict that correctly. Don't you remember Lee Iacocca's book and his wise words on changes in people's behaviour?'

Arthur interrupted the pundits' explanation of the ten avatárs of Lord Krsna, giving its significance in the evolution of human beings.

1. Matsaya avatár: Fish – Earth began as a water world; fish dominated.
2. Kórma avatár: Tortoise – Land emerged; amphibians evolved.
3. Varhágh avatar: Warthog – Marshland creatures evolved. 'The term 'warthog' emanated from the word Varhaagh,' said Arthur.
4. Narasimha avatár: Man + Lion – Humans evolved from animals.
5. Vámana (dwarf) avatár: First humans were like pygmies, from central Africa closely affirming the 'Afro-centrist' theory.
6. Parasuráma avatár: An uncivilised but talented human being.
7. Ráma avatár: An almost perfect human.
8. Balráma avatár: Powerful wrestler and intelligent ruler.
9. Krishna avatár: The most intelligent and an exemplary human.
10. Kalki avatár: The avatar yet to happen.
    'Kal ki' literally means 'of or for the future' said Arthur.

While these are the ten avatárs of Lord Vishnu (or Krsna), these clearly depict the various stages of evolution of the single cellular life forms into multicellular forms and finally into humans.

'Sadhá was so full of love for every creature on earth and even beyond, G. He pointed out that element in you after the only meeting he had with you. He told me, "Do not let go of this man, just be with him forever". He said that you are one of those few rare beings that practice love as a penance or habit. Don't you remember that couplet by Bárathiár about love which is so dear to me, G?'

'The "do penance" one? I remember the English version. Recite the Tamil one for me, I love that rhythm.'

Lacene recited both the versions, like she used to do in her regular meditation sessions. Her recitation was like a lullaby to him.

'Seiga thavam, seiga thavam, nenjey, thavam seidhál,

Eidha virúmdhiyadhai eidhalám – mei, ulagil,

Anbir cirandha thavam illai; anbúdaiyár

Inbúttru vázhdhal iyalbú'

Lacene always told George that 'penance' was nowhere close to expressing the full meaning of 'thavam'. Penance has a punishment element to it. Practice would be a better word, she had told George.

She preferred to replace

Do penance, do penance, O mind! If you do that penance . . .

with

Practice it, practice it, O mind! If you practice it regularly . . .

'Practice it, practice it, O mind! If you practice it regularly
You can achieve everything that you want to; true, in this world,
There's no better practice than LOVE; and for those practicing love
Living happily is just but natural!'

A practitioner of love, could Sadhá have embraced hatred?

———•:•◆•:•———

While with Lacene, Morgan feigned genuine interest in understanding the traitor whose name he spelt as 'Saddam'. After poring over the book, Lacene managed to get a page where Sadhá had narrated his 9/11 experience. It was in one of the pages that was hidden inside a fold and had to be split open. She called Morgan and without revealing that she had read it from a concealed page, told him in brief.

'Sadhá had jumped together with an injured Arab man from Floor 14 of Tower 1 using a fire hose till half way and had helped him out of the building before it fully collapsed. They straddled to the Arab's car parked in Baker Street. Sadhá shouldered the severely injured, large man to the car. He thanked Sadhá and after giving his address, fainted. Sadhá drove to that man's apartment in Baltimore and literally carried him to his room from the car.

'He also treated him for a fracture to his left fibula, besides attending to several bruises, and nursed him all night. When that man woke up at midnight, he was very happy to watch the breaking news on TV and was shouting in joy in Arabic. He thanked Sadhá profusely for saving him. Then he talked to someone over his mobile and urged that person to meet him immediately. Kabir came within an hour.'

'They both argued for a long time in Arabic. Sadhá understood that the Arab had asked Kabir to arrange a passport for him. After taking a few pictures of Sadhá, Kabir returned the next morning with a Saudi passport for him. "I made up my mind on what I should do".'

'Two days later, we took one of the special flights arranged for many Arabs to return home to evade probable reprisal attacks following 9/11. At the airport, a thorough check was conducted on about forty passengers only; all others were just checked for their ID and documents and were hardly asked any further questions.

'Sadhá was still helping the Arab with the crutches – which were thoroughly checked by security officials – and was allowed to pass security without any problem. Sadhá adorned Arabic robes with the 'keffiyeh' head cover.'

Morgan said, 'Amazing but quite possible! Although elaborate checks were made on the individuals who left the US on 9/13, I know that it wasn't thorough enough. So where did he go from there? Did he join them? Why did he go to the twin towers in the first place?'

'I have to read that, do not know where those details are written, it is in bits and pieces; I have to go through it fully.'

'Please do so, I am anxious. I need to know if he ever became part of their organisation. That is important for my mission,' said Morgan. 'Although I am sure he became one of them,' he said to himself.

'Let me read through,' replied Lacene.

Morgan wanted to move out so he could talk to Stuart in private. Lacene and George were glad when he excused himself.

'Looks like there are pages we didn't copy from that damned diary, Stuart! I do not know how many pages we have lost like that.'

'Can't we get that book from Lacene again?'

'I doubt it, unless we get it our own way. There are other contenders for it. Perhaps we may trade blames on them and pinch it from her.'

'Let's see how important that would be. Jaques has discovered a lot, and I need time to read. Wait 'til tonight. I'll send you a lot of material.'

'Sure. Good.'

The pundit objected to most of what Arthur had mentioned.

Pastor Biden was quick to point out that, while the theory of evolution was being contested by religions, there was truth in the theory, and he applauded the way that it was propagated subtly in the Hindu scriptures.

The bikku seconded him and said that he had never looked at it in this manner, although he had learned about the ten avatars of Lord Vishnu.

The pundit corrected him. 'Lord Krsna, please!'

The Pathan intervened to give his verdict. 'I learned that most of the Hindu scriptures tried to teach science through God and religion since most people – especially the illiterate majority – needed some form of divine intervention to understand and accept the laws of nature. Since Hindu scriptures also preach monotheism but allow for the practice of polytheism, it is quite possible that they all will one day embrace monotheism and convert to Islam.'

Arthur said, 'When you say that illiterate people needed some form of divine intervention to believe science, don't you agree that Islam's belief in the Angel Gabriel, Christian belief in the Virgin Mary, and the Resurrection of Jesus were all stories concocted just to legitimise their scriptures?' The Pathan looked at the clerics for answers. When none opened his mouth, Arthur thundered, 'Should I consider your silence as acceptance?'

'Sadhá had arranged for a gathering of members of a Tamil club in Tower 1 to commemorate the eightieth death anniversary of the poet Bhárathiár on 9/11. This was exactly a year after I last met him. One of the club members had booked a mini-conference hall in Floor 42. The meeting was scheduled for 4 p.m. but Sadhá had gone there in the morning to make preparations for the meet. No mention about the participants. You can find out,' said Lacene to Morgan.

'Will do that. Tell me something about this poet Bhárathiár and his fans – was he a Hindu radical?' asked Morgan.

'Not at all; rather, he was a freedom fighter and social reformer. His fans could only be patriots, not fanatics. Sadhá also has never exhibited any such radical qualities. He has always cared about the welfare of the entire human race and he had never shown discrimination against any particular race or religion or country or even class of people.'

'Well then, what was that Arab doing there at that time?'

'Only a brief mention about that. Sadhá had later learned that the Arab was there to place a signal, an indicator at the appropriate floor for the hijacked plane to hit the tower at the right level!'

'Jesus! So he was there to ensure that the tower crumbled! A few floors lower or higher might have had a different result! Osama's plan was executed to perfection, and these bastards had gone to any extent to accomplish that!' exclaimed Morgan. 'We have to establish whether Sadhaa had any prior links with them.

'We should also look at Sadhá's history – including the times he had interacted with you – and look for possible links with terrorist groups. He could have used this poet's anniversary as a ploy to have access to the towers! I must arrange for studying his past.'

'Incorrigibles, the intelligentsia,' Lacene felt.

Morgan left them with his mind frantically wondering how best to learn more about this Hindu Saddam and uncover links he might have established within the United States.

———————◆◆◆———————

The imam retorted, 'We don't have to answer such meaningless suggestions from an atheist like you! We believe what we believe and we do not require your approval!'

Arthur continued as though he didn't hear that comment. 'There are many other faiths to be discussed! We know that among those faiths, more heinous crimes were committed in the name of religion. Even today, racial, territorial, and language-based reasons together are far outnumbered by religious-based reasons in fostering hatred.'

The Pathan intervened, 'Are you saying Mr None, therefore, that religions ended up being the major cause of hatred and enmity in human history? That, they all claim hypocritically to propagate love and harmony, but in reality they only groomed hatred; is that what you say? May be you are right. Islam faced one of the worst assaults against it when it was still in its nascent stage.'

Arthur said, 'But everyone continued to believe that his way was the right way. Everybody wanted a "new order"– "my order"!

———◆———

'Our prophet (PbuH) never claimed that. He looked up to Allah as the one and only Almighty,' the Pathan noted. 'But of the rest, it was first Krishna and much later Jesus, who claimed almost in typical fashion, although under varying circumstances, "I am the way".

'So the onus is on you clerics to prove that Arthur is wrong. We will continue the debate tomorrow.'

The group decided to call it a day when the Pathan rose to leave. None was happy because the Pathan did not say a word about what was in store for them and what response his group had received from the UN.

No one dared to ask him, though.

———◆———

David could not keep up with Emily. She was full of energy and enthusiasm and had gone missing several times in the museum during that one day. She spent hours looking at and learning about the various crafts that travel on land, water, and air.

But David had coaxed her into sitting with him for more than two hours in a conference hall at 7 p.m.

'I am displaying Lacene's posters at this meet. Lacene wanted us to record the proceedings and relay them to her later. She was to have attended this conference, as you may know. So you should stay with me through this particular presentation.' Emily nodded.

Lacene's posters highlighted the issue of female infanticide in parts of rural India. She was keen to listen to Saraswathi's talk at the conference that evening. As a life-member of this women's group, Lacene had informed the organisers about David and Emily representing her.

David noticed and pointed out to Emily the arrival of a number of celebrities at the conference. A few of his female colleagues at Kansas University greeted him from afar.

David realised that the audience was eager to hear Saraswathi's speech. He wondered what would be so special in her paper. Unlike other presentations that took place simultaneously in different halls, her paper was slotted for a separate time, lasting an hour.

———————◦•◦◆◦•◦———————

As they entered the South Indian restaurant, Morgan received a message on Whatsapp, containing a link to an online article, from Stuart. He switched his phone off. He would read it later.

Their dinner at the restaurant lasted 'til midnight. At Abdul's behest, they had 'Fenny' for their drink. A popular drink from Goa and the Konkan coast, made from pure cashew fruits, it was rarely served in other parts of India and had become the 'trademark' drink of Goa.

Before Abdul could explain his choice of restaurant, Omar told the others, 'Naturally, Madrásis like to eat here; it is run by a Madrási. I love their fish curry!'

'Who is a Madrási?' asked Morgan, for the sake of being part of the conversation, although his mind was elsewhere.

Lacene asked, 'Madrási! Ya, what does that mean?' Pretending to ask that question, she looked at George meaningfully as they both signalled their understanding of the term.

Omar said, 'Oh, yes, you can't know that. A Madrási is from Madras, the capital of south India.'

Abdul said, 'C'mon, that's an old way to mark South Indians, Omar.'

Omar said, 'I must explain to the lady why you're called a Madrási.'

Omar wasn't smart enough to hide his soft demeanour whenever he addressed Lacene. Nor could he keep his roving eyes off her. George was bemused; Morgan didn't like that; Abdul was embarrassed!

While they were talking, Lacene recalled what she understood from the pages of the diary wherein Sadhá had narrated his first day with the al-Qaeda and Taleban chiefs.

News must have reached the top brass of the al-Qaeda and Taleban about this stranger brought in by Al Zawaidi, to the disapproval of many in the hierarchy.

Zawaidi had cleared the apprehensions of Omar Abdullah and Osama bin Laden on this stranger who had saved his life and had nurtured him back to good health, staying close by him for three months after 9/11. So when I was first introduced to all the four big men at their hideout in the Hindu Kush Mountains, our escort, Zawaidi's senior, named me a 'Madrási'. Omar was excited. 'Madrási? Is he a mullah or imam? Which madrasáh does he operate?'

'He is a Hindu, Omar,' Osama quietly answered him, 'and he is from South India. Madras is the largest city in South India, and during the British Raj, it was one of the three top cities through which they ruled the whole of India until they took over Delhi. So all south Indians were called "Madrásis" by the rest of India.'

'What? You are allowing a Hindu infidel to come so close to our fortress? He should be immediately sent out of our boundaries and never be seen again. I wouldn't be sad if he is beheaded. Well, a visitor and someone who helped our men need not be treated like that, but that doesn't mean he should be allowed so close to us all.'

Sensing that he was only half-serious about what he said, I politely told the audience, 'Some 400 years ago, when the British ship landed on the shores of what is now called Chennai, it was a small hamlet. Finding its shores most suitable for building a harbour, they decided to settle there. The first thing they heard on setting foot on its shores was the call for "namás" from far away, reaching their ears against the sound of the waves. When asked, the local fisherman told them that it was from a "madrasáh". And that is how they decided to call the place "madras" in their own style. That madrasáh is still in operation there. The whole world knows that city as Madras. Only recently did the local authorities revert to the old name Chennai. It was the capital of the whole of South India until 1950 or so. And that is how we South Indians came to be known as 'Madrásis'.'

'So a prominent south Indian city was named after a madrasáh? Very good!' said Osama.

'Do you know that our Indian Muslim brothers have always had a cordial relationship with the local populace there? Madrásis are much liked for their compassion towards outsiders – irrespective of their colour, race, language, or religion.'

Zawaidi had added this to change the course of Omar's thinking.

'And this man here, what a man he is! He knows so much about the world, so much about all religions, so much about nature cure, and what's more, he doesn't like the Zionists or the Americans at all! Not one per cent!' effused Imam Naseer, Zawaidi's mentor.

That settled it. I was given a ten-minute audience that evening and a permanent place in their hearts soon after that.

Both Lacene and George were pretty sure that Morgan would not have learned about that passage in the book from his team at the embassy, as that page was among the folded ones that needed to be slit open.

———◆◆◆———

Morgan enjoyed the fenny and the food. Abdul was hoping that his plan of offering fenny would work well in his favour. Morgan wouldn't be awake when meeting Lacene the next morning.

Morgan loved those south Indian dishes, mildly spiced to his palatable levels. So did the couple. For them those were familiar dishes.

Lacene wanted to go to bed early so that she could get up early and chat with her father and Emily after their return from the women's conference at the Smithsonian. She also remembered her planned meeting with Abdul in their room the next morning.

As Morgan appreciated the quality of the spicy fish curry, Omar narrated how Indian spices had essentially shaped the world, with Abdul aiding him intermittently.

Omar said that had it not been for the highly sought after Indian spices by almost all in Europe – *who were not happy paying a huge price to Middle Eastern traders* – the circuitous sea routes, would not have been ventured into. There was competition and rivalry among the European nations at that time for control over the seas, simply because they wanted direct access to these spices and to south India.

Their efforts enabled the discovery of the Americas, the West Indies, Australasia, and sub-Saharan Africa. The entire world as it is known today evolved into its present shape more due to Indian spices than any other single factor.

'Spicy world, this!' Omar said gleefully.

The three guests could easily gather that Omar had learned from Abdul this aspect of world history. It was quite an interesting argument for the trio, although they were quick to point out that Indians had a tendency to claim copyright over almost everything on earth.

Morgan was outright in saying that.

But mulling over what they heard from Omar and Abdul, they couldn't help admitting and admiring that Indian spices played a pivotal role in shaping the world.

Abdul had some more points to reiterate those views. Besides giving the world the number 'zero', India also gave it spiritualism and yoga. South India having been – and still continuing to be – the major source for such speciality spices, has had the lion's share in shaping the world.

No wonder that an eminent thinker like Mark Twain declared 'India is the cradle of humanity'. Then George put it succinctly, 'Well, that is all past glory. Where does India stand now in the global rankings?'

'That's too difficult to answer. Perhaps it is at its nadir, I would prefer to say' Abdul said in a low tone.

When they all retired to their rooms that night, George admired the fact that the two young Muslim men had won the confidence of the visitors, especially that of Morgan.

Reaching his suite, Morgan turned his phone to read Stuart's earlier message. Fortunately there were no missed calls.

> A damaged mosque in riot-hit Meiktila, central Myanmar, was visited by the local member of the national assembly this morning. He vehemently condemned such attacks on minorities and promised stern action on the perpetrators. Attacks against Muslims – who make up an estimated 4 per cent of Myanmar's population – have exposed deep fractures in the Buddhist-majority nation and cast a shadow over its emergence from army rule.
>
> While no one claimed responsibility for the attacks and damage to the mosque, some of the victims said that the attackers were wearing T-shirts with the Buddha's picture printed as a logo.

'This mosque is one among the sites in the list' Stuart had commented in his message.

———◆◆◆———

7. Eve's Rib

How can empathy prevail in those who eat,
To fatten their own, other creature's meat?

Six days in that godforsaken land was sufficient for the eight men to do some research. After debates and arguments, they came to the following conclusions.

- There is probably an airstrip just on the other side of the river or on the other side of the hill
- There must be a way for bringing all of them up to the cave; Crossing the river or coming around the hill carrying them up even one by one would not have been not easy
- The guard is in communication with the outside world; he also must have a storage facility for food
- He had changed his attire more than once; he may not be alone; it's a mystery why no other member of his group was seen
- There must be greater demands from the terrorist group in exchange for the release of all or some of them; the Pathan's silence on that was giving them a scare.

Their location yet unclear, they wondered which countries were talking with the terrorists and whether the UN was involved.

And, the most agonising question in all their minds was:

'How long are we destined to be here?'

Arthur said that he would ask the Pathan about their release and the demands set by his group; others agreed. There was certainly a softer side from this guard towards Arthur, and they decided to make good use of it. That morning seemed to be bright for them somehow.

There was a sudden buzz of activity at the top of the hill and everyone's eyes looked up. What they saw was an once-in-a-lifetime opportunity to witness a real hunting game! They saw a mountain yak being chased by a large cat! It wasn't clear what kind of a cat it was, though.

The pundit, of all the people there, identified it as a snow leopard.

For a moment, the two animals disappeared over the other side of the hill, only to reappear seconds later, the yak followed by the leopard. Twice the leopard reached close enough to scratch the yak's back but could not bring it down. Then sudden death befell the poor yak from another source.

What looked like a piece of stone, flung from out of nowhere, struck the yak on its forehead. The blow didn't kill the yak instantly, but it did shock and fell the yak before it gathered itself and began running again. That was enough for the leopard to gain ground as it lopped over it. Its sharp claws pierced through the yak's skin deep enough to cause serious damage and pain. The yak fell to the ground and as the leopard sank its teeth into the yak's throat, it breathed its last.

Only after seeing its fall, did all eight pairs of eyes turn to look for the direction the stone came from. The Pathan was already nearing the scene of the kill. While the spectators feared what might occur between the Pathan and the leopard, the man and the animal did not seem bothered by each other's presence at the kill.

The leopard released its grip on the throat to regain its breath and regularise its heartbeat. The Pathan slowly pulled the stone out, which was lodged in the yak's forehead as it had a sharp end. He then used what looked like a long, sharp sword to severe the yak's head with a quick slash of the blade. The leopard watched without any protest. Soon, the spectators realised that the beast and the man had an understanding of what they would do in such a circumstance!

The mastiff was barking with glee.

The Pathan looked at the men below as if expecting them to come to his help, but did not seem to call them. They were hesitant to move any closer to the leopard. The Pathan started slicing parts of the kill and removed the guts. The leopard, moving aside with the Yak's head as if to give clear room for the Pathan, slowly started enjoying its meal. Their cooperation was a sight to watch for the observers as the mastiff waited patiently, tongue and tail wagging.

⸺⸺◆⸺⸺

Thanking the audience for the warm reception and observing protocol, Saraswathi Wafula forthright plunged into her topic.

> We all like to know where we come from, our origin – Ádhi. Each region and every religion has speculated about that. I say 'speculated' because no one has really probed deep enough into our origins to find the real source of 'us'. Most of our ancestors – whichever region they were from, migrants as we all are – did not conduct as many scientific probes as our current generation does. Their findings were always relying on one God or the other who they believed created all of us. And the few that did really touch upon the truth failed in establishing it as strongly as they might have wished to.

> This was because 'might has been right' all along. The winner not only 'takes' all; the winner 'changes' all; winners distort truths in the losers' culture in order to establish the winners' legacy and beliefs. History has at least taught us this. Truth was consistently brushed under the powerful carpets of the mighty.

> It took three centuries for Galileo to feel vindicated when only two decades ago, the pontiff was kind enough to 'pardon him and accept his view on heliocentrism'. But the pontiff was not

kind enough to apologise on behalf of his predecessors to Galileo or to the thousands of victims burnt at the stakes or banished and excommunicated in the past for various unfair reasons.

In 2009, one and a half centuries later – there was a half-hearted and partial acceptance by the Vatican of Darwin's theory of evolution. Most other religions are yet to do so.

We do not know how long it is going to take for other such scientifically recognised facts to be approved by various religious leaders. We do not know how long they want to keep the 'weak minds' in the dark and subject them to accept their 'unproven but miraculously and divinely established' beliefs. Besides the Vatican, there are other religious bodies and leaders who are yet to turn a kind eye towards science.

Horrendous crimes have taken place throughout the history of this world in the name of religion. Quite unashamedly, the preachers of these religions have not had the humility to own responsibility for such horrendous acts and the honesty to vow never to let such acts take place again. The worst part of it is that most of them have proudly flouted their bravery in defending their faith with their lives and blood. Killing in the name of religion has never been a sin. Will it ever be?

We cannot estimate how many more innocent lives will be lost and put into everlasting suffering thanks to their vociferous opposition to science that contradicts their scriptural knowledge.

Almost all regions had been matriarchal, egalitarian societies over a long period in time of human history. They gradually changed into patriarchal ones. The Judeo-Christian tradition has only talked about patriarchal societies. A few examples of matrifocal incidents have been cited in their scriptures as exceptions that proved the law.

Biologists notice increasing occurrences of asexual births in other species. Although they discredit the possibility of such asexual conception and childbirth among humans, I have reasons to propound the theory that parthenogenesis had occurred in humans.

Societies in most regions were egalitarian when we were all hunter-gatherers. The concept of fatherhood and a patriarchal system came to be from 4000 BCE, according to research scholars. The advent of farming, agriculture, and settlements in waterbeds saw the beginning of patriarchal system in humans.

Sarah Grinke, of the nineteenth century, and Elizabeth Cady Stanton of the twentieth, spoke of an egalitarian society ruled by female leaders. The latter published a 'women's bible' with feminists' reading of the Testaments.

Genia Pauli Haddon wrote about the first woman 'Lilith', created before Adam, who was deliberately sidelined by Rabbanical versions of the Torah. She simply said 'you are she' to denote woman's presence in everyone. The Hindu Supreme Goddess Kàli is also called 'Lalitha'.

The patriarchal society conveniently ignored and continues to ignore their words. Unfortunately, even the feminists haven't fought hard, or well enough to establish those theories.

More feminists followed, but their voices have been muted by the vociferous patriarchal controllers of societies all over the world. D. D. Meyers wrote how women are better at the helm of affairs and how men would never want to give up their ruling positions. In most societies, we all know how women are suppressed and suffer silently.

If women were at the helm of affairs, they would certainly deal with burning issues in the same manner that Antoinette Tuff handled an identical situation as faced by George Zimmerman, who dealt with it as most men would.

The audience responded with thunderous applause.

Barbara Love and Elizabeth Shanklin wrote in their book '*The Answer is Matriarchy*', that it meant a society in which women define motherhood, determine the conditions of motherhood and also the conditions in which the next generation is reared.

No one paid any heed. Patriarchs wouldn't be happy to. But what are we doing, as members of NWO? *Own* our responsibilities?

Abortion is an issue to be entirely discussed and decided by women. Men can have their input but when it comes to deciding about a life, it's only women who should put their heads together. Women may have a voice in the United States of America, but mind you ladies, it is still not strong enough; nor is it good enough to support the entire female population of this world to stand their ground and be heard.

We begot them; we created them from our own selves and now they are ruling over us. We seem to have fallen too much of a prey to their all too important and fascinating reproductive organ that we primarily caused to evolve for our own betterment, to the sad result that we have let ourselves controlled by that very same tool. The simple reason is that we forgot that we can reproduce *without* them. Or we think so.

In the beginning, there were only women; we created the men out of us. We wanted someone to share our most precarious act of labour and childbirth. It was a simple process in the division of labour, in fact. When the first male came into being, we desired for more of him, as we wanted to ease our burden. Besides impregnating us, he would fend for us; that was why we created him. Then we wanted more and more of his kind because every woman wanted a partner of her own. They grew in numbers; initially, when they were fewer, they mated with many women. Then the ratio dwindled; they had to contend with fewer and fewer women to mate with.

Ultimately it became just one to one. But their testosterone levels did not proportionately dwindle in the evolutionary process of 'necessity causing a change'. They are coming down but not as fast as they should. This is the crux of our society's problem now.

We have men with more libido and polygamist DNA imprints but the present society is restricting them to stay with one partner. A solution is required for this. Immediately.

Religions have not found solutions to *this* problem. They set codes for regulated sexual behaviour, but all these are ultimately in favour of men. Yoga and meditation, those two very powerful and effective preventive treatments to this crucial problem, were designed by the wise old sages of India to combat this menace in particular.

Mind you, dear ladies. We describe sex-hungry people as animals and brutes. We name sex and lust as animal instincts. To be fair to those nobler creatures, we must admit that it is a unique human trait. Most animals have sex for the sake of procreation only. There are a very few cases to the contrary among animals. It is only *we*, human beings – both men and women – who indulge in excessive sexual activities for purposes other than procreation – sheer pleasure.

As long as we were quadrupeds, we behaved reasonably fairly in that aspect, perhaps. But from the time we became Homo-erectus and walked on twos, gravity has played a major role in trickling down the secretions from the relevant glands of our sexual hormones. The pineal and pituitary glands have become more active because of the earth's direct pull, I presume!

If we carefully analyse the science of yoga practices, we can realise the logic in its lessons to successfully defy gravity and to retract and regulate our sexual desires through controlled performances of our body glands.

Remember dear ladies. Men are designed to be fertile over a long period in their lives because initially they were fewer in numbers and we were dependent on those few for most of us to reproduce. We also insisted on getting more and more of the male progenies in order to mitigate our dependency on fewer men.

The yearning for a male offspring is so imprinted in our DNAs that it has not still been fully erased although we have enough – more than enough – of them. We have opened a can of worms that we ourselves are not able to control. Because they had so many partners then, they expect to have as many or at least more than one now. The best option for them would be to change their own desire levels, to learn to control their sexual urges. In my language, they say, 'tighten your loin cloth'. ('Langodai irukkik kattu').

In the early eighties, a team of anthropologists discovered the remains of an African woman in East-Central Africa whom they later named 'Eva'. That was the oldest human fossil ever found 'til then. They dated it to being more than 100,000 years old. As it always happens to such findings, believers in the so-called 'holy scriptures' rejected that idea outright, stating that it contradicted beliefs as laid out in their sacred scriptures. As powerful as it may seem, science indeed is certainly not mightier than those scriptures, unfortunately.

As described by the scientists, this 'Eva' had broad shoulders and 'should have been a gigantic, ferocious, black woman'. Mitochondrial Eve refers to the matrilineal most recent common ancestor (MRCA) of all currently living anatomically modern humans,

Several such discoveries have since taken place. Archaeologists, paleoanthropologists, geneticists, geologists, and other specialist scientists have brought their knowledge and hard works together to unravel the mysteries of our past. They belong to various nations, races, religions, languages, and cultures but they shredded their age-old beliefs to discover just one thing. The truth.

But the mighty leaders of those religions, the controllers of the minds of the majority of our population, do not want their powers diminished or their hold on the weaker minds to be challenged by the findings of these scientists who they brand as 'atheists', or 'a team of people bent upon misleading humanity'.

Most of you know that in the so-called 'pagan' religions, many believed in goddesses. Hinduism has many sects that revere goddesses. Yes, for one particular Hindu sect, the Supreme God is Goddess Kàli or Lalitha or Durgha or Sakthi. Briefly named 'Saktham' sect, this group is prevalent in eastern India extending to Nepal, Bangladesh, Myanmar, and Thailand. Such a belief in a female Supreme deity is not uncommon in other parts of India too.

With the revelation of so many facts about human migration from central Africa – where we all originated – we now know that we filled the earth from this first mother Eva or Kali. This particular sect in eastern India has not forgotten our true first mother, who must have been really a 'gigantic, ferocious' woman who was the mother of all our forefathers – rather, foremothers. They have remembered her from times immemorial till today and have aptly named her 'pure, black lady'. All the images and idols depicting her are in black.

Yes, the very name 'Kàli' means a 'black, pure woman'. We can wonder how in a country of mixed skin colours –where 'fair' skin was, and still is, respected as from a superior class – they came to revere a 'black woman' as their Supreme Goddess. But that is precisely how they remember her and worship her. She's appropriately named 'Ádhi Pará Sakthi' meaning, 'original, unequalled, force beyond us'.

Mind you – a force. Not a god or goddess.

Even some of the more popular Hindu male gods like Rama and Krishna have all along been portrayed as 'black or blue-skinned' avatars. Lord Vishnu, said to be in the centre of our Milky Way galaxy preserving our lives, is also depicted in black. I wouldn't be surprised if Lord Vishnu is a personification of the immense force at the centre of our milky way, the 'black hole' controlling the entire galaxy with its billions of stars. Lord Siva, the ultimate annihilator, has also been portrayed in dark colours! I am citing this just to highlight the fact that 'black' was our original colour.

While the first life emerged on this earth some four billion years ago, it took three billion years for multicellular, complex life to evolve. It has not been precisely assessed when the division of gender or sexual reproduction started. Asexual reproduction, in which the offspring was an exact genetic copy of the parent, a clone, was in vogue over a very long period in time. Also called agamogenesis, it was reproduction without the fusion of gametes.

Like how the multicellular organisms developed various organs to perform different functions that their bodies required for better longevity, at some stage they developed the sex organs for the process of conjugation to divide labour with different responsibilities.

Please remember that until then – until they started sexual reproduction – the parent developed an offspring within itself and delivered it through an organ that very much resembled the female vagina. When sexual reproduction first came into practice, the organ that was developed – rather evolved – to perform this function of 'transfer of genes or sperm' was the male reproductive organ, the penis. The vagina was already there; the penis came into being much later. Now tell me, who came first? Women or men?

Scientists have debated on this point: If the last person surviving is a man, can there be a chance of new life evolving from him? On the contrary, if only a woman survives as the last of the species, she has every chance to bring up a whole new population. She could then conceive on her own and then 'multiply'.

Many scientists have come up with answers to the question: 'Why do men have nipples?' All scriptures are silent about it. Perhaps they all know that raising that point or even commenting on it would stir up a hornet's nest. Science stops at saying that as an embryo, we could only notice that it is a female. As it grows, it develops all other limbs and we notice the development of the sex organ. At that stage, the nipples have already appeared.

I venture to assert that the genetic codes for the presence of nipples must have remained unchanged for the male offspring simply because the presence or absence of the nipples made no difference to the performances of what a male was specially meant to.

I have quoted from other studies as well; references are in my paper.

In a now-famous paper, Stephen Jay Gould and Richard C. Lewontin emphasize that we should not immediately assume that every trait has an adaptive explanation. The presence of nipples in male mammals is a genetic by-product of nipples in females. Men have nipples simply because females do.

The embryo follows a 'female template'. That is why nipples are present in both sexes. Nipples and breast tissue have no function as such except for protecting the heart and lungs from injury.

A certain level of the female hormone oestrogen is present in all men. Due to certain conditions affecting hormones, breast tissue in men can grow and men can produce milk. They could also get breast cancer!

All foetuses initially develop as females, the only prevailing sex hormone around. Hence the nipples. When the foetus' pituitary develops and estradiol converts to testosterone, then the male characteristics begin to show. Had there been no testosterone, the child would probably be a hermaphrodite.

The teats are left as they are in men because, should a need arise, the male may have to breastfeed too.

Men, who roam around with their bare chest and two nipples staring at us shamelessly but who consider women baring their breasts and nipples as obscene should remember that those nipples are the standing proof that men came from women.

Even if we have to accept the 'creation theory' as propagated by most religions, God – beg your pardon, Goddess – should have created a female first and from her, the male. There are still many species that produce without a male input. Humans should also have been capable of doing that until some stage in the evolutionary ladder.

Creation or evolution, or creation followed by evolution: Whatever the case, it was women first and men later. Much later, in fact! Would I then be wrong in concluding that, contrary to what the Holy Scriptures say, *Adam was made from Eve's rib*? Do we have the courage to rewrite the scriptures, ladies?

Please allow me to end here.

I request you to read my book *'Eve's rib'*. It has all the necessary research documents in place. Thank you for your patience.

A stunned and spellbound audience took a few seconds to come to terms with what it had heard. Then, as they slowly came to their senses, a lady in the front row put her palms together and rose, prompting the audience to give a standing ovation to Saraswathi Wafula as she took a bow and left the podium.

David Levite stood there motionless. Emily was shaking him vigorously trying to get him out of his trance.

She narrated his reaction to Lacene in an amusing manner over Skype a few hours later. 'It was like he had seen a ghost, Mom!'

The next morning Saraswathi called David on his mobile and invited him to her house for dinner the day after. Emily was delighted! She had learnt about Yuvan's cousins and was keen to meet them.

To Morgan, Abdul was certainly not from the breed of Taleban-like fanatics that Islam had somehow given rise to. Perhaps the likes of Abdul were the ones who would bring about the needful reformation within the Islamic world and make the radicals think like their peace-loving brothers.

In the same vein, Morgan could not trust Omar whose body language did not give him comfort. His years of experience at the Afghan and Pakistani warfronts had taught him to be mindful of such behaviour.

Omar seemed to be more like the wily informers he had encountered at the vicious borders between Pakistan and Afghanistan whose words and guidance could never be fully trusted. Many an American and NATO soldier had fallen prey to misleading information from those whom the NATO allies had to trust.

'Gadows', 'dowgas', 'wasdog' – Stuart told him that these terms had been used by a substantial number of bloggers and appeared on various religious forums online, according to Jacques. Morgan was still not sure as to how important the term was.

Jacques had been delving deeper and finding user data on some of the bloggers – especially Americans – in order to trace the history of any links between them and the holy sites. It was a mind-boggling exercise, requiring permission and help from federal authorities.

Morgan was doing his head in trying to decipher the term and had already roped in Lacene and George for their thoughts. The first reaction of all three was that 'wasdog' sounded like 'watchdog'. Lacene however suggested something very unique. She extracted an anagram 'saw god', a phrase George soundly recommended, But Morgan wasn't convinced.

Nevertheless, he passed on that view to Stuart immediately.

Morgan added to Lacene's dismay by bringing more revelations about Sadhaa's involvement with the terrorist outfits. Stuart had texted Morgan with disclosures from the diary, which clearly outlined how a number of second line leaders had been personally trained by Sadhaa on self-defence techniques and fitness regimens. Most of these young leaders had later assumed positions in Yemen, Iraq, Nigeria, Somalia, India and Syria, posing a dangerous threat to the Western world.

Morgan pointed out to Lacene that Sadhaa had unabashedly written down the names of leaders like Boko Haram's Momodu Bama aka Abu Saad, Irfan Moinuddin Attar, Zabiuddin Ansari, Abu Bakr al-Baghdadi, and many more. With the clues he had given her, Lacene hurriedly turned the pages of the diary. George and Lacene read those pages Morgan had mentioned that were written in Arabic. With a smug Morgan staring at them, Lacene shut the diary forcefully, distraught.

Back in their suite, Lacene and George watched with great interest the video that David had sent and agreed entirely with Saraswathi Wafula.

Lacene could easily relate to the Saktham sect that was popular in the eastern part of India, *historically named "Kàlinga" and 'Vangàl' (Bengàl) meaning "land of Kàli", she knew that Kàli was the Supreme Goddess* Ádhi Pará Sakthi. The male trinity gods under her are Brahma the creator, Vishnu the sustainer, and Siva the annihilator! **G**enerator, **O**rganiser, **D**estoyer – GOD!

"Bow out, gentlemen! Ladies *came* first!

Indeed, Adam was made from Eve's rib!"

With those words, Lacene showed George the way out, jokingly!

Back in his suite, Morgan found another message from Stuart. Another link to a news article. A column in a daily read,

> The latest casualty of the Syrian war: the minaret of the famed eleventh century Umayyad Mosque.
>
> The Ummayad Mosque, Allepo, Syria, built between the eighth and thirteenth centuries, is reputedly home to the remains of John the Baptist's father. It is located in Aleppo's Old City, a UNESCO World Heritage site. Heavy fighting during the Syrian civil war had ruined the holy site and toppled its minaret. The minaret collapsed amid fighting between government troops and Syrian rebels in Aleppo.
>
> Each side accused the other of being responsible for the damage. UNESCO director-general expressed distress over the destruction.

This is a disaster. In terms of heritage, this is the worst ever seen in Syria. Other videos posted online show the mosque, which is thought to date back to the seventh century, had been targeted in shelling for several days.

'It is not just stones that are destroyed but also religious and historic heritage cherished by the Syrian people,' said a resident.

International authorities including UNESCO have expressed concern that numerous sites in the country, including some classified as World Heritage sites, are being seriously damaged.

———◆•◆•◆———

8. Monogamous Rama

What is duly his, a man receives;
This law not even God can break;
My heart is not surprised, nor grieves;
For what is mine, no strangers take.

———————◆———————

Morgan was still in bed after their late night dinner and long sessions of communications with Irene, David, and Stuart.

The couple's morning meeting with Abdul lasted an hour. But neither of them noticed Abdul removing the transmitter from beneath the coffee table with the help of a tracking device even as he entered their room while Lacene went to call George.

Lacene asked, 'What made you look for us so specifically? Is it only the name Levite you found in my middle name? What do you know about the abduction of the clerics?'

Abdul said, 'The only reason is that our high command told us that you would most probably visit here looking for your uncle.'

The couple looked at each other signalling that Sadhá could have had something to do with the message from Abdul's 'high command'.

George asked, 'What is the intention of your group? Do you seek the release of any jihadists that are in Indian government custody?'

'I do not know. Our high command communicates directly with the UN or the nations.' Abdul replied, as he winked. 'Our group here works for peace. We are just the opposite of war. No violence.'

'How did you select these eight clerics?'

'Our high command decides, we only execute their command.'

Lacene then asked, 'How do you plan to take us to my uncle? What assurances can you give us that we also won't become hostages?'

'You have our word only. Our high command agrees to help you meet your uncle only because you have some vital information that comes from our hands!'

George asked, 'What is that?'

'The list, just that list. The long list of religious sites around the world. That's what we need,' said Abdul.

Lacene said, 'You could have forcefully taken that from us or even executed us. What makes you meet us and talk to us so kindly?'

'Like I said, we are the opposite of war, we want peace. Moreover, we do not know where you have kept that list. What's the use of harming you only to find that the list could not be obtained from your belongings?'

'Was it your men who tried to snatch Lacene's bag at the airport?'

George was blunt.

Abdul, taken aback, answered, 'Is that so? I have no idea. Maybe our high command tried to do that to avoid letting the issue get this far.'

The couple looked at each other again to convey their confirmation that they did not believe Abdul's reaction and words.

Abdul continued, 'Whatever it is, you somehow happen to be the only people to be accorded the special facility to visit the hostages. Morgan should not get a hint of what the background to this arrangement is.'

George asked, 'What is the link between your group and Mr Sadhá – Sadhá Sivam? Why should he send the list through us and ask you to collect it from us?'

'Sadhá, who? Haven't heard that name. I've no clue how the list fell into your hands. I was asked to contact you for it, that's all.'

His body language not showing any deceit, Lacene was gratified that Sadhá had nothing to do with any of these events. She even wondered if

Sadhá would be in trouble and whether he had given out George's name to this terrorist group under duress.

Abdul said, 'But if only you can give me that list now, I can reveal some more information to you.'

George said, 'How can you expect us to do that? What if you disappear after getting the list? You may even plan our execution!'

Lacene said, 'Give him a chance, G! What can you tell us Abdul?'

'I can tell you more about our group. What we are up to and why we need that list now. You have to trust me. You must appreciate that we took efforts to meet you and make your job easier. Or else, you would be wondering how to go about looking for your uncle.'

George looked at Lacene. 'True. Well, we do agree that you need us, and we need you. But why do you need it now? We agreed that we hand it over to you when we meet her uncle!'

'Yes, but once I go with you to wherever her uncle is, I cannot communicate the details of that list to the world. I would rather leave it with people here who know what to do with it while we go to the hostages. Time is of essence, hope you understand.'

Moving to their room together, Lacene and George talked between themselves and came back with a copy of the list.

Abdul said, 'Thank you very much; it saves a lot of my time. Just tell Mr Morgan, if necessary, that we were the ones who carried the clerics to Dharamshala and that on the way we were waylaid by another group that took them hostage. Chances are that we may encounter the same group this time again, as they always track our movements, especially when we are with foreigners like you.'

'Would you be able to come with us to Dharamshala and assist us in tracing the whereabouts of the clerics?' Morgan asked the floor supervisor Hritesh.

'I would be happy to, but they won't allow me to be away for two, three days at a stretch. I may lose my job here if I do so. Your money may help me, but I need a steady job to support my family.'

From Hritesh, Morgan established that the other guy seen with Omar by a hotel staff member escorting the eight men was called Siddhu.

'That other guy, Siddhu, was more active than Omar. My colleague would be able to identify him if shown. In fact, he had more interaction with Siddhu than with Omar,' said Hritesh.

As for Abdul, Hritesh said that no one had seen him on that day. Perhaps, he was inside the van and nobody could have noticed him.

With Omar's link confirmed, Morgan was quite pleased that he was letting himself get trapped by the same group that either abducted, or at the least transported, the clerics.

Information from Lacene and George about the extent of the duo's involvement in the abduction further strengthened his belief.

<hr>

Stuart kept sending messages to Morgan's phone with exciting information. Morgan realised that he needed to spend a lot of time analysing them all.

In response to one of Morgan's earlier apprehensions about Saddam's family members, especially regarding the credibility of Saravanan at NASA Stuart replied that an extensive investigation had already started at NSA headquarters. 'NASA seems to have reassured NSA authorities that his record has been immaculate.'

Jacques had come up with data collected from American participants on the 'gowdas' forum with a list of names spread out through the vast expanses of the country. Notable concentrations were in the East Coast, Midwest states and Californian belt.

'We also realised that the list has exactly 216 sites, equally divided across those two pages. We do not know if this number has any significance. The first 108 has about 50 per cent of the sites in Asia, 20 per cent in Europe, 10 per cent each in Africa, the Americas, and Australasia. The second one has 108 distributed evenly among all continents. We are breaking our heads trying to figure out what it all means, if it really means anything at all! Aziz

Azmi, our Indian correspondent, tells me that '108' is a significant number for Hindus. I will have to find out more about that.'

Morgan wanted to look into all these before his departure to Dharamshala. He wouldn't be able to do anything during those four or five hours of travel that evening. He buried himself into his gadgets.

The station wagon Omar brought for their drive that night had a special arrangement. The seats at the rear were attached to each side of the canopy, arranged to face each other. Four people could sit comfortably and chat. There was plenty of room for luggage and no partition between the driver and the passengers.

As agreed earlier, the three passengers hired a cab from the hotel and got dropped off at the IG Park. At 6 p.m. sharp, the station wagon picked them up from there. Abdul and Omar were particular that no clue be left at the hotel about their involvement in transporting the three guests.

While loading their baggage into the station wagon, Morgan received a call from Stuart. He moved away from the group to answer it.

'This nerd of a guy, Jacques, has deserted us, Morgan! Looks like he got paid until yesterday's work – Chris had approved it – and has vanished into thin air! No one can get hold of him. Since this morning!' shouted Stuart.

Morgan said, 'And you're only telling me now, Stuart? I am leaving for Dharamshala!'

'What difference does it make? What could you have done about it sitting in Shimla? Chris brought in another guy and – my gosh – the first thing he discovered was that Jacques himself has been an active participant in that gowsad or wasdog – whatever dog it is – forum!'

Morgan's heart sank. 'Oh no, not another Snowden!'

The station wagon started gliding past city traffic onto the highway.

George was curious to understand why there was a marked behavioural difference between Abdul and Omar in as far as handling Lacene was concerned.

He began, 'May I ask, are you both bachelors, Abdul?'

Even before Abdul could answer him, Omar replied with his voice raised so they all could hear him. 'I am an eligible bachelor, but Abdul already has two wives!'

Abdul was obviously embarrassed and shook his head in disapproval at Omar's interruption.

'Abdul is lucky! Not all of us get that blessing from Allah! I saw his second wife's photo. She is very beautiful, like Asin' added Omar.

George asked, 'Who is Asin?'

Lacene said, 'Should be a Bollywood heroine, right, Abdul?'

Abdul nodded shyly.

George asked, 'Is polygamy allowed in India? Is it not illegal here?'

'As long as no one complains. The law doesn't tend to these incidents uninvited. Both his wives, I am told, and their families are quite happy with that. So why should the police break their heads with polygamy when they have so much to attend to?' Omar answered.

Lacene said, 'But is it fair to your first wife, Abdul? Just because your religion permits it, can you do that?'

'Our religion is very fair to the fairer sex, lady! Our Prophet (PbuH) did not get these verses from Angel Gabriel without reason. There are always justifiable causes for guidance from Holy Quran,' said Omar.

George asked, 'Why are you so quiet, Abdul? I can see that you are a charmer but having two wives is a bit too much! Sorry if we are stepping too far into your personal affairs.'

Morgan was keenly observing the conversation around him without contributing to it. Besides reading the incessant messages pouring in on his smart phone, his eyes were keeping track of the route they were taking. Every little thing merited notice.

It was apparent that Abdul wanted, for some reason, to clear his image with these tourists. He answered them elaborately.

'I normally go more by reason than by religion or tradition, my guests. Our Prophet (PbuH) was very right in recommending that a man should marry one virgin as a prime duty. Hadith allows us to marry up to four women because during those times, frequent warfare created many widows and orphans. It was every man's duty to support those women and children. Social harmony would get imbalanced if those desolate people were left to fend for themselves. A marriage meant so much to them. They got honourable lives.

'Society had already reached a 50:50 man: woman ratio in almost all societies of the then world. Deaths of such warfront soldiers caused a gender imbalance with fewer men and more women. So a man's duty was to ensure that there were no gender imbalances in his community. If you can afford to, marry as many! And that is exactly what I did.'

George said, 'That's quite impressive, and a valid reason too! So your second wife was a widow. What happened to her first husband? He died in a war?'

'Well, it was during mob violence following a religious riot in which he was caught in the crossfire. I was his best man at his wedding and happened to be by his side when he breathed his last. I knew how much he loved his wife and how she would suffer thanks to society's misconception of his involvement in jihadist groups.'

Lacene and George noticed that Abdul's eyes were swelling and his throat choking as he said that. Morgan, sitting beside Abdul, looked at him in appreciation.

'I am blessed that my family accepted my decision. Until that incident, I kept promising my first wife that I would follow strictly the example of Rama, whom I consider a great hero.'

Morgan asked, 'Rama, who? One of your Prophet's successors?'

Bemused, Lacene said, 'No, Morgan, he is one of the popular Hindu demigods, an avatar of Hindu god Vishnu.'

Morgan said, 'I remember that name, is that not the name with which some Hindus greet each other? Ram, Ram! Why is he so special?'

George replied, 'True, chanting Ram Nám is by itself considered a noble way to attain the sublime state and the feet of the Lord. He was a very handsome and noble Prince whose father had three wives and many more mistresses. Rama vowed, if I put it right, that he would never marry more than once. He kept his word 'til his last. Sita was his only wife. This was not in line with the then-prevailing tradition that a royal prince should have many wives.'

Lacene said, 'In India, Ram was a standout hero in that aspect. Even when most Hindu Gods were depicted as having more than one escort or wife and when almost all men of royal blood and reasonable wealth had more than one, Ram promised his beloved wife Sita on their first night that he would stick to her only for life. He kept that promise.'

Morgan asked, 'But why should Abdul, a Muslim, follow a Hindu deity's example?

Abdul replied, 'Ram's act was logical, sensible, and humane. I am not prevented by my religion to adhere to a good principle wherever it may come from. I know many Muslims in India who admire Ram for his qualities. I found his reason for such a stand to be amazing given the environment he lived in.'

George said, 'Could it be that his own personal experiences in his family – what his father did – with three wives, each vying for his favour and attention, each wanting her child to receive greater share of his kingdom etc., caused him to decide so?'

Lacene said, 'Well, they were very respectful of each other, and they all loved Ram like their own son, according to the epic. It was just a quirk of fate that Ram had to go to the jungle for fourteen years. This vow of monogamy, Ram took long before he was sent to the jungle. He must have had some other reason. Maybe Sita was a beautiful, fabulous woman. There was no need to go for any other!'

Within her heart, Lacene was singing what George used to recite about his first sighting of Lacene.

To see her is to love her,
And love but her forever.

For nature made her so beautiful,
That men will seek no other.

George was actually singing it aloud to her blushing amusement. Abdul enjoyed that. Omar drew his ears closer to hear it as well.

Abdul said, 'Perhaps, yes! Sita was so adorable that Rama had no need to think of another. But there is a totally different dimension to his theory.'

Lacene asked, 'Different dimension? What is that?'

Her tone caused everyone to look at Abdul intently. Even Omar was sharpening his left ear to pay attention to Abdul's words. He was sure that something worthwhile or controversial was to be expected.

Abdul said, 'Like our Prophet Mohammed (PbuH) who had wise advice from Angel Gabriel on such issues like marrying more than one under such circumstances, Rama also must have had instructions or guidelines from the above. We must note here that as per the original *Ramayana* written by Sage Valmiki, there was no Vaishnavism by then. Lord Siva was the god of all gods – Mahadev. Rama quoted Siva's theory to Sita. His discussion with her – supposedly on their first night – should have run like this.'

Rama: Sita dear, I promise you that I will not even think of any other woman in my life besides you!

Sita: Oh, my Lord, I am honoured and so pleased to hear that. Perhaps you may be so good to me but will your royalty allow you to be so? Will they not pressurise you into marrying several princesses? Even the other kingdoms won't let you stay with one wife for long! They would want their daughters to be given in marriage to you.

Rama: No Sita, I would refuse them all. I have a valid reason. Look at Lord Siva from whom we have learnt so much about life. He taught us that after the emergence of the male species from unisexual beings over a very long period in time of life's history, gradually the male population increased and almost equalled the female population. The fact that an offspring is a product of both man and woman each contributing half of the child was firmly established by him. Until his disclosure of this truth, we all believed that it was all God's gift only.

Sita: So what has this got to do with your vow?

Rama: When the male-child production gradually increased – thanks more due to all the unisexual beings greedily wanting more male children to improve survival chances of their generations – such a desire became embedded in our genes. Every mother preferred a male child. There was great eagerness among all those surrounding a delivering mother to see the new offspring. Everyone wanted a male, the first person who saw the delivered baby instinctively looked at the groin to confirm its gender!

Abdul, breaking from the story telling, said, 'The term 'cocksure' came to be in vogue from such scenarios.'

Morgan did not like Abdul's mannerism of covering his mouth partially with his palm while speaking. Abdul told him that he was only being polite. Lacene intervened to explain to Morgan that when speaking at such close range, it's polite to do so to avoid sprays.

Abdul continued his act.

Rama: Such was the craze for a male child. Soon the male-female ratio reached par. But the desire for a male child didn't wane. Perhaps the DNA imprints were not erased. Earlier, with the shortage of males, it was but natural for one male to mate with several females to impregnate them. So polygamy was justified, it became our nature.

Now, with a 1:1 ratio of male to female, the logical combination can only be one to one. Men should learn to change their centuries-old behavioural pattern of mating with more than one female. Every man should learn to confine himself to partner with just one woman. Only then will the society be peaceful. Or else, those other men bereft of partners would cause anarchy.

Even females will be compelled to seek relationships outside of their marriages, as their husbands would be spending their nights between their countless wives or mistresses, and not doing enough justice to all of them. We would only encourage promiscuity in society.

Sita: How well said, my Lord! You are certainly an avatar purush. I am so proud of being your wife, and I would honour our perfect partnership with my total devotion to you.

Abdul said, 'This is how Rama came to be a monogamous Prince amidst such polygamous men. And the reason he gave for that is valid even today. The world's population is almost equally divided between males and females. Still that imprint in our DNAs of expecting a male child hasn't been erased. Even the DNA imprints on the males' hormones desiring for sex with more and more females hasn't fully died down yet.'

George said, 'Makes complete sense, Abdul. I am surprised that you guys come up with such mind-blowing ideas!'

Morgan wanted to ask Lacene if she knew anything about the significance of the number 108 to Hindus. With the topic hovering around a Hindu deity, he thought it appropriate to ask her.

Lacene said, 'Look at how his brothers and their wives maintained total celibacy until his return to pave way for his succession to the throne. Amazing qualities! I love this Rama avatar more than any of the other avatars of Lord Vishnu. How I wish every man followed his path. He is the seventh avatar, and seven is my favourite number too!'

Abdul said, 'I must correct you Madam. I told you that Sage Válmiki, who wrote Ramayana, the original story of the prince of Ayodhya, did not depict Rama as an avatar. Ram was inducted into those avatars by Sage Vyasa who wrote the Mahàbhàratham and *Sreemad Bhágavatam* centuries later.'

George said, 'What? Do you mean to say that Lord Rama was not one of Lord Vishnu's incarnations? How can that be? All pictures of Rama that I have seen and all books I read of Rama depict him only as Vishnu's avatar. There may be a few differences here and there in that long epic between regions. He sports a vertical mark in his forehead, a Vaishnavite symbol. Not a horizontal one, like Saivaites.'

Omar said, 'That is typical of Abdul. He always gives completely different meanings to scriptures. We are lucky that there is no staunch Hindu sitting here. He would have beheaded Abdul by now!'

Morgan interrupted with a 'sorry' and asked Lacene, 'Why is 108 so important a number to the Hindus? You have any idea? Google and Wikipedia only gave me limited information.'

Lacene said, 'Well, I have heard them using that number frequently in their casual talks in the same way we say 'umpteen' times. If my memory is right, there are 108 important verses in Upanishads the extended text to the Vedas and 108 holy shrines for Vaishanvites. That's all I know. You have any idea, Abdul?'

'Well, I also have heard them use that number especially when they want to mean "I have told you so many times", they say "I have told you 108 times!" I do not know any meaning behind it. Why do you ask, Mr Morgan?'

Morgan said, 'I also heard people saying so and wondered why.'

Abdul said, 'I vaguely remember someone saying that 1-0-8 represented one-none-infinity, meaning that the three different concepts about God are that he is one, or none or infinitely many.'

Lacene asked, 'Wow, That's a wonderful explanation! I have never heard that. Okay, tell me, Abdul, what makes you say that even Rama was misrepresented?'

'In the madrasáh that I went to, our imam was a staunch Hindu who converted to Islam at the ripe age of forty. He soon became the mullah and then imam at our mosque and school. He was the one who taught us that Vaishnavism spread across India much later – mostly from Greek and Persian migrants – with their beliefs blended well to suit the beliefs of the erstwhile Indians who only had Siva as their Supreme God by then. Some even portray Siva as a Dravidian God. Our imam would credit sage Vyása for popularising Vaishnavism.'

Lacene said, 'I have never heard anything like that. All along I believed – as most Hindus believe – that Saivism and Vaishnavism are the oldest of faiths practiced in India, besides Buddhism, Jainism, and many other occults. You know, I am a researcher in Hinduism and possess a doctorate on the bakthi movement in India. You are making a fool of me, Abdul.'

Omar was extremely pleased to hear Lacene disagreeing with Abdul like that. Now, here is a scholar – an Angrezi scholar, a beautiful lady at that – discrediting Abdul, the all-knowing Madrási.

Abdul said, 'Madam, you know that the Hindus love to chant Ram Nám – name of Lord Rama – as much as possible in a day. But this is the story of how they marked "námam" on-to Rama's forehead! Do you want to hear that story?'

Morgan, mostly engrossed in his smartphone, wanted to show that he was in the conversation. 'This guy seems to have a lot of stories to tell us, George! Let's listen to him!' He hoped this would draw their focus away from what he was doing on his phone.

Lacene said, 'Ràmarkey nàmamà? Ràmki bhi nàmam? Even Ram was cheated? Tell me, tell me. Also, you will tell me why that phrase came into practice. In Tamil they say "painted a námam" to denote that "someone cheated someone else". No other place in India speaks like that. Only among Tamils and a few other south Indians have I heard this word "námam" to mean as "cheating". Why so?'

Morgan said, 'What is this "námam" all about? Is it not just "name"?'

George said, 'There is something beyond that. Námam also came to mean the "vertical mark" on the forehead as sported by Vaishanvites to denote their faith.'

Morgan said, 'What about the horizontal mark that some use, then?'

George replied, 'Well, as far as I know, the horizontal mark is made with the ashes of some herbal mix to denote that we all will end up as ashes, the cosmic dust. The vertical mark denotes that we all end up as sand, interned in the earth. There are different kinds of strokes in that. I will explain that to you later. Let's listen to this, I find it interesting.'

Lacene said, 'They call it "shrisoornam" or "thiruman", meaning "holy earth". But why do they mean "námam" as "cheating"?'

Abdul said, 'Okay, let me first explain that. Only then the other story of "Ramki bhi nám" will carry some meaning.

'You know of the six holy temples of Lord Kumar or Muruga in the south. The Tirupathi temple of Lord Balaji, also called the "seven hills" was once considered the seventh temple of Lord Muruga. In that area, he was known as "Su-brahmanya". These seven temples would denote the seven sisters of the Pleiades cluster of stars in which Kumar or Muruga is said to have been created. A spark from the third eye of Lord Siva shot into the space and settled as the "Krithika" star – what western astronomy calls "Pleiades" cluster in our Milky Way. Even the term "Skantha" means "ejaculated or spluttered" giving authenticity to the belief that Siva passed on his sperm to give birth to Kumar unlike his brother Vináyak who was born directly to Sakthi.'

George asked, 'Is that so?'

Lacene said, 'Wait, G, let him continue. I know a little about it.'

Abdul said, 'The famous sage, philosopher, and saint Sri Rámánujar, who revolutionised Vaishnavism in the South and also propagated the "Vishishtádvaitam" philosophy, was instrumental in establishing that the Tirupathi temple was indeed for Lord Srinivásan or Báláji and not for Lord Muruga or Su-brahmanya. He, in fact, adeptly settled a dispute between the two claimants. He himself had later disclosed how deftly he handled that dispute. His followers have been showering praise upon him for that great feat.'

Everyone but Morgan, who was not interested in these stories and was following messages from Stuart, was keenly listening.

Abdul continued, 'Sri Rámánujar made both parties agree that two different flowers be kept one evening on the two shoulders of the statue or deity that existed in that temple – the same deity claimed by both parties as their own God – Srinivásan versus Murugan. Each flower would represent each deity.

'The sanctum sanctorum of the temple was to be immediately vacated and locked with multiple locks and would only be opened the next morning by those with the keys. Those who held the keys would not be allowed to meet in that night, so that no one could enter in the night without the other's knowledge. It was agreed that the deity would be decided by the flower that remained on the statue without falling.'

'As we all now know, Lord Báláji or Srinivásan, the Vaishnavite God's flower won the test.

'But the truth, as admitted or rather proudly claimed by the Vaishnavites much later, was that Sri Rámánujar had arranged for a trained snake to be sent though a drain hole into the sanctum sanctorum and push the "other flower" off the statue's shoulder!'

George said, 'Wow! Sneaky Snake!'

Abdul said, 'We all now know the roaring business Lord Srinivásan is doing in the Tirupathi temple! It is the richest Hindu temple now and has been so for a very long time.

'Tamil Vaishnavites piously call that mark as "thiruman" or holy sand but the vernacular term is "námam". From that incident onwards, the deity or statue in that temple has been adorned with the Vaishnavite mark on the forehead, which is the vertical mark of three lines as opposed to the horizontal mark of the Saivites or Muruga worshippers.

'That phrase "námam idu" or "námam pódu" meaning "mark the vertical námam symbol", came to be in vogue among a section of the Tamils to denote "foul play or cheating". Somehow it became so intertwined in daily usage that almost all people forgot its origin!'

Lacene said, 'Thank you so much for this, Abdul. Look at the irony, I am a research scholar and nobody in the South told me this much detail and I am destined to hear it from a Muslim.'

George said, 'Complete the story, Abdul. What about the námam for Rama himself?'

Abdul said, 'It is simple. During Rama's time in history, only Siva was the Supreme God as I told you earlier. All in his kingdom were only worshipping Lord Siva by then. There was no mention of Lord Vishnu in Sage Valmiki's original *Ràmàyana*. Saivites mark their foreheads with ashes horizontally. In the north, the practice is to mark with sandalwood paste or a red dot, called the 'tilak' mark.

'After Sage Vyása's books and the rising popularity of Lord Krishna, the Vaishnavites conveniently inducted Lord Rama into the fold of Vaishnavism and adorned Rama's pictures with the vertical "námam", and he became the seventh avatar of Lord Vishnu! Until then, Lord Rama and his pictures – if at all there were any – would have been sporting the horizontal lines or 'tilak' marks only!

'That's why my imam said that "Ramkibhi námam detha hai"!'

Morgan received another message on his phone, and called Stuart.

It was obvious that Morgan did not want the others to hear the entire conversation and that he had just received some shocking news. Lacene recognised the voice of Chris besides Stuart on the other end. She looked at George, who signalled her to keep quiet. Abdul stopped talking. Omar became attentive to overhear whatever he could.

In a very low voice, Morgan told Lacene, 'Chris confirms that the jihadist group is going to demolish 216 holy sites all around the globe if their demands are not met. Some have already been demolished! And the irony is that the term "dowgas or wasdog" has strong links to this group as they have discussed many of these locations in their online exchanges!'

George noticed a tone of sorrow in Morgan's voice.

'And the worst part of it that I can't tell you in the presence of these guys is that my daughter Irene and that wretched witch Uma -granddaughter of that devil Saddam- have been active participants on the forum until recently.'

Though he didn't say anything out loud, George could read from his face that something serious had disturbed Morgan. Lacene tried to bring everyone back to the discussion.

'If you scan through most old literary works in Indian languages, you will notice that the greatest challenge men faced and yearned to have complete control over, was the unending desire for sex. They have attempted all imaginable and unimaginable ways and means to combat this one invincible feeling – lust for women.

'Practicing severely demanding penance, becoming wandering mendicants, and leaving the household in order to keep away from their desires, were some of the common ways. Only a few succeeded in completely overcoming such a desire. Guidelines like "twice-a-month sex with one's spouse only" were unwritten codes for "gentlemen". Yoga and Ayurveda strongly propounded this theory.'

The topic was a good diversion for Morgan. He said, 'Only twice a month? That is not fair! Humans need to have sex as often as they can.' His mind rolled back to the numerous escapades that he had in the past two years. In fact, Florence separated from him blaming a few such affairs that she came to know of as the main reason.

Morgan participated in the discussion for the sake of it; his mind was elsewhere, and George could read that it was something very serious.

Morgan continued, 'Studies show that an average American has sex at least twice a week. You are giving instances of Indian men trying to suppress their sexual desires. But the worldwide trend – especially in the east – is that the craze for Aphrodisiac in one form or the other for which animals are poached – abounds everyday. India is almost branded a "country of rapists"!'

George said, 'Celibacy and restraint in sex were advocated as one of the main attributes to good health and longevity by ancient Indian sages. It is a pity that not all Indians follow that advice.'

Lacene said, 'Look at countries where the male female ratio is reversing! More females mean that in those societies, they will have to accept female polygamists! Where will the surplus men go if each woman is married to only one man in their society? At least some women will have to marry more than one man! And society should accept that. Already such incidents occur in China where the ratio is reversing in favour of males.'

George said, 'And soon this trend will spread everywhere.'

Abdul said, 'Sure, yes! New scriptures will be sent by the Almighty God to revise his laws on polygamy. Polyandry will be permitted! And men will get severely punished if they dare set their eyes on more than one woman. Angel Gabriel is coming to rewrite the scriptures!'

There was a smile on every face. Some even laughed.

The joyous mood continued, except for Morgan. Morgan's smile was wry, and he immersed himself into his phone, sending a message. His meaningful look at Lacene and George indicated that he was vindicated in his suspicions on Sadhá. There was also an element of 'why did you not tell me?' in that look.

Omar was totally unhappy at Abdul's new suggestion on polyandry, taking his frustration out by pushing down harder on the pedal.

Morgan was looking intently at the message from Stuart.

'Aziz says the person dealing with this case at Shimla for Research Analysis Wing (RAW) is called Thánu. His confidential number is 9786975499. Contact him for more information. I will send his photo now.'

And that was when Morgan felt the prick of a needle on the right side of his neck and swiftly raised his hand to prevent it. He could see Abdul's hand moving away from him as he felt the needle being pulled out. His other hand immediately went for his holster within his jacket but it was too late.

Abdul's action was a shock to Lacene and George too. Omar had timed his acceleration at that precise moment to take Morgan's upper body away from Abdul with a jerk. George and Lacene were also swayed by that change of speed. Abdul was obviously prepared for it and stood steady while removing his hand from Morgan's neck. His left hand had a .38 pointing at George.

'Don't move', Abdul instructed.

George tried to rise from his seat but a fierce look from Abdul kept him where he was. Morgan realised Abdul's treachery of bringing his hand near his mouth while speaking. While his mind was reeling to detect what kind of drug had been injected through his neck, he realised that he was losing consciousness. He could see and hear everything, but in a haze. The photo sent by Stuart was opening up on his phone when Abdul grabbed it from him. Morgan's resistance was ineffective.

'Do not worry my guests. I am only helping you not to see that which you should not see. Help yourselves with these injections. We hope you do understand that you all have to sleep for a while. I appreciate your cooperation.' Abdul stretched his right hand out with two syringes he took from a pouch behind his seat. 'You'll wake up soon.'

George quietly took one, and encouraged Lacene to do so as well, realising they had no choice but to comply.

Arthur, the pastor and the imam climbed to reach the kill and to bring some meat as directed by the Pathan. More than doing so on his bidding, they wanted the meat desperately for themselves. They knew that a missed opportunity would mean starving days ahead for them.

The Pathan sliced the yak up into perfect portions like a trained butcher. Having made two trips to its hideout to safeguard its share, the leopard came back for its third when the three men picked up the pieces Pathan gave them. No words were exchanged between them.

However scary the close meeting with the snow leopard was, it was equally thrilling for the three men as they eyed its graceful actions in picking its share with due respect to the Pathan and in retreating with a grateful glance at all the humans.

After disposing the remains by throwing them over the other side of the hill, the Pathan quietly left the place and walked to the southern end, disappearing behind the hills. The pastor commented that the stink of the meat should not reach them given the long distance. The others were not sure, though.

They didn't see the Pathan again that day. The group made plans to wash the meat in the river and smoke it together with the skin before consuming some of it and keeping the rest for the coming days. They had lots of challenges in executing their plans.

The topics of 'wilderness medicine' and 'IQ testing' were discussed and debated extensively between them. Arthur explained the phenomena, how a person's ability to overcome challenges under difficult circumstances and scant resources could determine one's level of IQ.

With the only vegetarian in the group again going to bed having only the rotis, the rest of the group had a field day. Arthur encouraged the pundit to eat meat for once, as it was not a sin. He told the pundit that all humans were omnivores once. Pure vegetarianism came into vogue long after farming and irrigation were invented and practised.

The pundit did not agree. 'The human digestive system resembles those of herbivorous animals and therefore we are all vegetarians.'

The pastor intervened, and explained that the position of our eyes would tell whether we are herbivorous or carnivorous.

The others were surprised to hear that. The meat was on the smoke, and the pundit placed himself on the opposite direction to avoid the smell of roasting meat. The pastor began.

'All herbivorous land animals have their eyes on the sides of their faces while all carnivores have them at the front. The former have to defend themselves from predators that may attack from the sides while the latter have to focus forwards on their prey to attack. All humans have their eyes like carnivores, justifying the theory that we evolved as carnivores and latter became omnivores or herbivores by selection.'

Others agreed that humans are omnivorous. All religions except Jainism encouraged both vegetarian and meat foods. Sub sects of some religions also followed strict vegan practices.

No one debated about kosher or halal. Extreme circumstances allowed violation of such stipulations. The debate on whether the yak was slaughtered conforming to any of the scripture-guided methods ended peacefully with that one excuse!

As the plane took off, Lacene opened her eyes and sensed that she was laid between George and Morgan, each in a sleeping bag. The chequered ventilated face screen enabled breathing and vision.

She hissed, 'Morgan must have some bad news. Saw his face?'

Before George could reply, they both heard Morgan's murmur. Lacene rolled herself closer to Morgan who uttered many words.

'Thánu . . . raw . . . Irene . . . wasdog . . . Uma . . . 108 . . . 108 . . .' were the words she could hear. Morgan went to sleep again. Losing hope to hear any further from him, she rolled nearer to George and tried to repeat what she heard.

Brooding over that admixture of unconnected words helped the two to drown into a deep sleep.

————•◦•◦•————

Omar, the ever doubting Thomas, had no choice but to tell the group that started haunting him late that night, almost everything that he had done so far together with Abdul and Ismail. The torture was unbearable for Omar.

At the airstrip, Abdul did not take help from Omar to offload the passengers. The station wagon was parked closer to the aircraft. Ismail came from the airstrip building. With Abdul, he carried them one by one into the plane. Omar felt that Abdul avoided him on purpose.

Omar hadn't seen Ismail since the last visit to that airstrip and believed that Ismail was with the clerics all those days. From the driver's seat, he just waved in reply to Ismail's gesture. Abdul had strictly told him to stay in his seat.

While Omar was as curious as ever to know more about the happenings around him, Abdul always kept him in the dark. Omar did not like that. Nor did he like the idea that he would not be travelling with the three hostages. A chance to be with this Angrezi– an infidel in his view, with such revealing clothes – a chance to 'know' her at least once was to be lost. He had fantasised about having intimate knowledge of her.

Abdul said, 'I shall stay with Ismail tonight. We both may go with the hostages. You leave the vehicle where I told you to leave it. I'll be in touch with you soon in the same discreet ways I have done before. Okay, bye.' His abruptness made Omar feel lonely. After clearing the station wagon of all baggage, Omar begrudgingly left.

It was during the lone drive that Omar encountered a scary intervention by the group. He had parked his vehicle near a tea stall at the turn-off from NH88 leading to Bilaspur. As he was sipping his hot tea and biting into the kebab, he sensed that some of the other patrons in the tea stall were repeatedly looking at him and talking among themselves. Not comfortable to stay there any longer, he hurriedly finished the tea and rose to leave for his vehicle.

That was when three of the gang members closed in on him and signalled to get into the car without a word or protest. One of them took his key and sat in the driver's seat while the other two walked with him around the car to accompany him in the back. The van moved and the other gang member followed them in a pickup.

Omar was not shaken much. All the gang members were Muslims, which gave him a sense of brotherly security, but the fear that they might belong to a rival gang did cause some jitters. The very first words of the man sitting beside him proved his fear coming true.

'Which jihadist group do you belong to?'

'Al Nusrah.'

'What? Al Nusrah doesn't operate here! We are the ones who handle this area, and there is no way Al Nusrah could have come this far without our knowledge! Are you telling us the truth? One word of lie will see you in Shaitan's hell, beware.'

'Which group do you belong to?' asked Omar, gathering some courage.

'You must know if you are from this region. We have thoroughly inquired about you. Who is your companion, and what were you both doing with those infidels? Tell us the truth. Al Nusrah cannot function here without our knowledge and approval. What did you do to those clerics from Hotel Shimla last week? Where are they now?'

Omar showed defensive signs at that question. He stammered, 'I do not know. I only drive the vehicles for them. Abdul and Ismail are the ones who involved me in this, but they have always kept me in the dark as to what they do. All I know is that they transported those eight clerics – and now these three – to a safe hideout in – they said – Hindu Kush. I dropped them at the airstrip not far from here.'

'That can't be true, no way! Heard that, Salim? You believe that?'

'No, it can't be true Javed. Either this rascal is telling a lie or he may have been used. We have been trying in vain all this week to trace which group had abducted those clerics, and now we have at least got hold of the vital link. Let us get the chain quickly. Should we not go to that airstrip he is talking about? It must be two hours since he had left them there, isn't it, Omar?'

'Yes, yes . . . yes,' stumbled Omar as the car took a U-turn and sped off towards the airstrip, with the pickup close behind.

When they reached the spot that Omar led them to, nobody was present. An open field with a small, dilapidated building in one corner was all that greeted them. The building did not look like having anything worthwhile inside it.

The only relief for Omar was the traction in the field clearly showing tyre marks of a vehicle to have rolled over the ground for a distance not too long ago, proving him right. They untied Omar and sat around him in the vehicle.

Then began the grilling, followed of course, by the spilling of beans!

───────•◆•◆•───────

A heavier meal that evening did show its impact on most of the hostages that night. Only the pundit, with rotis for a meal, slept well. Most of the others had one kind of a nightmare or the other.

- a herd of yaks attacked and killed a snow leopard but took pity on its cubs and left them.
- the Pathan came in pure white bishop robes preaching the gospel
- a plane landed and took off causing heavy disturbance to the air around their hill.
- they had visitors to their cave prompting them to share the yak meat with the visitors who gobbled up everything.
- three gunshots reverberating all around the hills were heard.

– starting from the rabbi, the Pathan lined up each one for a photo shoot, but each one fell dead after the click of the camera.

———•◆•———

Aziz Gulam Azmi, deputy Secretary, Ministry of Home Affairs, Government of India, was a tired man when he hit his bed that night. He wondered if he did the right thing giving information about Thanu to Stuart at the American embassy. Sometimes it worked well with such important diplomat staff to trade harmless information for some vital ones from the other side. That was a valuable trade-in because Stuart told him about Morgan Stanford from the NSA probing the case at Shimla. Aziz had sent a message to Thánu about him. Thánu had not replied. Aziz wasn't sure if Thánu got it.

When he checked his email before going to bed and noticed one from Stuart received a few minutes ago, he immediately opened it. 'There should be some vital information in this mail,' he said to himself.

The subject of the mail was 'one from the list'.

He noticed that it was a news item forwarded to Morgan with copies to several others in his headquarters. Sharing of information at the same time with such key US personnel and an Indian official impressed Aziz. He read the news.

A bombing occurred at the al-Askari Mosque in the Iraqi city of Samarra, 6.44 a.m. local time. The attack on the mosque, one of the holiest sites in Shia Islam, is believed to have been caused by al-Qaeda in Iraq. Although no injuries occurred in the blasts, the mosque was severely damaged.

The bombing was followed by retaliatory violence with over a hundred dead bodies being found the next day and well over 1,000 people killed in the days following the bombing – by some counts, over 1,000 on the first day alone. Explosions occurred at al-Askari Mosque, effectively destroying its golden dome and severely damaging the mosque. Several men wearing military uniforms had earlier entered the mosque, tied up the guards there, and set explosives, resulting in the blast. Two bombs were set off by five to seven men dressed as personnel of the Iraqi Special Forces who entered the shrine during the morning.

No injuries were reported following the bombing. However, the northern wall of the shrine was damaged, causing the dome to collapse and destroying most of the structure. Five police officers responsible for protecting the mosque were taken into custody.

No group claimed responsibility for the attack on the mosque so far.

---

9. Buddh Dharm Sangh

Knowledge is less than sense.
Therefore seek intelligence.

Global reaction to the news of the missing clerics had been quite muted so far, thanks to other burning issues in each country and region. But Aziz had his hands more than full with mountain loads of tasks to perform simultaneously.

To the ever-probing media, he had to say that everything was under control, that the negotiations with the jihadist group would end in the civil society's favour and that the hostages would all be released soon.

To the UN authorities and the concerned government officials of the six countries whose citizens were held hostages, he had conveyed the demands of the jihadists.

'The United Nations should convene an urgent session of its members to pass resolutions to incorporate all the new clauses we have suggested into the UN Charter. The UN should send strictures to all member nations asking them to immediately enact laws in their lands as demanded by the jihadists and in line with the new UN resolutions.

'All heads of nations are required to face the public in open arenas to declare their commitment towards fulfilling our demands. Until and unless the UN confirms to the public media that it has carried out our demands, the eight clerics will not be released. Furthermore, numerous religious sites all over the world will be destroyed by 9/9.'

All along, Aziz had advised all nations not to reveal too much to the public, as that would create global panic. Although those demands were conveyed only to the UN and the national governments with a firm request to maintain secrecy, the ever-inquisitive media publicised the demands somehow.

The flood of calls and correspondence from all governments were so overwhelming that Aziz repeated the same replies to almost everyone like a recorded disc.

There was no update from his source of contact from the jihadists. The name of the group was deftly withheld so far by that contact. There was no information on the release of the eight clerics. Nor was any scope of dialogue or negotiation viable. For him, the group's demand for a UN resolution was not unexpected.

Aziz was immensely disturbed at the unusual demand of the jihadists threatening with destruction of 216 religious sites through the contact.

This group appeared strange as their demands were directed at all the heads of governments, the Secretary General of the UN together with the Commissioner of Council for Human Rights. He had released copies of the list with 216 religious sites to the UN and several other trustworthy nations, including the USA, the previous afternoon.

He appreciated Stuart's response to it before the end of that day, with information on damages already inflicted on a few of the religious sites on the list. Besides the chilling realisation that the jihadists meant business, Aziz was greatly dismayed by the fact that his plans were going awry.

Since the previous night, his efforts at getting in touch with Thànu, his only source of contact with the jihadist spokesperson, were in vain. He had sent desperate messages to Thánu's phone, asking him to call back. He feared that things were getting out of control while he had to put up a brave face to the other governments and the UN.

Thànu hadn't replied nor had he called since the previous evening. The last message from him was that he would be busy that night and that he would deal with Morgan suitably.

Thánumálayan Pillay, Thánu to his colleagues, had been stationed in Shimla since the start of the religious conference. With reliable information that he brought in about the probable abduction of ten of the delegates to the conference by terrorist groups operating in the region, the Home ministry had made confidential arrangements to protect the clerics and to track the plotters.

Thánu had done a very good job so far, but Aziz believed that something was going wrong with the whole plan. From the time the list of religious sites that the jihadist group claimed to demolish was transmitted to his office, nothing had been heard from Thànu. His last message simply read, 'The set deadline for the destruction of most of these sites was moved from 9/9 to 9/11.'

Only six days were left for that.

None of the governments seemed to have taken serious note of the demands of this jihadist group. The UN responded by forwarding the demands to all nations and asking them to fulfil them and maintain complete secrecy until the resolutions were passed.

Aziz believed that the office of the UN Secretary General would have found the demand for the UN resolution to be reasonable. The office of the High Commission for Human Rights (OHCHR) did a commendable job in communicating with member states to respond as quickly as possible to the strange demands of this group.

Each government seemed to be handling this emergency in its own way. Perhaps they preferred to provide enough security to the listed holy sites in their countries than ceding to the jihadists' demands.

But the fact that a few of those sites had already been targeted for attacks bode ill omen. Thánu had never given any indication of that kind of a demand right from the time the plan was hatched until yesterday evening. He had simply explained that the list that he sent was just to 'legitimise' the abduction of the clerics.

Aziz felt a sudden surge of pain in his chest.

Whoever settles a matter by violence is not just.
The wise calmly consider what is right and wrong.
Whoever guides others by non-violent and fair procedures,
Is a true guardian of truth.
He is wise and just.

The Buddhist monk was reciting this sutta from the Buddha suttas. It was early in the morning, and the sun was still behind the hills. Most of the hostages were still in their beds but awake. No one had slept well that night thanks to a number of disturbances.

As each one got up from his bed and came out of the cave, they noticed some changes in their surroundings. There were marks on the ground, which were certainly not there the previous night. The drag marks were noticeable in and out of the cave. Sensing danger, the moulana ran in to see where it ended and to caution the two still inside to come out.

Hearing their calls, more than two people responded from the cave!

The rabbi and the pundit were the last two of the eight to get up and come out of the cave. But the additional voices that the moulana heard were coming from the northern side of the cave. It was an extension with a narrow entrance. As the moulana squeezed himself through the passage, he was surprised to see a beautiful lady's face peeping out of her sleeping bag.

That morning the eleven minds gelled so well that by noon they had connected all loose ends and deciphered how they all ended up there.

Within a short while, everyone conceded that Abdul had masqueraded as Ganesh with the clerics.

Morgan's investigative brain analysed the sequence of events. Arthur's knowledge of that hill and George's trekking experience provided support.

Tracing the new track-marks, they reached the riverbed at a point where the ground was flat like a platform. The river was at its narrowest point, like a fjord. On the other end of the river the ground level was slightly higher. The entire area there was like a playfield; large enough for a small plane to land and take off.

The field on the other side of the river had been noticed by the eight clerics earlier, but they did not decipher how they were brought to the cave from there, if they had been brought in an aircraft. They had assumed that they had been airdropped softly near the cave by a chopper. They were not sure, though.

Morgan explained that a ten or twelve-seat Douglas or Cessna that did not require a long runway could have brought them to that airstrip. All of them, still in their deep slumber, were probably sent over a slide connecting the two banks of the river, landing at the platform on the cave's side. They would have been carried all the way from that spot to the cave on a sledge or stretcher.

Morgan was sure that it required more than one person to carry eight men for the distance between the riverbed platform and the cave – an uphill task of over 100 meters.

With no clue as to their location, they could only assume that the place should be somewhere in either Pakistani or Afghan territory.

Morgan was at first happy to note that his transmitter was intact in his vest. But to his great disappointment, it was not functioning. Someone with good knowledge of such devices must have deactivated it, he believed, fuming at Abdul's trickery.

The rabbi and Lacene were in deep discussion and were joined by the reverend. The pundit moved between these two groups, partaking in their conversations. Lacene did not seem to be affected in the least by the happenings around her. She was calmly explaining George's miraculous escape from death on the slopes of K2 to the rabbi.

George continued to observe the restlessness in Morgan's demeanour and wondered what was bothering him. He could clearly sense that Morgan was bent upon capturing Sadhá, whatever it took.

Learning from the rest about the Pathan's visits and behaviour, Morgan and George decided that they should go around the hill to find where he would be coming from. With more than three hours to the Pathan's normal visiting time, they both decided to set off on their mission, much against the advice of the senior residents there.

Arthur did not join the duo. In fact he was among those who dissuaded the two from venturing onto that side of the hill.

An hour after their departure, the nine hostages heard two gunshots in the distance, most likely from the other side of the hill. Those were the first gunshots the clerics had heard since their arrival there. Lacene and the rabbi were shocked but tried to keep calm and looked at others. As nothing was heard for the next thirty minutes, they became anxious and worried. Arthur decided to go looking for the two.

When most others started advising Arthur against it, Lacene and the rabbi said that they would accompany him. Upon that, everyone kept quiet. They agreed to their departure knowing well that there was still more than an hour left for the Pathan to visit them. They appreciated Lacene's position and sympathised with her anxiety.

The trio had hardly reached the edge of the hill using the same route, when the others shouted to them to come back. They had seen the Pathan coming down from the top of the hill, alone.

No one was pleased.

Lacene raised her eyes to look at the 'monster' the others had described. The ease with which the Pathan glided down the slippery slopes of the hill did not confirm her expectation. This man's gait had no semblance to that of Sadhá. His face was much younger too.

———•◦•◦•———

Frantic efforts at communicating with the UN Secretariat and the UNHRC secretariat were driving Aziz insane. He had sent the list of the sites to both these offices and was expecting their feedback. He was aware that both secretariats had a lot of communication work to do besides persuading the nations to agree on an emergency meeting. Officials from OHCHR finally communicated that they had arranged for the convention of an extraordinary session of all its members within a week. They made it clear that their originally planned twenty-first session for 4 September had to be rescheduled to 9 September in order to notify its members of the new proposals that reflected the demands from this terrorist outfit.

They asked Aziz to convey their limitations in convening the session earlier to the terrorist outfit, and to press them to release the clerics. They also said that the OHCHR could only table the proposals but could not guarantee the passing of all the clauses as presented. Everything depended on how the nations reacted to those demands.

David was not only stirred but also terribly shaken by the revelation from Lacene and George that Jeremy had indeed tried to drown Lacene on that fateful night at the pool in the community hall in Lawrence, Kansas. He couldn't digest that truth.

With contradicting input from Lacene and Morgan, David couldn't help wondering if Sadhá was a good person or a wolf in sheep's clothing. He sent a message to Morgan about Jeremy's murder at the pool within minutes after Lacene spoke to him about it, but received no reply.

On the one hand, Sadhá was a simple Hindu priest with high moral values, an admirer of his language and culture. On the other he was a collaborator with terrorists and a facilitator of their anti-American activities – and most certainly Jeremy's murderer.

David had to admit that he had noticed a lot of positive changes in Lacene after her short period of interaction with that priest. If Jeremy did really try to drown Lacene, then Sadhá should be suitably rewarded for saving his daughter. And his son-in-law.

While replying to David on receipt of the video he had sent, George had requested David to get in touch with Sadhá's family and convey the good news of his heroism on K2 just a week ago. Recollecting the lecture at the Smithsonian, David looked forward to meeting Saraswathi to tell her how indebted he was to her father. He had, of course, conveyed his gratitude to Saravanan already.

Morgan had also wanted David to meet Saraswathi to learn more about Sadhaa's involvement with the 9/11 events. The appointment with her was that evening, with dinner at her home.

Emily was excited about the dinner and restless at the prospect of meeting Yuvan's cousins.

———◆———

Aziz was desperate to get in touch with Thánu to convey the message of the deferred UN council meeting and to find out when the clerics would be released. It had been more than twenty hours since he last heard from Thánu. He did not seem to have contacted any of the local intelligence officials he had normally been in touch with. The last contact they had was from Siddhu, who had given clues that helped the police apprehend four more terrorists the previous night.

'To keep everything under control, the clerics must be released the next day' Aziz thought. With the new threat on the 216 religious sites and Thánu's long silence, Aziz was getting nervous. 'Would our confidential plan be exposed? Would the PMO (Prime Minister's office) reprimand him for venturing into dangerous waters without approval from the top brass?' Of course, he had the Home minister's tacit approval for the detection and detention of terrorist groups in Himachal Pradesh.

As he reached for one of the most confidential files, code-named OWN, he knew he was plunging himself deeper down the rabbit hole.

The whole plan was Thánumálayan's brainchild. With reliable information about the intended abduction of ten clerics by more than one

Indian Mujahedeen group trying to set base in Himachal Pradesh, Thánu had made elaborate plans to nab all of them.

The Joint Intelligence Committee (JIC), to which his plan was presented by the Director of the RAW, immediately approved the project and nicknamed it 'Operation Wipe-out Now' (OWN). They gave the go-ahead for the coordinated execution of the project by Aziz Gulam Azmi and Thánumálayan Pillai.

Thánu would arrange the abduction of the clerics using his RAW teammates and a few trustworthy local guys. He would then arrange for sending the hostages to a safe haven. The outside world, including all terrorist outfits, would believe that the clerics had indeed been abducted. Each group would believe that 'another group' had succeeded in the abduction plan, and in the process of checking out on each other, they would give more opportunities for the authorities to decode their communiqués and trace them, monitor their moves, and eventually apprehend them all.

Once all the jihadist outfits trying to set base in Shimla and the rest of Himachal Pradesh were apprehended, Thánu's team would release the clerics. Until then, everything would be under wraps. Some false demands would be placed to legitimise the abduction.

So far, so good.

The demand for UN resolutions was not strange to Aziz. Thánu had already briefed him on that. But this new threat of the destruction of hundreds of religious sites around the world was not in the plan at all. Thanu did not explain the basis for such a demand. And he had been playing hide and seek ever since the release of that list by his contact.

'What if everything gets revealed, with the ever-snoopy US intelligence smelling a rat? Besides public outrage at such a misadventure and opposition parties' swipes at the government, there is the serious possibility of the UN and other nations deriding India for the uncontrollable monster it had inadvertently unleashed.'

Aziz felt palpitations in his chest and feared the worst when his pulse rate shot through the roof.

———◆◆◆———

For a change, the Pathan did not stay in his usual position for more than two minutes. He just glanced at Lacene once and then shouted to Arthur to collect the bundle that he threw. He did not wait to answer any queries. The rabbi asked him about George and Morgan. Lacene started to speak to him but just a single angry look from him shut her mouth. The imam went closer to him to attract his attention, but the Pathan did not show any interest in entertaining him.

The first one to pick up the bundle thrown at them was the bikku. He quietly opened it and found a bunch of papers, all of them copies of the same neatly printed two-page text. He distributed them to everyone, one each. They were all bullet points in a word text.

Their collective hearts sank as they realised that they would not hear about the two brave men. They could not believe that they would not get to know the fate of Morgan and George.

As each person reluctantly opened the paper, Lacene looked at the bikku blankly as she stretched her hand out for her copy. Realising that she was the last one to get a copy, she noticed that the bikku was left with some more sheets in his hand. Her look giving him a cue, the bikku opened the papers left in his hands. There were two more sheets left on his palm.

He looked at Lacene with surprise showing her the two sheets, and she responded with great joy, jumping in the air. They should be alive!

Just as everyone began reading the contents of the two-page sheet, they heard the voices of George and Morgan coming from the same route they had earlier taken. Lacene ran towards George.

The Pathan turned around to look at George and Morgan who had a look at him too. With about fifty meters between them, Morgan felt that the Pathan was staring at him as though deeply studying him.

In a minute, the Pathan was gone behind the ridge.

Morgan confided with Lacene and George that the Pathan was wearing a latex mask. The couple could not disagree with Morgan, as they could not observe as well as his experienced eyes did.

- Freedom of religion clearly indicates that every adult has a right to follow any or no religion or many religions, according to his/her personal preference. No member state shall sponsor or subscribe to any particular religion as its national religion. By expressing its affiliation to or endorsement of a particular religion, the state subtly denies the freedom of right to other religions of choice to its residents.

- Every child born in this world has a right to learn about all the religions of the world including spiritualism, agnosticism, and atheism. No one, including its parents, can thrust religious beliefs or faiths upon any child. All institutions of learning shall include in their secondary school curricula, a spiritual course about all faiths and non-faiths. The texts for these courses shall be designed for universal acceptance to be followed uniformly by *all* member nations. The UNHCR alone can design those curricula.

- All religious bodies shall, in their teaching institutions, educate its pupils with complete and unbiased knowledge of all kinds of faiths and non-faiths in the world. The preachers in these institutions shall undergo a special training course lasting six months to one year in order to prepare them on this universal spiritual course.

- At no stage shall this spiritual course be misrepresented by any section of the religious bodies by unduly projecting the negative aspects of the 'other' faiths or non-faiths. The information passed on to the pupils should be totally impassionate and without prejudice.

- All member nations shall reaffirm their commitment under the Charter of the United Nations to promote and encourage universal respect for and observance of all human rights and fundamental freedoms without distinction as to, inter alia, religion or belief.

- All member nations shall commit irrevocably to restructure their national constitution or supreme ruling text such that within the next ten years, they would give 50 per cent of the membership of their ruling councils to women. This shall be so at all levels of governance. Educating the women to reach these levels shall become mandatory. This commitment must be pronounced by all nations within the next six months.

- No religious decrees shall be pronounced by anyone from the member nations, such an act being severely punishable under each nation's restructured constitution. The UN shall have a right to subject such nations or its leaders to legal prosecution at the International Court of Justice.

- Centres for Interreligious and Intercultural Dialogue should be set up in each country in various important cities and towns for the regular conduct of such dialogue.

- All international, regional, and national initiatives should be aimed at promoting interreligious, intercultural and interfaith harmony and in combating discrimination against individuals on the basis of faith.

- Defamation of religion is a very vague concept and should be defined clearly and accepted by all nations. Any constructive criticism of religions or faiths should *not* be misconstrued as defamatory just because a section of the followers of the religion deem that to be so.

- Nations that do not adopt and conform to these new resolutions within the stipulated period shall automatically cease to be members of the United Nations. All the member states should ensure that they treat such nations who cease to be members of UN as 'pariahs' in both trade and cultural relations. Nations that fail to do so shall be subject to similar exclusion from the world body.

George explained to all what had happened.

Soon after they reached the other side of the mountain, Morgan and George heard growls of an animal at close range although they could not see any. As they progressed, hiding partially behind pieces of rock strewn on the slope of the other side, they heard two gunshots each flying past them at close range. After staying behind a rock for a while, they were confronted by a mastiff and a snow leopard when they stepped out. The two animals watched every move of the two men, not giving them freedom to advance any further. Long after losing their patience and hope that the beasts would move away, the men decided to return. The two beasts were stubborn and kept a constant vigil on the men until they retreated.

George told Lacene in private that Morgan was upset with her and George for not telling him the full details of her drowning episode and the murder of Jeremy by Sadhá as revealed in his diary. He had learned about it through a message from David while they were in the station-wagon with Abdul and Omar.

George also told Lacene that Morgan was furious with Sadhá, as it was his granddaughter Uma who had dragged Irene into the suspicious 'dowgas' forum, which seemed to have strong links to the destruction of religious sites around the world.

⸺◆⸺

Thánu had a tough time since his return from the hills. After a parachute landing on the damaged airstrip, he had to provide first aid to Siddhu and nurse him back to reasonable health. Before his collapse, Siddhu managed to narrate to Thánu the events that unfolded hours after the flight took off from the airstrip.

Noticing two vehicles approaching the airfield, one of which was Omar's station wagon, Siddhu hurried into the only building in that airstrip, which was used as the signals office.

Of the hundred and one ways to fight, the best was to flee. Or hide.

He knew he had to choose between a fight and a flight. Not knowing how many men came in those two vehicles and how well they were armed, the best thing to do was to hide from their sight and observe them. He locked the building from outside and got in through a secret passage, and hid himself in a corner of the attic. He watched their moves through a peep hole in the tin sheet between the wall and roof.

Four men got down from their vehicles and roamed around the area. Finding the building locked from outside, they looked for any sign of life inside by peeping through the glass windows. Not assisted by the poor lighting inside, their leader signalled them to blow up the building and to damage the runway.

Knowing he couldn't risk being seen, Siddhu took his chances as a grenade was tossed in through one of the windows. The explosion wasn't deadly, but was powerful enough to damage the foundations of the structure and cause it come crashing down. Siddhu staggered out through the damaged roof, after ensuring that they all had left. He was injured by the splattering materials and falling roof despite moving to a safer corner in the attic to hide, well away from the spot where the hand grenade exploded.

With the little energy left in him and the secure walkie-talkie, he conveyed the message to the DDGP of Shimla. He also needed medical help immediately but wanted to sustain and stay there to execute the other greater responsibility. Thánu would be returning anytime in that aircraft. The runway was certainly not landing worthy. From the dying flames of the explosion, he lit a cloth and waved it vigorously, standing at the centre of the runway as the aircraft approached.

Omar had checked in at Hotel Chandra early that morning to avoid suspicion. He feared that the police might have given his picture to many shops and hotels to enquire about him and to inform the police if they saw him. Before that exercise could begin in earnest, he wanted to place himself in a secure and convenient location. His room on the third floor overlooked the front yard of Hotel Shimla and from his seat near the window, he could hide himself, watch his TV and also the entrance to Hotel Shimla in the opposite direction. He was happy that he had done well so far. He didn't realise that sleep would win over him very soon that evening after more than ten hours of vigilant observation.

He had booked his friend Faizal Sheriff, Shahid's brother, at Hotel Shimla and had directed him to befriend the waiters there and pass information to him on his cell phone. His new mobile number was only known to Shahid and Faizal.

Faizal's room was directly below Lacene's. The second floor supervisor had already become Faizal's friend. Who would not like to befriend a plant engineer working for a hotel chain in Kuwait?

Abdul hadn't turned up until that evening; there had been no untoward or interesting incident at Hotel Shimla. If nothing had happened by tomorrow, he planned to go in there himself and search for the diary. Omar tried to continue his much wanted sleep. As he fell into it, the previous night's events replayed in his mind.

Though he was watching helplessly from his car, Omar was equally thrilled at the prospect of witnessing a bomb blast and hearing machine gun fire, for the first time in his life!

He wanted to tell those guys that the place might one day be useful for their activities too! 'Why couldn't they think like that?'

They didn't waste time at the airstrip. The heat of the burning building and airstrip hastened their exit from the scene. The two vehicles sped off towards Shimla. Omar was lying low between rows of seats.

When the car came to a sudden, screeching halt a little more than an hour after leaving the airstrip, Omar wanted to know what happened. His calculations did not show any stopping spot there. He raised his head slowly to look through the window but pulled himself down again in horror. His heart started thumping hard.

A check-post that was not present when they passed by earlier had suddenly cropped up a few kilometres shy of the Hazarpur junction. The two jihadists in his station wagon got down quietly and walked towards the police. The darkness outside helped Omar to hide well enough not to be seen, but he could see what was happening. He expected the jihadists to create a scene and fight with the police. He was surprised when they didn't do so. Omar could see that the guys from the pickup also walked out, very casually. 'Is this all a set-up? Is the policemen part of the jihadist group? Or, is it perhaps that the jihadists think there is no problem as they have proper papers?'

But within the next ten seconds, Omar realised he was wrong. Only two constables stopped them and they were both unarmed. With only a lathi (stick) in their hands, they did not pose any threat. That could be the reason why these four guys got down so casually and one of them spoke in a friendly tone, 'Hum Dharamshala se áthá hai' in chaste Hindi.

'Hán, hán, málum betá!' came a reply from inside the small hut on the left side of the road. Taken aback, the four were shocked to see an AK47-totting police officer emerging from the hut. Two more armed men revealed themselves from a hideout on the other side of the road. Realising that they were outsmarted, all four froze.

Omar was horrified at the prospect of being caught by the law. Plenty of thoughts ran through his mind in that fraction of a second. 'Is this not the voice of Abdul's friend Zein Allabudin? Abdul introduced him to me as an informer in the police. I've met him twice with Abdul.'

To see him as a senior officer in the police shocked Omar immensely. 'You traitor, Abdul!' he cried within himself.

He did not want to be caught by the police for several reasons. First and foremost was the physical torture he may have to endure. Without even knowing what he was doing, he quietly moved into the driver's seat and – Allah in his favour, the engine was still on – hit the accelerator, deftly avoiding all bystanders.

The machine gun fire hit the back of the station wagon twice, shattering the rear window but his speed and zigzag steering saved it from further damage. From the rear-view mirror, he could see a police jeep in hot pursuit. Not wanting to complicate his life further, Omar decided to get out of his vehicle as quickly as possible.

His vehicle having hit the parapet of the small bridge over a stream, he got out of the car along the wall, and jumped into the flowing stream. Abdul's face flashed in his mind, with that mocking smile of his. Omar wanted to wipe it off his face and rip it into shreds. As he plunged into the waters, as though plunging into Abdul and tearing him apart, he heard the sound of an aircraft in the air. Imagining how Abdul's aircraft would crash due to the damaged airstrip, his rage turned into delight at the image of a horrified Abdul inside it.

------◆◆◆------

The bikku was apparently pleased with the points in the paper and was showing his approval by reciting verses from Buddha sutta. The three tenets of Buddhism – Buddham, Dharmam, and Sangham were part of their daily chant.

Buddham Saranam katchaami.
Dharmam Saranam katchaami.
Sangham Saranam katchaami.

'It is only with intellect that one can analyse everything in this world. So I seek with surrender, buddhi, the *intellect*. The word "surrender" has its origins in "saran" or "saranam" from Bali and Sanskrit,' he explained to those around him.

'Dharma means righteousness, it is only with righteousness in mind that one can deal with everything in this world. I seek with surrender, dharma. The word "dharma" means much more than just righteousness.

'Sangham means association, it is only with the association of like-minded people that one can interact and serve everybody in this world. I seek with surrender, sangham, the *association of righteous intellectuals.*'

While everyone appreciated the appropriateness of those words in the context they found themselves in, Lacene, George, and Arthur went a step further and openly applauded the bikku. When the bikku opened his mouth to say something, they heard the footsteps of the monster. They hadn't expected another visit from him on the same day after he had dropped the papers and left.

———◆•◆•◆———

Morgan told Lacene and George in a soft voice, 'I'm pretty sure that this guy is wearing a latex mask to hide his face. He does not want to be identified, I swear.'

While they could not recognise anything of that sort, they both wanted to believe Morgan. His observation could not be wrong. Lacene was anxious to see the face behind the mask.

The Pathan, on nearing them, demanded that all must assemble below him immediately. He then bluntly told them that their lives depended upon the way the world governments and the United Nations responded to his group's demands. The points in that paper he gave them were a part of what the UN was expected to pass as resolutions in its global meet, which was to be held within the next few days. All the nations must accept and pass them as laws in their national legislature bodies immediately. Only then would all be released.

Arthur was the bold one among them to ask, 'What do you think the governments will do? This is too much of an asking or demand. Each nation has its unique make-up and cannot easily comply with what you ask. The UN may be willing to go along with your request but not many nations will. What made your group come up with these strange demands? You don't appear to be like the other jihadists.'

'Indeed we are a special group; we want to bring about religious harmony throughout the world – one of the purported objectives of your international religious pseudo-conferences. However amiable you may all look to be in such gatherings, have you not noticed that the differences among each religion, sect, race, region, language, etc., are so highlighted by humans in their daily lives that they end up in – if not hatred of – indifference and suspicion towards each other? We want those differences to be brought to an end.

'I cite an example to showcase these differences.

'A snake slithers its way through the yard inside a household. The father claims that the snake had five heads, but when his own son claims that the snake had six heads – just one head different from the father's claim – then their hearts break apart. They remain enemies for a very long time! The number of reasons for divisions among people is immeasurable.

'Such is the nature of our people. Even the slightest difference cannot be tolerated and accepted, especially if they offend one's ego. Most differences in religious beliefs stem from such clashes of ego. A 'Why can't you accept the God that I have accepted?' kind of ego.

'That is precisely why we want a uniform code for religious beliefs all over the world. Every group should understand that the other group has sincerely attempted to understand God and creation, and created laws for peaceful living. It is imperative that future generations are not raised in such suspicious and hate-filled environments.

'Religious teachers like you are the culprits. The pundits, the rabbis, the bishops, the pastors, the imams, the moulanas, the bikkus. You are the ones who sowed the seeds of hatred amongst humans – seeds that thrive beyond science, technology, and communication, seeds that tear apart the human population from becoming one.

'You are the ones who, in your zeal for promoting and marketing your beliefs, deride the other beliefs stereotypically and poison the minds of the ignorant and the innocent people.'

There was total silence among the audience.

Before turning to go, the Pathan commanded Lacene, 'Follow me.'

Shocked at his words, the rabbi came in front of Lacene and shouted at the Pathan that he could only take her after his death. George came forward too to question him.

Lacene had been deeply looking at the Pathan for a while. When he called her she just walked towards him as if to accompany him. Although he was at first taken aback, George allowed her to go, having noticed the resolve in her move. The rabbi was devastated and pleaded with Lacene not to go. He was worried that the Pathan and his mates would not return her alive, or worse could happen to her.

Lacene turned towards her uncle. 'I will take care of myself. Do not worry about me. I know what I'm doing.'

With those words she walked alongside the Pathan with absolute confidence. Morgan saw his suspicions coming true. 'This woman cannot be trusted any more. I have to be cautious with George as well,' he thought to himself.

At his room on the third floor of Hotel Chandra opposite Shimla hotel, Omar woke up when his phone rang incessantly. Annoyed, he answered it. 'What the hell do you want?'

Shahid said, 'How long can we keep calling you? The floor supervisor was about to break open the door, worried that you might be dead!'

'No ways!' Omar retorted. 'I needed rest. What's news from Delhi?'

'I'm sure we will get something very soon. They have spotted the wife and have located her apartment.'

'Good; don't disturb me unless you have news for me.'

Shahid understood and disconnected. He called Riaz, the floor supervisor, to assure him that Fakhrudeen was sleeping in his room.

Omar tried to continue his much wanted sleep. But he also remembered to set his alarm for 6 p.m. He was happy that his team of friends who helped unsuccessfully in retrieving the diary and list from Lacene and George in Delhi at Abdul's bidding were available to help him trace Abdul's family background.

Although Omar did not know his Delhi address, he had a photo of Abdul and Sairá Bhánu taken immediately after their wedding, which Abdul had not bothered to take back from Omar.

Through Shahid, he got the photo scanned, emailed and faxed to Shahid's friend in Delhi, asking him to trace them and give him feedback. He sent some money through Western Union to the contact in Delhi for his services.

Omar's mind was on the diary. He was sure that Abdul would certainly go to Hotel Shimla looking for it which – Omar remembered clearly – Lacene told Abdul she had left in her room.

'I must track Abdul's moves from now on. I must possess that diary; it must be of extremely high value. And, take my revenge, Inshá Allah!'

Finding that his family and neighbours had already been rounded up and questioned late last night, Omar decided not to venture into his locality and put them into more trouble. He relied on his friend, the saloon owner Shahid Iqbál, to assist him.

The money Abdul had earlier given him for his expenses and for safekeeping was still with Shahid.

***

Although everyone sat there with the paper in their hands and their mind on Lacene, the bikku told them not to worry about anything. He could see Lacene as a strong person with adequate intellect and morals, very much in line with Buddha's teachings. He explained to his fellow hostages what the essence of Buddhism meant.

Gautama attained self-realisation and enlightenment under a bodhi tree – bodhi literally meant 'to preach'- that gave him those three steps to be taken in unison to attain peace, harmony, and happiness in this world – a world beset with woes of numerous kinds.

Buddha realized the truth in the age-old belief of the four kinds of people in the world:

1. Those that know and know that they know.
2. Those that know but do not know that they know.

3. Those that do not know but know that they do not know.
4. Those that do not know and do not know that they do not know.

A Supreme power created everything but that does not control our lives here. It has set off a system that we understand only partially. Our lives are all run by that system. Using an interfering and punishing God as a tool to keep others in ignorance was one of the many means the elite adopted to stay in control.

Buddha wanted every individual to learn these truths, to come out of the shackles of traditional beliefs and seek enlightenment through intelligence, righteousness and association with such people.

Having realized the immense truth in this theory and understanding people as they were, Buddha concentrated on the dissemination of this truth to the last three strata of people in that classification, and helped them attain the same enlightenment as the first stratum.

He had also noticed that each of the first three in the list was exploiting the rest in one way or the other – sometimes the three together exploiting the fourth. And one of the main instruments they used in such exploitation was religion.

Feeling a vibration in his pocket, Stuart pulled out his phone, and saw that he'd received a Whatsapp message from Aziz. The message shocked him as it revealed the outreach of the terrorists. He could not believe that it could be their work but the name of the church was on the list in the second page.

Lourdes, France:

The Lourdes flooding has damaged the Sanctuary of Notre Dame de Lourdes and forced officials to close the site. Heavy storms have created serious flooding in the area, which has been closed and evacuated.

A popular pilgrimage site because of the sighting of Our Lady of Lourdes in the area, it is believed the sanctuary has healing powers and can restore health. About six million people visit Lourdes every year. Officials are concerned that the flooding will threaten pilgrimages this year. The floods are having an impact on the Gave de Pau River, and it has gone up by fifteen feet.

Early estimates of the damage have already reached more than $2 million. Although the water has not receded, and evacuations are still in place, the sanctuary has started to request donations to help fix the damage. In 2012, Lourdes also suffered from flood damage, but officials believe the destruction this year will be greater.

The local population in Lourdes, however, griped that their demands to strengthen the foundation of the Cathedral were never heeded by authorities, and they suspected sabotage by vested interests in the failure to protect this holy site.

10. One-Night Stand

Does history support a belief in God? If by God we mean not the creative vitality of nature but a Supreme Being intelligent and benevolent, the answer must be a reluctant negative. History is full of injustices committed by man against man.

———◆———

'Are you really going to destroy the 216 religious sites?' was Lacene's first question as soon as they were away from earshot of the rest.

'Sure I am, Lacene,' was his terse reply, to her great disappointment as he removed his latex mask together with the wig. His face had not changed much, Lacene felt, but he had lost some hair.

'I can't wear this mask any longer. It's such an irritant.'

The moment they were away from others' eyeshot, Lacene clung to his arm and leaned on his shoulder. 'I can't express how grateful to you I am for saving George and for saving me on the happiest day of my life. I had never realised it was you for so long!'

She took his right palm in her hands and pressed it to both her eyes in respect, as Indians do to show their reverence. It was as good as touching his feet for paying her obeisance.

Sadhá stroked her head with love. 'I just happened to be there Lacene, that's all. It was in George's case that I went a bit out of the way. I saw him at base camp on my return from K2, accompanying another group whom I had escorted. His team was about to start their climb for C2. Of course, he didn't recognise me – how could he?

'It was just some uncomfortable feeling I had that made me follow his team. Conditions in K2, I had noticed, were turning worse unusually early in the season. Well aware of the merciless savageness of K2, I never expected I would be saving George; it could have been anyone else in his team, or none of them at all.

'After leaving him at C1 early the next morning, I had to rush to this spot through a shorter route. That was a hell of a journey. I had hardly three days to reach here as the clerics were supposed to land by then. I covered 180 kilometres in two and half days and am happy I made it.'

'Where are we and with whom did you arrange all of this? What is all this about, guru? Is there no alternative to your plans? Should it happen, the repercussions would be catastrophic!'

Lacene realised that they were descending towards his abode on the other side of that hill. Her mind was calculating 180 kms from K2 to determine her location but wasn't sure if they were south, southwest or southeast of K2.

'If there is no positive response from the UN and all the nations by this Monday, yes, I have no alternative.'

Lacene looked at her watch. Only five days till next Monday.

Besides the disappointment, Sadhá's reply was also shocking to her. Lacene hesitated to ask him further when Sadhá spoke by himself, sensing her dilemma.

'I have been in a completely different world altogether in the past decade, Lacene. It is not only the al-Qaeda and the Taleban; there are numerous minds out there in this world that have been corrupted by religions, Holy Scriptures and blind beliefs. The so-called developed countries are no exception.

'Education doesn't really mean that people get enlightened with true knowledge. There has been a disproportionate rise in stupidity and idiocy despite the developments and advancements in science. It is so heartbreaking to see people still mired in millennium-old beliefs when nature has consistently been showing us the way forward.'

'Is monotheism not the solution to the problems? Are not the religions of the Middle East – the Abrahamic faiths – the answer?' asked Lacene.

'They are no better. In fact, they are also mired in irrational beliefs. Moreover, they are already divided into three religions, each on the other's throat, and into further numerous sub-sects. Even if the rest of the faiths and non-faiths unite, I do not foresee any chance of these three coming together. They've sealed the fate of humanity forever.'

'I saw your conditions given in the print out yesterday. I am sure those papers must have come with us on that flight. I don't think we will see any positive response from most of the nations. May be the UN would agree as they are also striving towards a similar goal but not many of its member nations. If they do not fulfil your demands, what do you hope will happen by destroying all those religious sites? The repercussions are going to be catastrophic!'

'Let us talk in my cabin, come!'

Sadhá's abode was also a cave-like structure, a natural, huge dent in the rock modified by human hands to make it a decent living space. At the outset, an antenna could be seen. Lacene could not determine if it was just a radio antenna. The inside looked like a campsite, with all the facilities required of a sentry post. The mastiff was sitting outside the cave and was happily wagging its tail. She could see the snow leopard in the distance, basking in the sun.

'Do you have my diary with you here, Lacene?'

'No, I didn't want to take chances, wasn't sure where we were heading to. Abdul did give some hints, but at that time we could not trust him fully. George also advised against it, so I have left it in our hotel room.'

'I don't think it would be safe there. The other jihadist groups may be spying over that hotel. I believe they are all going to be rounded up at any moment. Does Thanu know that you have left it there?'

Lacene could not understand who these jihadist groups could be. But she could sense that Abdul and Thánu was one person. 'Who is Thánu? Do you mean Abdul? I think he knows. I mentioned it to him.'

'Let's hope Thánu retrieves it.'

———— ◆ ————

'The first place we checked for our dad after the 9/11 disaster was at the Kauai Hindu Monastery in the Kauai islets of Hawaii. His last visit to that Monastery was six months before 9/11. His last phone call to them was on 8/11, telling them that he would be with them by mid-September that year. They didn't hear from him after that. They didn't make efforts to contact him either. I checked with them first because he was always telling us that he would like to settle down there.

'His aim was to bring about religious harmony and, if possible, to restructure all scriptures into a combined one that could be taught at all institutions as the basic universal religious holy text. The UN would play a major role in effectively implementing that idea.

'His earlier attendance at two World Religious Conferences gave him the hope that such a restructuring would not be an empty dream.'

Saraswathi told David about her father's preferences. David had agreed to spend the night in their home when Saraswathi and her husband John Wafula asked him to. Emily was delighted to be in the company of Lucky and Innocent with whom she built an instant rapport. They showed her wonderful worlds in their rooms.

Innocent's was like a cabin inside a spacecraft! Lucky's room was like a secret garden – something Emily couldn't imagine possible.

Both Innocent and Lucky kept her fully entertained until they all went to bed. The elders discussed matters in the lounge, drinking green tea.

———— ◆ ————

Lying on his bed in Hotel Chandra opposite Hotel Shimla, Omar replayed the events of his last twelve hours.

Omar's previous night was a mixture of varied experiences. The villagers who sheltered him near the stream treated him with so much love and concern for his health that he was deeply moved by their hospitality.

Swimming for only ten minutes in those cold waters, he decided to seek the shore to prevent an attack of pneumonia. He also had to ensure that he was getting out far enough from the bridge to not be spotted by the policemen on his tail.

Abdul! Omar hated Abdul for leaving him high and dry in such a situation. Had he been sent with the hostages, it would be Abdul facing all that trouble. On second thought, he felt, 'Perhaps not'.

Abdul did advise him to return using the other route. 'I decided to have a cup of tea in that junction before reverting to the other route. Maybe I should have followed his advice,' he mused.

But the image of Zein Allabudin in police uniform brought back his anger towards Abdul.

How did the police officers arrive there in such a short time and set up that post? Omar didn't see them on any of his three trips on that way. Unless the blast in that airstrip alerted the police, there was no reason for them to be there. There was nobody in that airstrip building to inform them nor could anyone have survived the explosion. Such swift reaction by the police – if it was in response to that incident – was highly unusual!

The senior police officer that came out with his aide carrying an AK47, sporting a badge -'Vijay Malhotra'- was certainly the same Zein Allabuddin, a friend of Abdul.

Omar had seen Zein Allábuddin in Abdul's company twice in the last three months. He was introduced to Omar as an informer from the HP Police, on their group's payroll.

'Either this Vijay Malhotra has double-crossed Abdul or Abdul has used me. Did Abdul see my desire to join a jihadist group to help the Kashmiri cause and hooked me into his trap? If my suspicion proves true, then Abdul deserves death by my hands,' he fumed.

Shahid called just then; the information he provided about Abdul's family in Delhi shocked Omar. Abdul's real name was Thànu; his only wife – the same one Omar had a photo of – lived in the Senior Central government employees' staff quarters in Delhi with her two sons- one from her first husband and the other from Abdul – no, Thànu. The realisation that an Indian government official in the guise of a prospective Indian Mujahedeen had used him enraged him so much that he smashed the coffee table in front of him. He ended up bribing the room service person heftily to get that coffee table repaired without the knowledge of the hotel management. He didn't want his identity to be questioned by any one at any level at that point in time.

'"Thánu" means "on its own". The term "Swa" which also meant "on its own" got disfigured into Siva or Eswa as many people could not pronounce 'swa' clearly. Lord Siva, whose place is at the centre of the universe, is the origin of everything and is called "Thánu" in Tamil. From him sprang all galaxies including our Milky Way.

"Mál" means "the black god", Lord Vishnu whose abode is the centre of the Milky Way and can be equated to the "black hole" at the core that controls everything in our galaxy.

"Ayan" or "Ayyan" means "the Enlightened or Superior one", but here it denotes "Lord Brahma" who, having arisen from the navel of Lord Vishnu, is the source of life. He created all beings on our planet.'

That was the explanation he got when Aziz asked *Thánumálayan Pillai* during their first meeting, wondering what his long name meant.

'Is that so? I haven't heard a similar name in the north combining all of the Hindu Trinity!' Aziz admired. 'What's your father's name?'

'My father's name is Sámbha Sivam Pillai. Sámbhal in Tamil means 'ashes', from 'asthi' in Sanskrit. It represents the cosmic dust and my father always jokes that I was born of 'dust'! My community surname is Pillai, which also means 'son'. Thánu-mál-ayan Pillai. I am son of the Hindu Trinity.'

'I've to be careful with you, Thánu. You're a powerful person!'

Aziz took Thánu's confidential file and wanted to spend some time sipping his strong, hot coffee, poring through it.

Thánumálayan Sámbhasivam Pillai.

Thánu came from a small temple town called "Sucheendram", near Kanya Kumari in the southern most tip of India. His Tamil dialect was quite different from the other Madrásis. It had a strong Malayalam accent. Thànu always claimed that his dialect was the purest of all Tamil dialects – as did everyone else.

He got into the Indian Air Force (IAF) through the National Defence Academy (NDA), admission into which was through some very tough competitive exams and physical tests. Being one of the youngest to become a flight lieutenant, he was soon absorbed by the National Security Services unit that protected VIPs and strategic defence power centres spread across various regions in the country. Soon after that he was sent to Afghanistan to support India's various projects there in the development of their client nation's defence establishments.

Thánu became a star performer in RAW under the PMO. He

- Worked at different levels after serving in the air force for five years.
- Was sent to Kabul to work for the success of projects undertook by the Indian government.
- Specialised in penetrating into the rival's strongholds and breaking them apart dextrously.
- Was summoned urgently to New Delhi six months ago from Kabul to undertake some adventurous, top-secret missions.

He was one of the few who had strongly forewarned of the 26/11 attacks in Mumbai thanks to sources he had reared in the dangerous realms of Kabul's suburbs. It was in that attack – he was distraught that it was allowed to happen – that his close friend Raheem, husband of Saírá Bhánu, niece to Aziz, was fatally injured. Since that fateful incident, Thánu had been shuttling between Kabul and Delhi.

He was the one to first uncover a plot by two jihadist units based in Waziristan of abducting and holding hostage a team of religious clerics attending the Shimla Conference. That group was believed to have aimed at demanding the release of Ajmal Kazab, the lone assassin captured alive from the 26/11 attack, who was awaiting execution.

He was instrumental in drawing up an elaborate plan to thwart the attempts of those groups without raising any doubts in their minds and in the minds of any other group. His plan was approved without second thought by the authorities thanks to the very good record he had created for himself with his exemplary service thus far. And, thanks to the unmatchable perfection of his plan.

Personally, he was a saviour to Aziz, whose sister was devastated when her only daughter Sairá Bhánu became a widow while delivering the family's first third-generation child. Thánu married her on Raheem's insistence before his tragic death after those injuries in the 26/11 attack.

If there was one person Aziz was most indebted to, it was Thánu.

Despite elaborate and many times open operations in Jammu & Kashmir state, the arms and wings of terrorist groups were never allowed to spread in Himachal Pradesh. At least that's what the central and state governments sincerely believed.

And that's precisely why they did not want to allow any event like the abduction of innocent civilians – that too visitors, some pious, peace-loving clerics – to take place in that state.

The clerics were abducted by Thánu and his team, a day earlier than planned by the two jihadist groups, who were misled into believing that another group had already abducted them. Their movements were tracked so that all their links in Shimla and erstwhile Himachal Pradesh could be traced and nipped in the bud.

So far, so good.

The so-called demands of the current group that had seemingly abducted those eight clerics were communicated to all concerned nations and the UN. The media and public were purposely kept in the dark with limited and doctored releases of information that aimed to reach – not only them – but also the jihadist groups.

Until such time that the entire network of terrorist outfits trying to establish base in Shimla and Himachal Pradesh were completely rooted out – that was promised to happen within a week from the day of abduction – all terrorist groups should remain in a state of confusion and belief that 'another group' was holding the hostages and making the demands. No news from any source should cause them to doubt the effectiveness of the particular group holding the clerics hostage.

'The Indian government would, naturally, not reveal to the public or media that the abductors were demanding the release of Kazab. No way,' that would be the line of thought amongst all terrorist outfits. They would not doubt that there were no strong demands from the abductors. A section of the media had already raised doubts if the abductors had demanded such a release, though!

Everything had worked well so far. Numerous clandestine talks and coded messages were interrupted and their sources identified. RAW and state police worked in tandem to trace those groups and drew up a plan to nab all of them in one sweep – Operation Wipe-out Now.

But this latest demand – and threat – with a list of 216 holy sites around the world, did not figure anywhere in the plan projected by Thànu and his team. More irksome was their demand for the UN, OCHRC, and all nations to immediately convene an emergency session to pass resolutions that would bind all nations on a number of issues relating to religious freedom – rather, freedom from religion.

Why was this new development causing so much anxiety now? What was Thánu doing?

Aziz had to resort to the last option he had. RAW Directorate also had no information about Thánu's whereabouts. Their team in Shimla was busy rounding up several jihadist gang members in and around Shimla. Without Thànu, he was sure that the whole drama would end up in a great mess. He had to get approval from the home minister immediately for the next steps he would take. He must prepare a top-secret dossier and ensure its quick passage through the home ministry.

News had just arrived from the RAW office that one more flight trip was made the previous night without any prior approval or permission. It was still not clear if the information was true. Aziz awaited further communiqué from the base in Shimla about that. He had already ordered an inquiry into that reported flight trip. He also ordered that another capable sleuth be sent immediately to Shimla to contact Thànu and handle the release of the eight clerics.

Thánu's silence caused him real anxiety, worry, and palpitations.

Lacene got Sadhá to agree that she would call him 'Guru'.

'You won't believe me, Guru! You may have saved me from drowning in that pool, but you literally trapped me into this whirlpool of Tamil and its literary treasure. I am dwelling deeper and deeper into it and do not see any hope of coming out of it! It indeed is an "amudhak kadal" (Ocean of nectar)'!

Sadhá was delighted to notice that Lacene spoke fluent Tamil, much better than most Tamilians! According to her, she had spent almost half her life in the past decade in Tamil Nadu and India. He was particularly happy that she had read Thirumoolar's *Thirumanthiram* in its entirety. 'That single book would suffice for true enlightenment, Lacene.' She agreed with him wholeheartedly.

'Why do the Tamils claim Lord Siva as "thennádudaiya Sivan" as though he "belongs only to south" of India? Even Siva has another name "Dhakshina Moorthy" meaning 'Icon of the south'. Does he not belong to the whole of India? Is it because North India has more Vaishnavites?'

'Not at all, Lacene. That term "then-nádu-udaiya" or "Dhakshina" means the land south of the Himalayas and not just south India or south of the Vindhya Mountains. People distorted words and diffused the original meanings. In fact, Lord Siva's abode has always been believed to be the Himalayas. And it is true that he was not popular in Tibet, China, Mongolia, or even central Asia, which all lie north of the Himalayas. He was the prime deity in all the lands stretching from Thailand to Afghanistan – almost the entire belt to its south protected and enriched by the great mountain range.'

'Now I get it! I have so much to ask you that this single night is not going to be enough. Would you mind that we spend the whole night talking? Do you have a lot to do tomorrow?'

'Would be happy to do so, Lacene. I insisted that they bring you here so I can spend some time with you. I know Thánu must have taken a great risk in bringing you here. Well, forget all that. Let's clear your mind of all its doubts.'

'Soon after 9/11 we were resigned to the idea that he was gone forever. I'm not surprised but happy that he is alive. But I won't be calling him here. If he has chosen not to contact us for all these years, he must have a reason. He has always been an independent person. He will come to us only if he feels that **we** need him. Give and forget has been his policy. He has always described 'home' as the place 'where if one has to go there, the people there will have to take him! I reckon he has not reached a stage where he felt compelled to come to us!'

'I am impressed! Can there be such a person who had loved his family so much yet not visited them for more than a decade especially in his old age? What kind of a mindset is that? Does he consider himself a messiah, serving the lot?' David wondered loudly.

'He doesn't believe in messiahs. No messiah had delivered the perfect panacea for all the ills humanity suffers from. He never believed that there were divinely recognised messiahs. I believe so, too.'

'What makes you believe so? A plethora of messiahs have treaded..'

'If you count the generations from the times of Adam and Eve until the period of Jesus of Nazareth – I quote him here just for the known number of years from his era, two millennia plus years – we can estimate the number of centuries between them. For almost every in-between generation, your holy scripture the Torah has recorded divine intervention with someone in the hierarchy.

'Then how is it that your Lord Yahweh has not had some means of interaction with anyone in the last two thousand years? Or at least sent an angel on his behalf? How is it that, when you were actually and finally handed the "promised land" by the then US President – figuratively, no Messiah was present to glorify that occasion?

'Why do you still continue to extol your scripture so vehemently? Unless you claim that you have your own secret interactions with your God that you wouldn't like to share with the rest of the world – I mean your Jewish community,' said Saraswathi.

Taken aback, David Levite tried to explain to her that one should read the Torah and the Talmud in their entirety before raising such queries. 'There are a lot of things to be studied and understood before coming to such irrational conclusions.'

'You are clearly running away from the problem, Mr Levite. This is exactly the way the Israeli spokespersons or Jewish leaders answer difficult queries, you are no different!'

John chided her. 'You can't embarrass our guest like this, Sara! Can't you talk of other things?'

'The number one burning issue in this world today is the Palestinian crisis, honey. You can't lay claims to a land that most of you have abandoned for sixteen or seventeen centuries and then aim to drive away the very people who have lived there for that long! And you can't declare them second citizens in the land you claim is the "Promised Land" in your holy text!

'Will the whites agree to cede the entire Americas or Australia to the original sons of the soil, on the very fair grounds that these whites have only been there for the past five centuries or less? And, will all the whites eventually return to Europe? They will not, isn't it? Is it because those poor aborigines do not have a Torah or Bible to prove that the Almighty was always in touch with them and promised them those lands only to them?'

David could feel his brain and body stiffening. Saraswathi was looking like the monstrous Kàli that she spoke about at the conference, ready to devour him and his clan. He tried to open his mouth but could not. Only his eyes showed his total contempt for the way she spoke.

'It would be good for your people to do this, Mr Levite. Besides the Palestine issue, the Muslims in the world may have a dislike for the Jews because at some stage in his life their Prophet is said to have uttered words that signalled his disapproval of Jews for whatever reason. So the resistance from the Muslims can easily be projected as just that – religious hatred.

'But among the rest of the world – of the 80 per cent of non-Muslim people – clearly more than half do not approve of Israel's stance on the Palestinians. This is not a view of a doctorate scholar but of simple common folk who regularly read some news about the world. World media also is not on your side, as you may tend to believe.

'It is better you all wake up to that reality now than when it is too late. The holocaust did happen and the whole world – barring a little – does sympathise with the Jews. But they will not have the same sympathy if any calamity befalls your community in the future for any reason. If you have not read that so far, then you are living in a fool's paradise.

'And remember – there is no Yahweh. There is no Allah. No Jesus. No other God. All that this god - or goddess as I may propound-, does here is what we humans do by ourselves – individually and collectively. If the history of this world has not taught you this lesson and if you stick to your Holy Scriptures forever, then you are still in a dream world.'

'You have spoken very offensively to our guest, Sara. I am not happy about it at all. How do you say that history has taught the absence of any God? I haven't read anything like that anywhere! I haven't heard you saying this before, either' said John.

'In real history, John, which God has come to rescue anyone in such a way that the reign of that person or tribe or religion had lingered long enough to be remembered or admired? No nation that has a state religion – from times memorial – has proved to have flourished or ruled with milk and honey flowing in its streets or with all its citizens living blissfully forever! On what grounds then can anyone claim that there is a God and he would redeem us all? There may be many a story from mythology or scriptures to such effect, not from history.'

'But you have a Judgment Day or afterlife, heaven or hell,' said John.

'For how long are we going to fool ourselves with these theories, dear? And, if there are such things, who cares? Who would prefer an unknown angel, the life after, to a known devil, the life here?'

'Then how can goodness prevail? What motivates people to do good deeds if they are not assured of a reward or refrain from bad if there is no threat of a punishment?'

Saraswathi's response was swift. 'By continuing to educate everyone that we are all one, that no differences exist between us, that we have to fairly share to be happy, that our conscience and sense of social responsibility would do well to keep us away from wrong deeds.'

'Madam, you are into a utopian world that we cannot fathom. We have believed in certain things and will have to continue to believe in them because that is how our ancestors have taught us to live and believe in. For me to digest what you have said and to change my mindset to that level, my lifetime will not be sufficient.' David spoke at last.

On David's insistence, Sara began to detail what made her arrive at such strange interpretations and conclusions. John Wafula bade them 'Goodnight'. He knew that for those two people to solve this world's problems, one night wasn't going to be enough. When David and Sara decided to end their discussion, it was almost dawn!

Thánu deliberately avoided contacting Aziz for the next twenty-four hours. He did not want the plans and strategies adopted by him and Sadhá to be thwarted by anyone. After rescuing Siddhu from the airstrip and admitting him to a private hospital, he had to take care of a number of issues that he had to do.

The previous night was a nightmare for him. He didn't expect the airstrip to be so badly damaged. Finding that the aircraft could not land there thanks to the signal from Siddhu on the runway, the pilot gained altitude at the last moment and discussed a plan of action with Thánu. Thánu then decided to take a short rope jump to see how badly Siddhu was injured. The aircraft took a U-turn and flew low enough above the grass for Thánu to jump off without much damage to him.

After getting Thánu's signal, the pilot moved on to the next airstrip and messaged the relevant authorities for help. Help arrived after almost four hours. In the meantime, Thánu tended to Siddhu to save him from grave consequences. He had to remove – with Siddhu in great pain – as many as seven shrapnel from his body. Siddhu had lost a lot of blood. Only after he was assured by the physician on night duty that Siddhu was out of danger, did Thánu leave the hospital. It was already dawn by then, and he needed to sleep desperately. But time was not on his side.

He got the message that more than twenty members of four different terrorist outfits in and around Shimla had been rounded up so far. Four were apprehended last night from their vehicles on the Shimla-Dharamshala highway, but he did not get full details. He was sure that Omar was among them. More arrests were expected soon.

He was smiling to himself and wondered how Omar would be reacting now inside a cell. Would he suspect his mentor Abdul? 'No. Perhaps he would be hoping I would come to his rescue. Well, I should do that. I should get the least sentence possible for him. He had not – at least so far – partaken in any subversive activity other than those initiated by his most trusted, but wily Madrási, Abdul Allah Pitchai. I have eaten from his mother's hands, and I can't bring distress to that poor, noble lady.'

The ten men at the foot of that hill, on the other side, were seriously discussing the demands of the abductors to the UN and all the nations. There were practical difficulties in the implementation of those demands, even if passed as resolutions at the UN. Most of the nations would call that outrageous and seek to capture the group and eliminate them for making such atrocious demands in the first place. Many nations had declared Islam or Christianity as their state religion. Israel was a Jewish state by design and creation. Some had taken Buddhism as the national religion. None of these nations would rewrite their constitutions on those secular lines.

George told them that he fully supported the demands of the group as they bode progress and prosperity in the long term for all of humanity, and would love to join them. He countered by asking the others to show one reason why the group should be punished when it had not subjected any of them to any form of torture except, of course, confining them against their will in a remote place.

When the others raised issue about the Pathan taking his wife alone for probable torture or abuse, George sternly replied that they did not need to worry about that. Lacene was an adult woman capable of defending herself against any form of abuse or torture and had gone with the Pathan on her own will. There was no force or violence in that move.

Including the rabbi, no one was happy. Morgan was convinced beyond doubt that George was a part of the whole plan. Although Lacene and George did not expressly tell him that the Pathan was none other than the Hindu priest Saddam, he was certain that it was him.

Morgan wondered if George could have spent considerable time on K2 discussing this abduction plan with Saddam. If not for David's call and email, Morgan would have missed a great opportunity to capture one of the world's most dangerous terrorist groups.

Long hours of discussions until late in the evening ended without any firm conclusion as to what their stand would be on those demands. The clerics agreed in principle that the suggestions were all worth taking good note of and worth a referendum in each of their countries. But they were quite sceptical about all nations accepting and implementing them. They all went to sleep knowing very well that they would not sleep peacefully. Those demands would torment them throughout the night.

———◆•◆•◆———

George felt the absence of Lacene in the cave and wondered what kind of a bed she would have got at the other end with Sadhá. He fondly reminisced how Lacene would time and again excitedly relate to him the reasons for her mad love of Tamil.

Lacene would wake up suddenly from deep sleep and shout, 'How did I not tell you this? Do you know that the word "culture" stems from Tamil or Sanskrit "kala áchár"? Kala is art. Ácháram denotes "discipline, practices, regular habits, traits, applications in daily life of practices that have been followed for ages by our fore parents". How stupid the westerners were in not capturing the essential meaning of the words in their languages? They even use it in science!'

George learnt to be patient with her during such occasions and would tease her with 'can one example like this suffice to put your point across?' He knew that she would be eager to be challenged.

'What do you mean? I can bombard you with hundreds of them! Circle came from "chakar". We didn't even have a word for killing or murdering others. Kill came from "kol" in Tamil. Even the mouse that we all use like an extension of our arm nowadays was 'moushikam' in Sanskrit or 'moonchooru' in Tamil. That's the rodent Lord Vinayaka rides on. Such a tiny one carrying the huge elephant!'

'I thought "mouse" came from its whiskers that were like a "moustache".' George would giggle.

'Don't be silly George. Tell me, what has the word "curriculum" got to do with a person's career record or bio data?'

'Don't tell me it has anything to do with "curry", the Indian spice!'

'Kárya means work or career; kramam means "in an order" or "in sequence". "Kárikramam" is a term used to mean the "order of events". Even TV channels

210

use this term to denote programs of the day. "Curriculum" came from *kaari-kramam*, the career sequence.'

'You say that the Europeans did not know how to set the events of their lives in a sequence until they got this word from Indians?'

'I don't claim so, but the etymology of that word speaks for itself. If we go to the origin of such words, we find that they have emanated from somewhere in India. That tells us that after its migration from Africa, mankind must have settled for a long while in parts of India; after gaining intelligence and language they moved to the rest of the world.'

'I agree if you say India was the cradle of mankind, I have read that from great scholars; but why do you insist that Tamil was the cradle of civilization?'

'You are losing patience, G, I know. But listen to me carefully.'

George would curse himself for raising a point like that but had no choice but to listen.

'"Kal" is a wonderful word. In Sanskrit – as in Hindi and most Indian languages – it means both "the past/yesterday" and "the future/tomorrow". In Tamil it denotes "past", "stone", and "ancient". "Karkálam" means "stone period" or "stone age".

'Again, as a verb, "kal" means "learn", we "learn from our past"!

'"Kalai" is the "act of learning" that graduates into an art. "Kalai" simply means "art".

'Mind you, George, don't get offended – even "nation" comes from Tamil's "nádu". A person from a certain place, say a hill is called a "malai nádan" meaning "highlander". From "nádan" came nation.

'Now, the rest of India used to call the plains south of the Vindhyas as "karnád", meaning "kal nád" or "ancient land". One of the states in that region is named after that as "Karnátaka".

'British transformed "karnátak" to "carnátic". The rest of India called this region "karnátak" or "ancient land". It goes without saying that this was one of the oldest "developed" regions of India from where people migrated to other parts of India and therefore fondly referred to this place as their "ancient land"!

'Even in those ages, outsiders came in with curiosity to learn art and literature from this land.'

George certainly didn't want to prolong her talk and would say, 'Quite possible. I don't want to dispute that as long as you promise you won't keep adding more and more proofs to drive that point home!' George was obviously tired of hearing such claims.

Fourteen years of celibacy!

Morgan spent a sleepless night with those last messages from Stuart and mixed feelings arising from recent events tormenting him. Lacene's words about the near-divine qualities of Rama's three brothers and their wives who remained purely celibate for fourteen years waiting for the return from exile of Ram, Sita, and Lakshman – spending their prime youth in a penance – kept haunting Morgan.

'Did such people really live? Are they real life or fictional characters? I could not stay without sex for two weeks at a stretch!'

George had seconded Lacene's views while they were hiding behind the rock with the two animals watching over them earlier that day. 'Even considering them to be mythological, such characters leave messages for us to emulate.' George had said.

The bottom of his heart told Morgan that Florence started neglecting him only on suspicion of his one night stands – one too many.

He also felt very sad that the love about to blossom between him and his online girlfriend had to be nipped in the bud. Her bombarding messages after his failure to join her in Hawaii reeked of desperation and ended that affair.

He regretted the separation from his wife Florence that had resulted in Irene losing direction and ending up a pawn in the hands of the witch that Uma had proven herself to be. Morgan had faced many such situations in his life and was strong enough to withstand or even overcome all of them. But anything adverse happening to Irene was too much for him to bear.

He realised that he was sobbing. Florence and Irene were repeatedly appearing in his nightmare.

━━━━━━━━━◆•◆•◆━━━━━━━━━

Thánu slept the whole day except for the two visits he made discreetly to see Siddhu. It was very important for him to ensure that there was no laxity at the hospital and also no suspicious visits that could endanger Siddhu's life. From the information he gathered at the hospital, he had no reason to believe that anyone could have known about Siddhu and his condition following the attack at the airstrip.

Only after he was sure of Siddhu's safety and good medical care did he start thinking of his next assignments.

He had to contact a few trusted members of the media for the timely release of news about the clerics and the threat to the religious sites. Besides that, he also had to send off an advertisement for a death anniversary for the classified columns in select newspapers.

His mind thought next about the diary. 'I must go in my original form – trim moustache, a summer crop but no goatee, jeans and a t–shirt. I should not be identified by anyone there.'

He had been there thrice – in different get-ups – once as Ganesh and twice as Abdul. Nobody had recognised him as the other. This time around he planned not only to succeed in his disguise but to also get access to Lacene's room. 'The diary is important for the good of the world. I know its worth in full measure.'

━━━━━━━━━◆•◆•◆━━━━━━━━━

Aziz decided to visit his niece, Thánu's wife Sairá Bhánu, and find out his whereabouts from her. That was the only reliable source, and he was confident that his niece wouldn't hide anything from him. He hadn't met her and the kids, Sulaiman and Patanjali, for more than three months. That gave him a good reason to stop by Thánu's flat unannounced.

The Intelligence Directorate reported that while there was significant breakthrough and progress in cracking the terrorist networks in Himachal Pradesh, they had not heard anything from Thánu. The last contact was from Siddhu, the previous night, purportedly from the airstrip. Later, the police found the airstrip totally damaged but no human soul there, only bloodstains. Investigations were on.

That was not pleasant news. Could anything have happened to Thánu?

Aziz found himself at Thánu's apartment in Dwárka in the next hour, in southwest Delhi. No phone call was necessary. He was always a welcome visitor to Sairá's home; a surprise visit would also ensure a sumptuous dinner with Kaima dosa and varieties of chutney.

He ate to his heart's delight, but he also ended up spending the night in that apartment. True to what she told him over phone, Sairá was a concerned wife at the long silence of Thànu.

Besides that she narrated - with fear in her eyes – about the movement of strangers around her complex and the visit of two men in the guise of electronicians who came to check the security alarm system installed in the apartments.

She had later realised that the security company did not send anyone. Aziz grew suspicious and started contacting the relevant people to increase vigilance. He decided to spend the night there, just to make Sairá feel secure. He called his wife to inform her of his decision.

———◆◆◆———

'I couldn't believe it. I started thinking in Tamil, Guru! And the flow of my thought and words were always spontaneously in Tamil. It was an effort for me to revert to the language of the person in front of me. After reading, memorising, and regularly reciting some of Arunagiri Náthar's *Tiruppugazh*, my fluency in Tamil almost reached perfection.'

'I can see that and I love the way you speak!'

'The bakthi movement that started – like you rightly told me – among Tamils had really shaken the entire subcontinent. There was a devotional tsunami that swept over India! Sage Vyasa's famous literary works gave a missionary zeal to its adherents. The rapid spread of Vaishnavism throughout India changed its entire face.

'*Sreemad Bhágavatam* played a huge role in percolating that concept. It all started with Sage Vyása's amazing feat of compiling and publishing the Vedas in the form we know them today. This person – forget the controversies raging that it could be more than one person to have accomplished so much in a lifetime – realising the wealth of knowledge in those four Vedas and the Upanishads, and the need to disseminate that knowledge to the common man, had set about writing the great epic *Mahábháratha*,' Sadhá continued.

'That single work is by itself larger than any other literary work of any single person anywhere else in the world. Besides that, he is believed to have compiled all those eighteen puránas (epics) besides *Sreemad Bhágavatam*. In my humble opinion, he is the wisest person ever to have lived on this earth. The terms "wise" and "wizard" must have sprung from "Vyás"!'

'I can't agree with you more. I realise that too, what an achievement! But why do you claim that Vaishnavism sprang to life only after Sage Vyása? Did it not exist before him?'

'Maybe, but he gave the impetus. The *Sreemad Bhágavatam* told of the ten avatars of Lord Vishnu, in that came the two most popular heroes Rama and Krishna. Vyasa's whole idea was to propagate the theory of evolution through this work – *Sreemad Bhágavatam*. But as it always happens, people idolised those heroes just as the modern generation idolises its celebrities.'

'I did hear about the similarity of the dasavatharam concept to the evolution theory. I only understood that people noticed that similarity but never thought that it was intentional. Do you mean to say that Sage Vyasa created the whole *Sreemad Bhágavatam* to drive home the concept of evolution?'

'Absolutely. Why else should he bring the other name "Naràyana" into that book?'

'What has that name got to do with this theory?'

'Just as in *Rama ayana*, meaning "the path or journey of Rama" and in "uttara ayana or dhakshina ayana" – meaning the northward or southward path/travel/journey of the Sun depicting the two solstices, Nara-ayana simply means the path or journey of Nara, the human.'

'Gosh! It is Nara ayana and not Nára ayana?!'

'Of course, like most words that get distorted in spelling and then in meaning, this word lost its true essence along the way.'

'So the theory of evolution was nothing new to Indians when the west was slowly waking up to Darwin's new theory, that too after two millennia!'

'Yes, to the learned Indians, it was a theory as old as the oceans.'

'So from the fish to the amphibians, to the half man-half beast to the stunted man, to the ferocious or barbaric man to the well-disciplined and almost-perfect man to the wily and schemy man, well, yes, the *Sreemad Bhágavatam* has laid bare the concept of evolution almost perfectly!' Lacene sat on a meditation for a while.

'What is your observation and comment on the current-day Tamils, now that you know to a reasonable extent the minds of our past thinkers?' Sadhá asked her.

'Honestly, I can't say that I am pleased. While I do see pockets of shining light that keep the hope alive, the general picture is one of gloom and disappointment. Materialism is eating away at the excellent culture that was so painstakingly built by your ancestors.

'For me personally, as one who had observed them from the outside and then from within, this is the lament, "Eppidiyirundhavanga, ippidi ágittaangaley!" (what – *how exalted* – they were then and what – *how denounced* – have they become now). Village folks still maintain the good old tradition and culture to a great extent. I admired the common folk during and after the Tsunami that devastated their coast in 2004.'

'That's what worries me too, Lacene. The equanimity in the outlook of most Tamils has shrunk to very little horizons of caste, wealth, and political power. To me, redemption is not in my visible horizon. We lost that 'guest quest' that was so embedded in our veins.'

'Do you mean the *Tirukkural*, "The one who waves goodbye to the just-then-entertained guest and eagerly awaits the next at his doorsteps is himself eagerly awaited at the doorsteps of heaven"?'

'Precisely, not only the Tamils, the entire Indian culture were such. You must have heard the quote, "máthru devo bhava, pithru devo bhava, ásán devo bhava, adithi devo bhava".'

'Yes, I do. Devo is God, an adithi is a stranger, right? And one is to revere his mother, father, and guru as equivalent to God and in that same order, a stranger comes next. That's an amazing culture!'

'Perfect, "bhava" here means "to consider or treat like". The term adithi has a special meaning too, not just a stranger. "Date" comes from "dithi", in the same sense as used in "'Do you have a date or appointment'"?'

'Is that so? That means an adithi is one without an appointment?'

'Next only to your parents and teacher, the most important person in your life is a "visitor without an appointment". A person knocking at your doors without an appointment must be in some urgent need of help, and must be attended to on top priority like you would to God! How noble a perception that was and what an amazing culture we had. And we lost all this to this neo-culture of materialism!'

Both fell silent perhaps in mourning or meditation. Lacene came back.

'Why should you – at this age – risk doing something like this? As much as I understand your concerns and forward thinking, I do not see any hope of most of the nations and its people accepting your demands or proposals, to put it mildly. And the consequences of the destruction of holy sites would certainly be disastrous! Razing so many holy shrines will only lay grounds for a world war. A religious war that will have no mercy, a war where compromise is sin!'

'That's exactly what I want, Lacene. Many believed that the world would end by 2012, right? Let it happen now because of me! Let these people die in millions! I just don't care! Then the remaining ones will see the light and truth. They will start afresh, a new world of peace, understanding, and harmony. I am pretty sure about that.'

Lacene was horrified to hear that from Sadhá; she could neither accept nor digest that, and didn't know what to say in response.

Their night extended beyond daybreak; they talked and talked about language and religion. At dawn, upon Sadhá's insistence, Lacene got into a sleeping bag and closed her eyes, trying to sleep; and sleep she did, for the whole morning and afternoon.

------◆◆◆------

Madras filter coffee has its own unmatchable flavour and aroma. Aziz admired and enjoyed every sip of Sairá's coffee. As he turned on the TV, news of an unusual religious attack in Finland appeared.

> The attack by arsonists on Friday of a Buddhist temple in Turku's Moisio's district is another worrisome sign of how a deranged group of people can undermine Finland's good name. Fingers point at some Finnish politicians who have fuelled such acts ahead of elections by their populist statements and shameful lack of leadership.

> Immigrants in Finland are being singled out by some opportunist politicians as scapegoats for the country's economic woes. Some MPs make anti-immigrant statements bordering on racism.

> One MP made the incredible remark recently that immigrants would fuel racism because they would take jobs away from Finns. The other MP likes to call asylum-seekers as 'refugee shoppers.'

A spokesman for the Vietnamese Buddhist Community said that it wasn't the first time Buddhist families have been targets of attacks by racists.

Finland was recently named by the press as the best country in the world in social and economical terms.

With attacks of the Buddhist temple serving as a rude reminder of what racism or religion can do to a minority community and society, we should ask newspapers to include how open a society is to cultural and religious diversity in their surveys.

11. Six-Pack Goddess

The splitting apart of man from man
Dooms more than that of an atom can.

———◆◆◆———

When a 'Baboo', a high-ranked government officer, like Aziz Azmi- stations himself in a place – be it a residential apartment – and gives directions, things happen at lightning speed in India. With the identification given by Sairá, Sulaiman, and Patanjali, Aziz got the sketches of the two suspicious electronicians made out and approved by the trio. Patanjali had taken a picture of one of them using Sulaiman's Samsung Galaxy S4 while he was checking the alarm monitor pad. Although not revealing his face in full, it helped in the sketch work. Relevant teams were dispatched immediately with those pictures for tracing them. Aziz appreciated a delighted Patanjali, who was earlier chided by his mother for misusing Sulaiman's Samsung phone.

Assuring Sairá of continued vigilance and protection from any possible harm, Aziz left the apartment in the morning and headed straight to his office. Anxiety compounding every minute, he was bewildered at the networking capabilities of the terrorist groups. Apprehending a score of them in and around Shimla in the past three days was not the end of it all. 'Many more are still out there,' he worried. More worrisome was the lack of news about Thánu.

———◆◆◆———

Omar got more information from Delhi through Shahid quite late in the afternoon. Although he was angry with Shahid for not waking him up to convey the message immediately after Shahid got it, he calmed down when Shahid explained that it was Omar who did not respond to his several calls and messages.

TV news flashing about the abducted clerics did not talk of the release of any jihadist in Indian prisons at all – not even a mention of the release of anybody. It only talked of some demands to the UN and other nations. There was mention of some threats to blow up some religious sites or shrines. But why was there no talk of prisoners?

It was clear to Omar that he had been totally fooled by Abdul. All the information he got from Shahid through his Delhi contact baffled him.

Sairá Bhánu and her two kids – one from her first husband and second from Thánu – were all living there quite happily and safely. There was no sign of Thánu having visited them in the past month; maybe he had spoken to them. Omar's contacts could not tap phones. The two spies who visited his apartment could not find any trace of his first wife.

Furious by that treachery, Omar instructed Faizal and Shahid as to how they should keep a vigilant watch on Lacene's room and be in constant touch with him. He was sure that the traitor would show up. The damaged airstrip would have certainly delayed his return and forced him to look for alternate landing spots. Perhaps he was dead by now, perhaps not. If alive, he must be keen to get hold of that diary. 'Wait patiently. Act at the appropriate time.' He told himself.

Seeing the Pathan coming alone, all eyes looked for Lacene behind him. That she did not accompany him caused concern for most of them, especially the rabbi. George showed a stern face and hid his emotions. Morgan looked at him curiously. George just signalled him to calm down. Arthur raised his voice to ask something.

'Where is the lady?' It was the pastor who gathered courage to ask.

The reply was sharp from the Pathan. 'You are not responsible for her, you better mind your business.' To George, he signalled that she would come. George nodded in response.

That was when everyone noticed the change. The Pathan looked completely different. They did not notice the absence of the beard until he unveiled his half-hidden face as he drew closer to them. With a fully shaven face, they found it much older than they believed it was. And his features were much clearer!

When he removed the cloak around his body, they were surprised to see him scantily clad! Wearing a vest and a loincloth, both made of some animal leather, and with a thick lock of grey hair, he was a completely different person from the Pathan they knew.

'Which is his real face, and who is he? Is he the same person?' As the others looked at one another with questions, he started.

'We have not got any response from the UN for our demands. We have decided to move you from here. You will be transferred tonight to another safer location – not safer for you but for our group. Your fate will be decided there. Prepare to leave after sunset.' It was the same voice as that of the Pathan.

Recollecting the similarities between him and the one in the 9/11 photo, Morgan was sure. It was the devil incarnate, Indian Saddam.

'I am feeling sick,' Morgan told George. The sleepless night had given him a weary look that legitimised his claim. George advised him to go to the cave and take rest. Morgan left the place after getting one last glimpse of his nemesis. Sadhá did not seem to be looking at him.

'Don't we deserve an explanation as to what is going on? Who you are and what your group stands for. What is the meaning of all these strange conditions and demands laid down by you to the UN?' The reverend decided to ask these questions lest they would all leave without knowing why they were brought there in the first place.

'I told you about the five-headed and six-headed snake spotted by the father and son, how such a minor difference even over a false claim that too between father and son could tear them apart. Each of you has a false claim about God and each of you hates the other for not believing in a God or scripture the way you believe in! Here is another analogy to answer your query, Father Guillerimo.

'Have you all heard of the poem 'the six blind men of Hindostan' in which the parts are claimed to be greater than the whole?'

Those who have read it wondered why he was referring to that; others just gave a blank look.

'Just as you represent various religions, there existed numerous faiths in India. From the worship of immediate parents to ancestors, it extended to heroes and heroines of the clan and beyond. That was the case in all regions of the world too. Besides the five elements, visible celestial bodies including the Sun were worshipped; anything that was deemed more powerful or dangerous was also worthy of worship.

'Consolidating all these numerous faiths into six major sects over a very long period of time, learned sages of India preached harmony and appreciation of such beliefs. Each of these six had been dominant in one part or the other within India, rivalry prevailing between them. But rival sects created relationships between their favourite deities and amalgamated to become one faith. Religious meetings of the kind that you now hold have taken place in India before outsiders invaded it.

'The six sects lay in different strata in the universe.

1. Sun being the life-giver to our planet, a daily visible God, was the chief deity of one sect – Sooram.
2. One of the clusters of stars – Pleiades – believed to have been sent directly from the centre of the universe to mingle with our galaxy also got importance – Son of God or Kumar sect – Kaumáram.
3. The black hole at the centre of Milky Way – Parent galaxy to the Sun, offering life on earth – Naràyan-Vishnu – Vaishnavam.
4. The force believed to be keeping all the celestial bodies afloat and the universe expanding – the invisible and most powerful dark matter, dark energy – Ganesh – Ganpatham.
5. One of the two main sources of everything in this universe – the Matter or God particle – Siva – Saivam
6. The other main source, the Supreme force or power or energy – Sakthi – Saaktham.

'It makes complete sense when you designate levels in the cosmos to reach the ultimate God. Such strata do not in any way degrade the ultimate source, the origin of everything that is immeasurably far off at the centre of the universe. One must cross each stage to reach there!

'When the mindset of the commoner was embedded in idol worship, the sages of the past thoughtfully wove science with people's beliefs. They

educated them to accept all these six forms of the ultimate God. Images
were created to symbolise the six strata.

'The Supreme Being which caused the big bang was called "Ádhi Pará
Sakthi" – literally meaning "the original, mega power or energy". Matter,
space, and time were by-products of the big bang; the God Particle that
enabled the formation of matter in the universe is what scientists laboriously
and diligently search for in the Large Hadron Collider project by CERN in
Switzerland – the Higgs Boson particle.

'These two inseparable matter and energy were named "Swa Sakthi"
since the power that caused the big bang, Sakthi, came on its own – Swa.
There is no known creator of this power that caused the big bang. So that
term "Swa Sakthi" symbolises the same God of the monotheist Abrahamic
religions. The only difference is that the Hindu God "Ádhi ParáSakthi" is
a woman who split herself into a man and a woman, representing matter
and energy. A great difference, that is!

'One of Goddess Sakthi's names, "Tripura Sunthari" means "three-
dimensional beauty". We have a state in eastern India with that name
'Tripura'. In that single term, the sages explained the creation of space and
its three dimensions, which were not present until the big bang. "Kàla"
meaning "time, is also another name given to Lord Siva, as he created
"time", the fourth dimension, with the big bang. Epics specifically state
that this creator "lit the three dimensions". "Káli" can also be interpreted
to mean "time" in a feminine form.'

Sadhá gave a break.

'Well, we understand what you say. But why do you talk about these
six sects here? We also know that, besides these Hindu sects, India gave rise
to Jainism, Buddhism, Sikhism, and many spiritual movements. So what?'
This was from an irritated Yahya, the imam.

'There is need to mention all these here, if you want to hear what our
group is up to and what we intend to do with you all!'

Silence from the audience meant acceptance. Sadhá continued.

'The six sects also had their own internal wrangles, each one trying to outsmart the other; each one vying to be 'numero uno' among the followership. That prompted the emergence of the fable of the six blind men who wanted to see, feel and understand an elephant. Each one saw only a part of the whole and fought with the others saying that his part was the whole. Incidentally, elephant also symbolises the vast dark matter, an analogy to the understanding of Lord Ganesh.

'Originating in India, this story was widely diffused and used to illustrate a range of truths and fallacies.'

Sadhá recited that famous nineteenth century poem by John G Saxe.

'After years of wrangling, the six parts came to an understanding. Communication and compromise paved the way forward.

'They all amalgamated into one and became relatives to each other, harmony set in gradually. This underlines the need for communication and respect for different perspectives. Even the other religions that Yahya mentioned did thrive, although minimally. Then came in Islam and Christianity. Jews, Persians, and others came too.'

'And then?' It was Arthur who asked.

'They all lived peacefully in India, despite attempts by colonial powers to divide them and rule them. Yes, there were big shake-ups in the form of independence from foreign rule that split the whole subcontinent. In spite of that, Indians have proven to the world that religious harmony is possible in democratic, secular governance if the national constitution embraces secularism and the people are educated on that. If such peaceful coexistence is possible in India, a diversified country with a huge illiterate public, it must be possible in the world.

'You clergies claim that you try to bring about harmony among religions through communication, dialogue, and conferences. But you do not address the root of the cause of religious disharmony.

'To bring in such religious peace and harmony among all humanity, world nations must de-link the relationship between the state and religion. This is of utmost importance. All nations must declare themselves secular.

Even if a religion is by itself secular – as every religion falsely claims – this declaration of secularism is the first step in achieving religious harmony.'

'What religion does your group follow? Where does it operate from?'

'What is the name of your group? Who are its members?'

Lacene was seen descending from the corner behind Sadhá to the great relief of the rabbi. Everyone noticed that there was dot on her forehead like most Indian women.

'"Secular World Angels" was formed by a group of pantheists in Afghanistan six years ago. It has membership all over the world touching three millions now. We have been very discreet since formation and have decided to announce ourselves with your abduction and the destruction of religious buildings around the world! Our ultimate goal is to convert all religious sites into "meditation and yoga centres".'

This message of destruction to build meditation centres confounded the audience. Looking at each other and wondering what to say or do, the clerics started talking to one another.

'Eat, drink, and be merry! For tomorrow you shall die!' shouted Sadhá as he placed a bundle on the ground and left.

The clerics found a bottle of wine, dried and salted meat, and roasted tree nuts and peanuts. They started opening the packs long after the Pathan left. And as usual, the pundit could only consume the nuts. The Muslims did not touch the wine.

George exclaimed, 'Oh, biltong from South Africa, great!'

<hr />

'Fourteen years of abstinence! How can that be possible? I can't wait for fourteen days without sex! These guys must have been idiots – in a spell!' Morgan muttered as he walked towards the cave.

While biding their time behind the rock at the hill for the two animals to go, George had elaborated on that point of fourteen years of celibacy by Ram's brothers and their wives as remarked by Lacene during their conversation in Abdul's vehicle. In fact, Morgan had asked for an explanation.

He realized that, although he feigned sickness, he was really yearning for sex. More than three weeks had passed since he had his last dig. The thought of how many encounters he had had in the past few years in the absence of Florence, and the question as to how Florence would have spent her nights in his absence, made him feel sick.

People were different 3,000 years ago, or so he thought. Culturally, Indians were much different from others, perhaps. Why from others, even amongst themselves, they must have been different between then and now. Can we expect Indian men of today – so famous for their rapist mentality – to follow such a celibate culture? No way, he told himself. In this modern world of glamour and promiscuity, celibates would be looked upon as naïve, conservative aborigines!

'But could it be true that just because the elder brother – that too, a stepbrother – was sent on a mission of fourteen years of aesthetic life in the jungle, his three stepbrothers and their wives vowed to remain celibate until his return? What kind of characters could they have been? Why would those young wives agree to such a torture? Could the love and respect for this prince Ram have been so overwhelming?'

As he opened his baggage and calmly took out its contents from every nook and corner to pick up the intricate components of his airgun – which he found to be intact despite the pillage of that baggage by Abdul and his team – his mind was reeling over what Florence would have done all these years to keep her passions under control. 'Would she have practiced celibacy over the entire period?'

He cursed himself for fumbling so many times while assembling the airgun – although it was indeed a challenging task – which he would otherwise not have found so difficult. His mind was roving over Florence and her fidelity quotient. He was confident that she would never have slept with another man. That very thought sank his heart every time he thought of her. That was the first time in all these years that he not only realized that he missed her but that he had not been true to her.

'Was it just in my nature to be so promiscuous? Or is it culturally all right for men to be so? What about women who are also promiscuous? Can the world survive peacefully without extramarital affairs? Or without sex workers who keep the passions of insatiable seekers of pleasure under wraps? If men were to contain their desires, why should nature give them such libido? There is certainly something wrong in the equations. God has been making serious mistakes.' Morgan was sure that celibacy was unnatural.

Although he took a longer time than he estimated to assemble the parts for making the whole pistol, he was confident that the gun wouldn't fail in doing its job. If nothing else could be done to escape from that place, at least killing the traitor wouldn't be a mistake. He appreciated his own skill in precisely remembering the many complicated and tiny parts of the gun and assembling them dexterously. 'I hope to sleep well tonight,' he said to himself.

When he inserted the airgun into the holster in his jacket, he decided to get back to join the others and look for an opportune moment.

George and Lacene were seen talking privately when the others were discussing the 'Secular World Angels' and their plans. Nobody seemed to have bothered about the absence of Morgan, but George's mind was wondering what Morgan would be doing alone inside the cave. He paid keen attention to Lacene's description of Sadhá's miraculous feat of saving him from the slopes of K2. That was a marvellous story for him.

Candid exchanges of information between Stuart and Aziz enabled both of them to reduce their anxiety levels. Stuart's concern about his inability to communicate with or even track Morgan was allayed with information from Aziz about the unauthorised flight the day before, the damage to the airstrip and the injuries to Siddhu, Thánu's deputy. The location of that airstrip matched the coordinates where the GPS lost track of Morgan.

Aziz did not, of course, tell Stuart about project OWN. That would be too much of a revelation at that stage, he knew.

Recollecting the exact coordinates where they lost track of Morgan, Stuart was sure that Morgan had to be with the hostages. Fully satisfied that Morgan was on the right track, Stuart stopped worrying about him and concentrated on the massive piles of data collected by Craig, Jacques' successor in the snooping process on the religious sites and the endless list of bloggers discussing them.

Latest information on one of those 216 locations rallied his concerns again, and he immediately forwarded that to Aziz.

> Residents of the Palestinian Authority town of Jabba, southeast of Ramallah, reported Tuesday that a town mosque had been damaged in an apparent arson attack. Graffiti at the scene said 'The war has started,' and 'You will pay the price.'

> Locals in Jabba said they believe the vandalism was part of targeted attacks on PA Arabs. Residents expressed surprise that their town was targeted. Jabba is a quiet town, and its residents are not involved in the rock attacks on Israeli motorists in the region, they said. Yesha Council head condemned the attack.

> Rabbis and other local leaders in Beit El have called on supporters of the Ulpana neighbourhood to avoid violence and damage to property during their protests against the planned expulsion.

12. Know Space

The whole problem with the world is that the
Fools are cocksure — and the
Wise are full of doubts!

Sunderlal Nahata IPS, the Deputy Director General of Police, Himachal Pradesh state, was startled to hear the name Aziz Azmi from his secretary. He was leaving his office to go home for lunch, passing through his secretary's office. 'He's holding the line, sir. Shall I put him through to you or will you take it from here?'

'Sure, sure, put him through.' He ran back to his office. 'My lunch with family is at abeyance,' he thought. 'Yes, Mr Azmi, I am fine,' he stammered. 'How are you, sir? What can I do for you, sir?'

Aziz Azmi was instrumental in placing Sunderlal there against political pressure, by citing nefarious activities in the suburbs of Shimla and in the state. Sunderlal was longing to get a posting there because he hailed from Sanardh, north of Shimla.

'I am concerned about our guy Thànu, Sunder. He has not contacted me for the past two days, which is very unusual. How far are the arrests of the potential terrorist gangs you have been talking about? How helpful were Thánu and Siddhu?'

'Oh, they are gems of sleuths, sir! Excellent job they have done. We have rounded up more than a score of these elements; some of them are avowed LeT branches and twigs. No IM (Indian Mujahiddeen) involvement. I am

231

particularly happy that we have nipped them in the bud. I can't thank you enough for placing me here and supporting me with the likes of Thànu and Siddhu. It is only unfortunate that Siddhu was badly injured in the airstrip blast. I believe Thànu is looking after him. After that incident I have not personally met him yet. I wanted to ask Thánu about the other guy who escaped.'

Sunderlal did not take breath until he finished. Aziz showed his genuine concern for Siddhu. 'What a pity! He is such a wonderful boy! No wonder Thánu did not contact me, he must be very upset. Raheem, Thánu, and Siddhu were all from the same batch and were close friends. Raheem lost his life unfortunately in the Mumbai 26/11 attack, that is when Thánu married…'

'I remember Raheem well, sir, he married your niece. It was a pathetic situation.' Before he could finish, Aziz began, 'Is Siddhu married?' and then cut himself. 'Why am I asking this silly question now?'

'I think so, sir, I'm not sure. I can check for you.'

'No, no. No need, not at all. Let us see how we can end this fiasco without much embarrassment to anyone,' said Aziz.

'I believe all the clerics will be returning tonight, sir?'

'Yes, they should. I hope all goes well. Thánu may not be participating in the moves, looks like, but you do not need him anymore, do you?'

'Sure we don't, we can manage. The IB and RAW will be there to take care. Media will not be allowed to meet them. News will be out only from the Home Minister's office – your office, I mean, sir.'

'You told me about one guy who escaped, who is it?'

'I am not sure if he is a dangerous person. His name, I believe, is Omar Sherfuddin. Thánu was seen with him several times. We do not know if Thánu was using him or befriending him to learn about this gang. We have kept his family under house arrest; his neighbourhood is under surveillance, no sign of him.'

'Was he caught along with the other terrorists?'

'Yes, sir, but it looks like he was in their captivity when our officers confronted and arrested them. I believe they had destroyed one of our old airfields – the one used for flying the clerics.'

'So we do not know if this Omar is a dangerous guy or just an informer. Maybe he is looking for Thánu to take refuge in him!'

'Probably, sir, we have our vigilance unit watching the hospital and Siddhu's ward in particular. We are not sure if Thànu knows that this guy is still at large. Thánu took Siddhu to this private hospital and got him admitted there with my help. It was wise of him to have chosen that private hospital. I have done the needful. Hope the specialists are doing their best there.'

'Thanks for that, Sunder. You please make it a point to somehow inform Thánu about that Omar. Most times, our people – even the smartest ones – slip in vigilance when they are personally affected. Trace Thánu, ask him to call me immediately. Take care, good luck.'

'Sure, sir, thank you, thanks for calling, sir. Yes, that is why they are our chosen..,' Sunderlal blabbered.

Sunderlal was pleased that he could go home for lunch as promised to his family. His home front would turn into a war front especially if he did not go home for lunch when his wife's siblings were visiting his home – no matter how busy he was at work.

He had to try and get hold of Thánu and caution him about Omar before he set his hands on his meal and to ask him to call Mr Aziz.

But he also did not succeed in reaching Thánu.

———◆•◆•◆———

The entire scenario at the post-operative ward where Siddhu was lying in his bed in that private hospital was exactly the same as in Jaslok hospital in Mumbai years ago with Raheem in a similar condition. Thánu could not control his tears. 'I don't want a repeat of that fateful day' were words he couldn't help uttering loud enough to be heard. The nurse in the ward got startled at his sudden utterance of those words. Thànu apologized to her.

At least Raheem could speak to him. 'Siddhu can't speak now,' the doctors had said.

Raheem was sensing death and was desperate to talk to Thánu. It was at his stubborn insistence that his doctors allowed him to talk.

'I know you treat her as your sister, Thànu, but after I'm gone she must be your wife. You know our past and only you will accept her. I can't leave her with anyone else. I know you will be the best father for my child.' Even without waiting for Thànu's confirmation – so confident he was – Raheem went into that last slip of coma. He never came out of it again and was gone in a month.

Thánu recalled how Siddhu was excited about his first meeting with 'Guruji' while leaving the clerics at the hill a week ago. He and pilot Danny McCarthy were meeting Sadhá for the first time and were very impressed with the whole plan. They must have spent hardly two hours with that 'sage' as they described him but seemed to have learned a lot. Siddhu received plans from Sadhá for onward actions.

But how did Guru forget? His failure to send the list through Siddhu did upset the whole plan and caused a lot of inconveniences. Perhaps this trip would not have become necessary. 'I need not have wasted my time tracking Lacene and George for the sake of that list. Anyway, what could not be helped has to be endured.'

Thánu left the room quietly. 'If only Sadhá did not put that list inside that diary and into George's bag, things would have gone smoothly. Siddhu need not be lying here like this. Sadhaa will regret it if he comes to know of Siddhu's condition. Hope all goes well.'

He recollected his meeting with Sadhá the night before on the hill. It was a like a reunion of a mentor with his most favourite disciple. At least he had another chance to meet his guru thanks to Sadhá's forgetfulness! Thánu likened himself to Arjuna and Sadhá to Krishna! He had learned a lot from this man he met five years ago in Kándhahar. 'Queen Kàndhàri of the great epic *Mahábháratha* hailed from this kingdom,' Sadhá had told him.

234

Grief still overwhelming him, Thánu looked at the time; it was nearing six in the evening, and he had one more task for that day. Only McCarthy had his other personal contact number. News arrived from him that the aircraft carrying all the hostages would land in the other strip 60 kms south of Shimla by about 8 p.m. Thánu was not sure if Lacene would make it to Hotel Shimla that night. 'Probably tomorrow.' He said to himself.

'All of them may spend the night in the nearby government guesthouse facilities. I must move now. Perhaps I can go as a diner to the restaurant at Hotel Shimla and bide my time to look for the diary in her suite. The time at the restaurant will give me a chance to see if someone recognises me or not. That's a gamble I must take. Will it still be there, though? Should be, no one knows about it. Omar is in custody. He wouldn't have taken it. I'll hand it over to Lacene after making a copy for myself. I should go now.'

'Would it be impolite if I ask you how your night with them went, Lady?' Arthur did not want to mince words.

'It was wonderful, Mr None. Not them, just only one. This old man here. His name is Sadhá. And I decided to join his group – the Secular World Angels organisation – without a second thought.' The rabbi could not digest any of what she said, although George had briefed him about Sadhá. 'You're joining a terrorist group?'

'No, this is not a terrorist group. They aim at making the entire world population secular. I invite you all to join us so that you'll feel free to embrace any religion of your choice – not necessarily the religion you have been following for reasons other than intellectual choice! I admire their ideology and will work towards achieving their goals through non-violent means.'

'What is this costume this Pathan has come with? It appears like he is playing Lord Shiva?' this was the pundit.

'I noticed it, yes, that's like one of those gods I have seen in the pictures,' muttered the pastor. 'What secularity is he talking about?'

'That's just a costume he wanted to show you all – especially my husband – that it's possible to roam in the Himalayas with the least of outfits and with some natural leatherwear only! It's also the supposedly regular costume of Rudra or Shiva, yes. Maybe Sadhá wanted to imitate that saint he so admires – a god for Saivites, famous for roaming half-clad in this abode of snow – Hema álaya!'

'That's what I am asking, how can you claim to be secular and also admire a particular god? It defeats the very meaning of secularism!'

'On the contrary, that is what secularism is all about, dear pastor. You have your favourite god or deity and still you appreciate every other person's favourite god too, without claiming that your favourite is the best. If you only say that "I like this god the most" you are fine. But if you say, 'my God is *the* best' you automatically deride the others' preferred gods. It is like in music – I like Michael Jackson, and you like Kanye West. I can recommend to you to listen to MJ, but I can't tell you "MJ is the best, so don't listen to KW"!'

'That doesn't justify his costume. You can't claim to be secular and yet adorn symbols of a particular religion or sect,' said the pundit, obviously not pleased at Sadhá's Shiva costume.

George came to Lacene's rescue. 'Perhaps he wants to show that we should not believe that only gods can do so, can walk in these cold, high-altitude conditions with the bare minimum of clothes. Ordinary folks like us can also do that with proper training, yogic practices, etc.' Turning to Lacene, George continued, 'Does Sadhá try to imply that the person whom Saivites believe to be Rudra of the Himalayas was just a human and not Lord Shiva himself in human form?'

Lacene looked at him thankfully. 'George, very true, thank you! My guru always maintained that the Himalayan dwelling Rudra who married Parvati was just a human being. His disciples elevated his status to divinity – just as the four apostles did to Jesus Christ! Siva's disciples did that to him simply because he was the first one to propound the formation of this universe from time zero with the big bang and three-dimensional fire.

'He called the force that created this universe, as "Swa Sakthi", or "a force on its own". His disciples named him after that same original force – Swa. That word got distorted over time to become "Siva or Eswa" etc. There are many such firsts to his credit, making him certainly one of the best, scientific-minded human beings that treaded on this earth.'

'So you also subscribe to that big bang theory and not to any creator God? The only omnipresent, omnipotent, and omniscient God we all talk about (he looks at his Judeo-Christian-Islamic members of the group) does not exist, according to you too?' And, what does this dot on your forehead signify? Have you converted to Hinduism?' The pastor raised this question, with a hint of anger in his voice.

'I don't think even science questions these qualities of the creator of this Universe – the three 'omnis'! Your description of the Holy Spirit rhymes very much with these big bang and Swa-Sakthi theories. I am not disputing that. As long as it was described as a spirit, all religions go together. But the moment they assign a gender to "it", all religions become "pagan" in our opinion. That is the essence of our message.'

George was amused to notice that Lacene had already become propaganda secretary to Sadhá's group!

'But you call it a male-female mix!' said the rabbi.

'That is certainly much better than assigning only the male gender to it! Our argument is that it can only be a neutral gender. The terms "Ádhi Pará Sakthi" or "Swa Sakthi" do not represent any gender. If at all we have to assign one, then it is a female.

'The difference between the monotheist religions and our group's claim lies at the very origin. Is God a "he" or a "she" or just an "it"?' There was a huge silence on that hill; to Arthur, the lone atheist, it appeared that they were all listening to a mount sermon.

'Islam believes Allah to be a formless, omnipotent God, it doesn't assign a gender to him,' the imam came in.

'There you go. You said "to him". What gender is "him"?' asked Lacene.

'That's because we speak in English which doesn't translate well. Hu or Huwa means "that" or "it" only, not "him".'

'Each one of us believes that our scriptures are God-given, either from God directly to messiahs down here, or through angels to prophets, or gods themselves descending here to proclaim those scriptures to us as avatars. The divine aspect of these scriptures cannot be questioned nor ridiculed,' said the pastor.

'Exactly, that would amount to blasphemy.' The moulana nodded.

'But your scriptures do repeatedly hammer onto your heads that only what they say is right, they specifically say that the others are wrong. I see an element of fear in such assertions,' said Arthur.

'Fear? What nonsense are you talking about? My God fearing another's God?' a chorus of ferocious voices arose from everyone!

Lacene was startled at the angry response and was wondering how to react when she heard a supporting, equally angry voice from behind.

'Yes, each of your Gods is afraid of other Gods! A true God would love all humans preaching love, non-violence, kindness, forgiveness, and universal brotherhood/sisterhood. It should not promise only a particular group a piece of land or a particular people a place in heaven on the Judgement day,' Sadhá's voice was unusually loud.

'A true God doesn't have to claim "I am the only God, trust no other", talk of Satan or Devil who should be under its control, send angels to sing his self-praise, demand "total surrender" to him, claim "I am the way, whoever follows me shall reach the heavens" implying that the others would go to hell, sow seeds of jealousy between brothers by showing a preference for meat offered vis-a-vis fruits/vegetables and leading one to kill the other, annihilate a child in a fit of fury, brand anybody as an infidel and declare 'fatwa' on anyone, or slay a crocodile in order to save an elephant just because the elephant cried for his help!

'More than all, a true God doesn't side with one group and work towards the annihilation or the surrender of another group. I can give you millions of such points as to what a true God would not and should not do that your Gods have done – rather, "claimed by you all to have done." Does God really have a religion?'

Sadhá's voice was louder than ever before and his tone, furious.

'The truth is that we created God in our own image. The plethora of prophets and messiahs and seers – they all sincerely meant to do well to their society but had to drag God into their lives to either legitimise their services or to fortify them.'

'You mean they "cheated us by projecting a non-existent God"?' asked the moulana. His voice was no less loud.

'Yes. They cheated us either with or without intent. Perhaps they cheated themselves too. The God of Moses was a God for his clan only; it was not a universal God. It is quite unclear why, despite realising the pantheist nature of truth like other sages did, Moses decided to present it to his people the way we all know he presented.

'Jesus Christ was just a human being like all of us performing social service to his clan. He was a social and religious revolutionary. Unfortunately for him he was eliminated by the clerics of his time. Full credit goes to his apostles for projecting a Jewish reformer as *the* Son of Universal God. If not for their propaganda, Jesus would have just been a Jewish reformer.

'All stories of virgin birth, three wise men from the east, and the resurrection of Jesus, were concocted by those ardent disciples. While everything in Islam is full of earthly events with no miracles of any kind in the life of their prophet, the very mention of an Angel Gabriel sent by Allah makes the whole episode appear more like the other religious beliefs. The scriptures of Islam would be much more valuable if they were understood as manmade and not as god-sent.

'So is the preaching of Jesus Christ – more valuable if he was not the Son of God as purported to be.

If I have to believe in the miracles of Jesus Christ or in the visits of Angel Gabriel, then I have to believe in all those divine interventions claimed by other religions. Either no religion is pagan or all religions are pagan. Period.'

There was silence but not one of acceptance; it was one of defiance. But, the bikku had something to say.

'You can never find any such intervention in Buddhism. There may be later insertions but as far as Lord Buddha himself was concerned, there was no miracle in his life.'

'I agree with you, Bikku, Buddha was just an enlightened soul like most other prophets. What sets him apart is the absence of miracles.'

'Then you must admire Sage Mahavir of the Jain faith, Mr Sadhá! There was no miracle in his life either, as far as I know,' said Arthur.

'Well, yes, there wasn't, maybe. We may group Tao and Confucius also likewise. But then such faiths were pushed aside by the icon loving, pagan-minded faiths that slowly subdued them. However, polytheists are more tolerant and respectful of other religions than monotheists. That's what history has taught us.'

There were murmurs and ruckus among the audience but when Sadhá continued with a thunderous voice, all became quiet.

'I know what you all are grumbling about. I include the pundit among monotheists because he believes only in Krsna. To understand God in its real glory, the first thing you all must do is to travel into space – a far distance in space so that you can have a wholesome look at the earth. You must know space to know God.'

'You are digressing here. What has space got to do with belief in God or understanding God?' asked Arthur.

'To perceive the elephant in its entirety than in a piecemeal. To look at the six continents as one earth. Unless you go up there and look at the world as one habitable planet, you will never understand that we all are one. You will never appreciate why pantheism is the only philosophy all of us must embrace; only pantheism can bring peace and harmony on earth.

'The same scriptures that you quote to project your religion as a peace-loving, all-embracing one, are quoted by the fundamentalists who cause destruction and commit violence against people of other faiths and sub-sects. You are not doing anything to change their mind-set or change their understanding – rather misunderstanding – of your 'glorious' holy scriptures. Just a few lip services here and there, a few superfluous condemnations of violence are all that you do. You do not take sincere efforts to go to their midst and preach the real meaning – as you claim to believe – to bring about the required transformation in them. Do you? Rather, you blame people of other religions and faiths that they "do not understand your religion properly"! Why don't you make your house in good order before you blame others?'

Silence amongst the audience again.

'Think of yourselves as God or God's angels, sent to solve this world's problems. Meditate upon your favourite God and wish to be transported to such a place in space. Look at the world from there and see what is going on in various parts of this globe. If you were a messenger of God or an angel, what would you do? How would you transform those hate-filled minds into peace-loving ones?

'You will find not just six but six billion "blind minds" contradicting each other and ready to devour one another. Even the most broad-minded follower of a religion would be longing at the bottom of his heart that the whole world should convert to his faith so that harmony and peace would prevail. Will that happen? Will that truly solve the world's problems? How will you change his mind-set?

'Yoga and meditation are erroneously believed to be linked to Hinduism or Buddhism by many. They are the only practices with no link to any religion that can bring about such a mind-set in us. You can transcend to space – space where you gain true knowledge – through yoga and meditation. You will realise the oneness of all beings. Go there. Travel now. Know space. You will know God.'

The audience was listening to Sadhá in absolute silence but not necessarily in agreement.

'You are adorning the costumes of Shiva, a Hindu God. How can you do that when you claim to be a pantheist?' The pundit didn't like to budge. For his sect, Shiva was a lower-level deity.

'Because Siva of the Himalayas was not a Hindu, nor a Saivite. He was a scientist, a true pantheist. He invented or discovered so many scientific truths about this universe – the galaxies, the solar system, the planets, life on earth, the gender split, yoga and meditation. Just because his followers elevated him to God-status does not mean that I worship him as a god. I just respect him for his many "firsts".

'Siva invented yoga practices to primarily learn to regulate sexual desires and maintain good health. His reasoning was that since humans became Homo erectus from being quadrupeds, gravity has played an important role in facilitating more frequent and excess secretion of sexual hormones. Quadrupeds and other creatures have lesser sexual urges than humans, he claimed. Yoga is an amazing practice which helps streamline one's sexual desires and in utilising their energy towards better health and agility.

'In all the communities where civilization developed in this world, people were classified as good or trustworthy and bad or untrustworthy. In South India, from time immemorial, there have been only two divisions based on the goodness of a person. An "ayogya" is not a good person; a "yogya" is a good, honest person.

'Obviously, you can deduce that a "yogya" is someone who practiced yoga regularly! Such was the value given to yoga and meditation practices that, unless you practice them, you cannot be classified as a good person! This notion had nothing to do with any religion. However exalted you may think your religion is, if you do not practice yoga, you cannot evolve into a good person.'

Arthur and George looked at each other meaningfully. They observed that those with a half-belief in the goodness of yoga seemed convinced. But those with strong religious views linking yoga to Hinduism and Buddhism remained sceptical.

Sadhá continued.

'Siva spent most of his time in yoga and meditation, especially after the episode with Parvati's child Ganesha.

'It was then that Parvati is said to have regretted begetting an offspring without Siva and longed for rewarding him with a child of his own. Seeing him adamantly practicing yoga and meditation, showing no interest whatsoever in procreation, she is said to have taken help from Cupid – Manmathan. That is eventually how Kumár aka Skantha, aka Murugan, aka Saravanan, aka Karthik, was born to both of them.

'Skantha – or Kantha as Tamils call him – means "ejaculated" or "thrown out". Lord Siva is said to have enabled the birth of Kumar to essentially tell the world that "it needs two – man and woman – to procreate"! The famous literary piece *Kumára Sambhavam* by Mahàkavi Kàlidoss – his name meaning servant or ardent follower of Goddess Kàli - narrates this story in very engaging Sanskrit verses.'

'Who is this Kàlidoss? A saint or a prophet?' asked the imam.

'Only a poet but he has one similarity to your prophet. He's another one to become a learned person overnight. He was an ordinary person with very little education and linguistic skill. He was a stupid man – so stupid as to cut a tree branch at its base while sitting on it.

'But it is believed that with the grace of Goddess Kàli, he became a great lyricist and poet overnight, authoring some famous works admired in the same vein as those of Shakespeare. Your prophet, who was until then possessing limited language skills, also is believed to have been blessed with such skills by the grace of the Almighty, am I right?'

Just a quiet nod was the response from the imam and the moulana.

Without waiting to listen to any other questions that anyone might have wanted to pose, Sadhá swiftly turned to go back to his abode. Before leaving, he said,

'You will all be leaving by sunset. Stay near the riverbank, and you will know what to do at the right time. Remember, we are not going to force you or coax you to leave your religion and become like us. You don't have to become one of our Secular World Angels but at least become secular-minded. Instead of preaching your scriptures, preach yoga and meditation. People shall then learn to think and live better.'

'We are all secular-minded and well aware of the existence of other faiths, there is no need to abandon our religion and embrace other new groups.' This was a stern reply from the moulana. 'We have never disliked anyone just because they do not belong to our faith.'

Sadhá spun around faster than a tornado. 'You as an individual or a few in your faith may be secular-minded like you have said dear moulana! And you meet regularly to exchange your sweet tongues and disperse. You do not really carry the same sweet tones to your parishes or ministries or monasteries or madrasáhs. And there is a vast majority who, overtly or covertly, nurture this disbelief in, this dislike of and this hatred for, other faiths in varying degrees.

'As learned clergies you do nothing to change this. A large majority of your imams, moulanas, bishops, pastors, rabbis, priests, and bikkus teach hatred and **nothing but hatred**.

'This is prevalent in every religion and sub-sect. This is precisely what our group aims to address. It would be very effective if you, as leading personalities in your faiths, address it at the very source from where such indifferences arise in the first place – your scriptures and the way your preachers misrepresent the facts to the common man. They are the root cause of all the problems in this world.'

There was pin-drop silence; the sound of the slow moving water in the stream was audible.

Sadhá continued in his raised voice. 'We do not equip ourselves and our children to face a borderless world, which is an inevitable destiny we are all heading towards. The greatest barrier is the blind belief in our scriptures. We do not have the courage to question them, the honesty and humility to accept that they may not be "perfect".

'We only have the audacity to hold on to whatever we were told to follow. We do not realise that this strict adherence to the "words" in the Holy Scriptures as sacramental is the main stumbling block to the progress and elevation of humanity.' Sadhá stopped.

'I agree with your views on the need to rewrite the scriptures. I would also recommend that we scrap all of them altogether. But how do you hope to succeed in your mission of preparing the people for a borderless world?' This was from the rabbi.

'We formed this society, the Secular World Angels, a few years ago and we aim at educating the entire world population in understanding the need for secular beliefs. All we want you to do is to – as you preach your religion to people – lay stress on the secular contents in your scriptures and desist from speaking so high of your beliefs at the cost of other beliefs. *Only a secular world will be a secure world.* Ensure that *all* clergies in your religion speak alike.'

'I agree with what you say, and I shall try to do my best. Although I cannot predict what the reaction will be in our circles.' This was from the reverend himself, to everyone's delight!

'I do hope that your Pope will bring in the required transformation among the Catholics. I call him "the Pope of good hope". That is the only sect which has a central leadership and can lead from the front for the rest to follow.' Sadhá's tone was pleasant for once.

'But then, what is this threat of destruction to so many holy sites in the world? Is it true? Is it going to help? Will this not have a negative impact on the entire world?' The rabbi asked with sincere concern.

'Let it have! Let them all see what hatred can bring about upon us! Let each one blame each other and bring about an end! An end to this great misfortune that we have in our midst in the name of religions! An end to all the sufferings that we have endured so far!

'If there are survivors after that catastrophe, they will get it all right! It is better to live with no religion but with love for all than with religions and hatred!' Sadhá's voice became unbearably louder, with his whole body dancing like fire, his eyes burning with fury!

He was a very different person to the Pathan who had never shown this much animosity or hate in all these days.

Sadhá retreated stepping backwards, and resorted to a kind of dance as he moved. A strange, ferocious dance, moving all over the rising hill, without any misstep. While the audience was gaping at him in awe at his tenacity, dexterity, lightning speed, gracious movement of his torso, he disappeared behind the peak after performing a fiery bit.

Morgan was a dumbstruck listener all along, totally forgetting what he intended to do. His right arm that slid into his jacket to retrieve the airgun had remained there for all those moments. He suddenly realised that he should act.

Lacene's eyes were fixed on Sadhá and she was obviously spellbound by the display. She beckoned George towards her and pointing at Sadhá, told George, 'He is performing the 'Sapta natana' – the seven forms of dance. This last one is the 'ózhik kóthu', the dance of total annihilation, depicting how this expanding universe would eventually collapse and converge into its origin, all in flames!'

That was a scene so engraved in their minds that it would always replay time and again until they closed their eyes permanently.

Morgan could not find a good aim at Sadhá as he was jumping from one place to another while performing that strange, awkward dance. He was getting increasingly frustrated at his failure.

———◆◆◆———

When Sunderlal received a message that the only escapee among the captured lot of jihadists, Omar, was spotted at the restaurant in Hotel Shimla, he decided to go there immediately. He advised his team not to create any disturbance to anybody there but to keep a watch and report to him every five minutes. The message was from the area inspector of police; it was from a single informant posted at that road with many commercial complexes in the vicinity. The informant had to keep moving all around that area, but Sunderlal instructed the inspector to let him stay around Omar for another hour.

There was no news from Thánu as yet. He got confirmation from the private hospital that Sidhu was out of danger and about Thànu's departure from the hospital a couple of hours ago.

———◆◦◆◦◆———

The long wait at the riverbank gave them ample time to mull over all that had happened in the past week. The only begrudging soul there was Morgan. Everyone else seemed to at least condone if not admire the SWA group and its mission so far. None, of course, approved the group's intended plan of demolishing hundreds of religious sites all around the world. That had to be stopped somehow, they all opined. They hoped that the UN and its member nations would do something about the resolutions that this group was demanding to be passed.

Pointing to the dot on her forehead, Lacene explained to the pastor:

'I owe you a reply on that, pastor. I did not convert to Hinduism. This dot does not necessarily indicate any religious affinity. I totally concurred with my guru - Mr Sadhá, when he explained last night the real significance of the dot on the forehead as adorned by many Indians.

'It simply represents the 'black dot' that existed on its own before the 'big bang', turning red as its inner pressure mounted and finally it burst into the 'big bang' setting off the creation of the three dimensions, time and this universe. This is simple science. Not religion.'

The entire group was astonished to hear that. No one had explained the significance of the forehead dot in that manner to them. George also was perplexed to hear that. But Morgan considered that it was all part of an identity tactics of the group Sadhá belonged to.

They all heard the sound of an aircraft and turned around.

Everything happened as if they were in a dream, minutes after the aircraft landed with a thundering noise on the other side of the river. The touchdown was at the tip of the plain field on their right and the taxiing was until the middle of the runway. Morgan was appreciative of the pilot's skill at bringing the aircraft to a halt within seconds after the touchdown.

The two men who came out of the aircraft ran towards them giving instructions. One end of the rope holding the string-ladder they brought was thrown at the group, which George and Arthur caught. Pulling the rope slowly, they grabbed one end of the ladder and laid it on the ground. The two men placed its other end on the other bank of the stream. The unwound ladder looked like a slide on its surface. With elevation on the other side, each person was asked to climb the not-too-steep pathway it created. George and Morgan were the last to walk across it, with Lacene ahead of them. Others who had crossed started loading their baggage into the aircraft.

'Look behind,' Lacene shouted, and everybody looked at their one-week-home-hill; on top of it stood Sadhá. The descending sun's rays off the opposite cliffs reflected a dim twilight on him; the third crescent was glittering behind as if bedecked on his head, sitting comfortably on the right side of his dreadlocks.

'Chandramouli!' Lacene exclaimed. 'How does she know this name?' wondered the pundit who couldn't help raising his palms in prayer at the image of Rudra, Lord Shiva.

At that moment, Morgan did something that shocked everyone!

<hr/>

Omar had no doubt. 'That clean-shaven man with the French cap and sky-blue T-shirt must be the traitor Abdul-no-Thànu, who cheated me as Abdul,' he mused. He had seen Abdul in that unique T-shirt with the Victoria-Falls print on its back. Omar could see that Abdul did not want to be identified by the hotel staff. 'He must have come for the diary, no doubt,' he said to himself. 'I can identify you in any garb, even if you show only your back to me, Abdul!'

He was very happy that his long wait by the window paid off. He sent Shaheed a description of Abdul in his present avatar. After getting a glimpse of Abdul, Shaheed was to go and wait on Floor 3, watch over Lacene's room, and update Omar.

Omar then freshened up and left for Hotel Shimla across the road. He estimated that Abdul must have returned from that trip alone – perhaps only today; hence his delay in coming for the diary. 'It means Lacene is still with the clerics. Now it doesn't matter to me what happens to them,' he smiled.

———◆———

The only connection at Hotel Shimla that Sunderlal could think of for Omar was the American trio who Thànu was said to have airlifted a few days ago. Intelligence reports and Thànu's instructions to his colleagues both indicated that there was no other player staying in or visiting the hotel. So he could not decipher what made Omar come out of hiding and roam in that hotel. The only other clue his informant gave him was that the Americans had not vacated one of the two suites in Floor 3. 'Could there be something of interest?' he wondered.

As he passed through the revolving door to the restaurant, posing as an elite guest, Sunderlal noticed that Omar was leaving the restaurant through the same door. His contact, sitting at one of the tables, nodded at him with his eyes marking at the exit door. Sunderlal signalled to him to stay put and after spending a minute as though looking for his dinner partner and at his watch, left the place through the same door. He could see Omar climbing the stairs briskly, texting on his phone.

The large lounge demanded at least a minute for crossing over from the restaurant to the bottom of the staircase. Sunderlal did not want to follow him through the stairs. His attire did not suit such a climb! He had to use the lift. As for tracking Omar, he asked his informant to do that. Giving himself a few moments to casually look around the lounge, he waited at the lift. When he got into it, he did not know which floor Omar was going to but his instincts made him press 3.

———◆———

Thánu certainly did not expect to see Omar there. After he comfortably entered Lacene's room and pulled the drawers open for the diary, he found it and tucked it under his armpit. He suspected that somebody was watching him and came out carefully. As he closed the door and turned, he saw Omar closing in on him from the other end of the passageway. Grinning at him and shouting 'you betrayer', Omar raised his arm to hit him.

Although he could defend himself from that onslaught and send Omar to the ground with his blows, the hit on his head from an unexpected third person from his back with a club destabilised him for a moment. He managed to recover from the fall and send this third man tumbling down. But Omar picked the club up from the floor as Shaheed fell and flung it at Thánu's head. A second hit on his head flattened Thánu. Just then, Sunderlal emerged from the lift and walked towards the turn of the passage cautiously. Hearing the sound of the scuffle, he saw them and shot at Omar as he raised his hand to strike at Thánu's head again. The bullet hit his arm, and Omar fell in pain, while Shaheed froze. Sunderlal's contact had reached the floor climbing the stairs in big leaps and jumped on the two to apprehend them. Thànu had fallen on the floor carpet; Omar looked at the book fallen on the floor.

Sunderlal neared them and leaned to have a look at Thànu who remained motionless. Sunderlal saw blood oozing from his ear; there was no apparent external head injury. He feared that there could be some internal damage.

———◆———

A few hours ago, Morgan could not succeed in getting a clear shot at Sadhá. By the time Morgan was prepared to do so after clandestinely taking out his airgun, Sadhá had started dancing and moving with unexpected swiftness. And he disappeared behind the ridge after a few minutes. Morgan had lost hope that he would ever see Sadhá again. So he was naturally delighted to see him at the top of the hill. For him, it was a god-sent opportunity!

The single compressed air bullet that Morgan shot from his silencer did not miss its target. It managed to travel more than 400 meters, at almost forty-five degrees along the slopes against gravity and hit Sadhá just below his neck. Everyone below could see with horror-filled eyes Sadhá falling on his back from the top of the hill, over to the other side.

Morgan was pleased to see that his aim did not fail him. He knew very well that wherever the air bullet could have hit a person, it would burst and the three-bar pressurised air would play such havoc into the blood circulation system that the person's heart also would burst instantly.

Lacene shrieked in horror. George held Morgan's arm preventing him from taking another shot – which was not necessary. The intended target had already fallen off the cliff. No one showed any joy whatsoever in Morgan's act. The two pilots, who were also shocked, came closer to Morgan and said, 'On behalf of the President of India, we put you under arrest. You have the right to remain silent; anything you say shall be used against you. You will explain your action to the appropriate authorities.' They didn't even point a gun at him!

It was obvious that they had never arrested a person before!

As the plane took a U-turn at the far end along the curve around the hill and returned along the same track for take-off, the entire group inside the plane turned to their right and took a last glimpse at what was their home for the past ten days. To their great surprise they noticed that one person from their group was running towards the hill. He must have jumped off the plane using the sliding door they all got in through, even before it started taxiing. George's guess was correct.

They all saw Arthur Kingsley running towards the stream!

'What is he doing?'

'Has he gone mad?'

'Can he hope to see him alive?'

Loud utterances and murmurs showed how upset they were. Lacene and George glanced at each other meaningfully. Lacene's eyes were swelling with tears.

The co-pilot came to the cabin after take-off and ordered everyone to get into the designated sleeping bags. He tied up Morgan and also gagged his mouth. 'We do not want any trouble 'til we reach our destination' were the only words he uttered.

———————•·◆·•———————

Stuart was happy to see the text message from Aziz. 'Al wel with clerics, v can meet them tmrw.' Morgan should be back soon. Stuart replied Aziz with news about New South Wales.

> New South Wales, Australia: A Buddha statue stood out among the charred wreckage of a temple mysteriously damaged by fire in Sydney's west at the weekend while its residents were overseas.
>
> Police suspect arson may be the reason behind the blaze at Jamisontown, near Penrith. Media understands that vandals have targeted the building several times in the past year.
>
> The Korean Buddhist temple was well alight when emergency crews arrived about 2.30 a.m. on Sunday.
>
> Fire crew managed to contain the fire to half the premises. The remaining structure sustained significant smoke damage. It was still smouldering when NSW Fire and Rescue crew returned to investigate the cause of the blaze on Sunday afternoon.
>
> A prayer room adjoining the kitchen suffered some of the worst damage, including a collapsed roof. A charred collection of prayer books lay near a burnt-out doorway.

A nearby resident said, 'I've been living here twenty-two years, and we never had trouble with nobody. A neighbour's dogs had sounded the alarm about 2.30 a.m., and I saw big fire. The building had stood empty for about three months. Its residents, originally from Korea, had gone there for a holiday.'

Police said investigators would check the temple for security footage.

———————◆•◆•◆———————

13. On its own

So many Gods, so many creeds,
So many paths that wind and wind,
When just the art of being kind
Is all this sad world needs.

———◆●◆———

At the Intensive Critical care unit of the All India Institute of Medical Sciences hospital, New Delhi, Lacene and George stood by Thánu's bed. Aziz came with Siddhu, apologising for keeping them waiting.

Siddhu nodded at both of them in recognition. He had carried them in sleeping bags to the airstrip from the station wagon a few days ago. They were seeing him for the first time.

'Two days ago, I was in a hospital bed in Shimla, and he was caring for me. Now here he is, not in a position to recognise anyone. But for him, I wouldn't be standing here alive,' his voice choked.

George held Siddhu by his palm and patted him on his shoulder. Aziz hugged Siddhu and said, 'He has accomplished a great task and has a lot more to do. I am hopeful Allah will spare him for us.'

Lacene said, 'I couldn't believe that all would end so soon and like this. I was so worried about my uncle and the other clerics. With Sadhá's name etched somewhere in the whole episode, it always gave me some kind of reassurance that no one would be harmed or die. But I am now concerned about the religious sites. How do you think Abdul . . . er . . . Thánu would have known Sadhá?'

Aziz said, 'You mean who Thánu and Siddhu refer to as Guru Baba? I have never met him. I believe that he saved Thánu from near death in Afghanistan when Thánu was on a mission there under RAW.'

George looked at Lacene with a 'I told you so' fervour. He had interpreted the meaning of 'opposite of war' that Abdul had mentioned twice with an emphasis in his private meeting with them.

Lacene said, 'Oh, there it goes again! So Sadhà also saved Thànu? Was Sadhá a rescue-mercenary of sort in his last birth?'

Aziz looked at Siddhu.

Siddhu said, 'Well, Guru Baba didn't directly save Thánu or meet him face to face on their first encounter. But he had left Thánu – with a hint – a Tamil verse written on a rubber pipe when a NATO army unit was misled by an informer into entering a building projected as a hideout for a Taleban sect. Thánu was with that team by default.

'Once they were all in, Thánu noticed one of the militants throwing that pipe towards him. It was as though the man came there under the pretext of ensuring that everyone of their team was inside. Peeping through a passage between the external staircase to the building and the access passage to it from inside, he threw this piece at Thánu and disappeared.

'First Thánu took it for a bomb, then seeing something written on it, boldly took it. It read, "In a minute get into attic above toilet". Trusting the Tamil writing, without a second thought Thanu rushed his mates to do so. That same moment, the militants detonated the bomb inside the building. Thanu was the last among the four to slide into the attic when the structure imploded. All five survived with only minor injuries. By staying anywhere else, that building would have been their cemetery.'

Aziz then handed the diary over to Lacene and said, 'I believe that Thánu went to the hotel to prevent this book from getting into the wrong hands, and that is where he met this fate. He had left a note to that effect in his official log before he left for the hotel. The DDGP of Shimla, Mr Sundrelal Nahata, recovered this from the scene. Had he known by that time that Omar was at large, I am sure Thànu would have exercised more caution on that occasion.'

Lacene said, 'That is very unfortunate. This is a very important book, yes. Not only for me, but for all those who wish the world well. I have a mammoth task on my hands, Mr Aziz. Guru's 'whereabouts and howabouts' are not clear. Thánu is in this condition. I do not know how to do justice to my pledge to him. I have to launch the service organisation that he was keen to start functioning openly.'

George said, 'I understand that there are three million people spread all over the world – connected through the net – ready to launch this organisation. They are all waiting for the signal from Sadhà. When I look at the zeal with which this old man has worked towards it, it is astounding! Especially when you realise that he had no access to the Internet most of the time, wherever he was. No, we must not let his dream remain a dream. I'm sad that I left him in such a precarious state. I wonder if he would have survived that fall, if indeed he survived the bullet hit.'

Lacene said, 'I get down whenever I think of that moment. Why did we not jump like Arthur did? What made Arthur do so? Was he already aware of Sadhà and his plans? Siddhu can shed some light on that perhaps (looking at Siddhu). I may have to interact with you to fulfil Guru's wishes, Siddhu. My first task is to officially launch his dream organisation of all "secular" minds through SWA on 9/11.'

Siddhu nodded in agreement.

Aziz said, 'There are hardly two days left for that. Well, I must admit that we haven't taken adequate efforts to trace your guru's situation. The low-flying aircraft could not trace any sign of him moving alive at that hillside camp. Nor could they spot Arthur Kingsley anywhere near the hill. I have to send a team for that. It's in Kargil and was one of the sentry posts during the war with Pakistan. There are other priorities for us at the moment. Already we are under pressure to explain our actions and our involvement in this operation so far.'

George asked, 'How did it go with Morgan Stanley?'

Aziz said, 'You mean Morgan Stanford? He has been deported already. The two governments are negotiating a deal. Nothing has been made public, and no other nation knows anything about his visit and his attempt on your guru. With no information on your guru's present nationality, Morgan may be released on technical grounds from the clutches of our laws.

'I have only heard about this old man through Thánu and a little more from Siddhu now. I really don't know what I should do about him. My mind is not on that now. All eyes are now on tomorrow's UN General Assembly EGM. Will the destruction of these religious sites really take place? That is our concern at the moment. Do you have any clue on that? Is there anything you can derive from this diary?'

Both George and Lacene felt that the Indian officials must also have taken a complete copy of that book. They must be lucky to have been able to get all its pages copied unlike their US counterparts!

Lacene said, 'Not from what I have read so far, Mr Aziz. I shall read more today for your sake, if that will help. We are also very concerned about it. Though he wouldn't cause such destruction given his nature, I can't rule out such a possibility.'

George intervened, 'His behaviour, talk, and body language were all very strange last evening when we all departed. It appeared that he was anxious to do something – anything – to attract worldwide attention and create an awakening.'

'Let's hope that he hasn't already given instructions to all his executioners in those select locations. Unfortunately for us, unexpected events have caused the disappearance of guruji and incapacitation of Thanu, the only two people we know to have control over this catastrophic project.' Siddhu's tone was one of lament.

Everyone agreed with him. Thánu's blank stare at Siddhu gave them no indication of what the day after had in store for the world.

'You need to clarify many things, La. We didn't speak enough about your night with Sadhà. You said that you'd learnt a lot.'

'Ask me, G. What's your question number one?'

'Numbers. You told me Sadhá explained the significance of numbers and Thirùkkùral. What of this 108, or 216?'

'Well, let me narrate it the way we discussed, it's easier for me.'

'What is the significance of 108, Guru?'

'What do you think, Lacene?'

'I learnt from some scholars that it could only be the least common multiple of 9 and 12 – the nine planets and twelve zodiacs. Hindu Astrologers quote that number frequently to denote that these two factors – the planets and the zodiacs control all our lives. It also signifies the twenty-seven stars that the moon crosses over in its cycle, with each star divided into four parts – feet or paadhaas as they are called, numbering to 108 star-pádhás, imposing themselves over our globe in a regular cycle. We are all born within these 108 star pádhás.'

'That is the popular belief. The truth lies somewhere else.'

'You said Thirúkkúral has something to do with numbers and colours.'

'Thirúvalluvar is believed to be from the fabric-dyer class. Some say he was a launderer. His collection got the name "kúral" meaning "short or condensed verse".

'Whatever he was, he divided his work – the collection of short verses – into three divisions to signify the basic three colours. Then he used seven words for each verse to mark the seven colours of the rainbow.'

'Is that so? No one told me that! Then what about the 133 topics or 1330 verses?'

'In his time, the dyers in the Tamil speaking region managed to develop or produce shades of colours that totalled 133 distinct varieties. Then each had ten sub-shades. 1,330 in all. Some people claim that they reached 1,400 shades and that Kúral had 1,400 verses of which seventy could have been lost. We do not know.'

'Amazing! Could that be true?'

'I do not have any proof, so I can't be sure.'

'So tell me about this 108. I know that the beads in a rosary are 108; it's the same with 'rudráksha' beads in the garlands worn by Hindu saints; for most Vaishanvites, there are 108 'Divya sthalams' or holy sites. Abdul —er, Thánu gave a different meaning to 108; he said it denoted the three different philosophies about god. The 'one-none-infinite' beliefs. I had never heard that before. Is that correct?'

'Correct; this 108 denoted the Advaita philosophy so simply.'

'Advaita? What releveance does it have? Does it not mean 'not two', stressing on the oneness of the creator and the created, as against the monotheist belief that the creator is distinct from the created?'

'You said it! 'Not two — what does it mean? It could be one, as in 'the creator and the created being one, or none as in 'soonya', or 'infinite as in 'the multitudes of gods' as believed by the major civilizations!'

'Now I get it. It's perfect. 'Not two' means 1 or 0 or 8!'

'Let me give you the other important meaning for 108. By the turn of 2000 BCE, Indians have identified 108 elements on earth. I am talking of the basic, independent standing elements of the periodic table. Learned people had known that everything in the world was made of 108 basic elements only. That's why they used that number so frequently — especially to denote "I have covered all". The true reason for the usage of such a number was completely lost with time. People came up with their own stories.'

'My God! So many elements were known by then to these people. I must also assume that the 108 special Upanishads have a significant correlation with the 108 elements!'

'You are right. They do have.'

———————◆◆◆———————

The UN general Assembly convened on 9/9 for an extraordinary meeting and passed a few resolutions on Human Rights, freedom of religion and non-religion, and more empowerment of women, among others. The meeting ended at 8 p.m. NY time on 9/10.

Lacene, David, and the rabbi sat in front of the TV in the rabbi's Tel Aviv apartment. George had taken Emily to Auckland as he had many backlogs to clear. Since his K2 climb, he hadn't met his colleagues at his office and friends at his hiker's club.

Lacene was on her iPad, eagerly reading the news online from the UN and UNCHR web sites for the latest update on that meeting.

The twin brothers discussed at length about Sadhá. Lacene pinched in intermittently.

Estimating him to be older than them by at least a decade, they admired the several known feats that he had performed - the underwater struggle at Kansas, the 9/11 escapade, the rescue of George from the K2 avalanche. There could be many more that he might have performed but they would never get to know about.

'Give and forget' was his philosophy, Lacene had told them.

'I have heard 'give and take' policy generally adapted by most people. I have come across some people who 'give, give and forgive' while most others 'get, get and forget'. But this is the first time that I hear a person following a principle of 'give and forget'. Unique.' David told the rabbi.

The rabbi nodded. 'Look at his vision of a world without religious animosity! We have to work towards it for the welfare of humanity, David. Future generations will never forgive us if we let the world implode itself into a religious world war that looks quite imminent!' the rabbi's tone was quite feeble.

David briefed the rabbi about Saraswathi's strong views on the essential recognition of Palestinian statehood by Israel and the need for reconciliation and integration for lasting peace in the Levant. Lacene listened to him with keen ears and nodded quite often.

The rabbi agreed entirely with those views. He had been working towards a similar peace initiative and was longing to see the two communities live in peace and harmony before he breathed his last.

'The rest of the world will never support us or even sympathise with us if we fail to reconcile. But, will the vested interests ever let it happen?' was his sorrowful query.

The imam, moulana, bikku, pundit, bishop, and pastor were back in their respective countries, each experiencing a memorable reception in his hometown. Each one was glued to his television watching news of the resolutions being discussed and passed at the UN meeting. They were in constant touch with each other. The bonding and experience of those ten-days had miraculous effects on them.

———◆◆◆———

Only forty-six nations participated with their UN ambassadors representing them. Most other nations sent written commitments on the various points demanded by the SWA group.

Only 75 per cent of the proposed resolutions were adopted by the close of the day during that crucial apex meeting of the world's only League of Nations. Contacting each other, none of the eight clerics expressed satisfaction. Some were resigned to the probable catastrophic aftermath of the general assembly resolutions. Some were hopeful that sanity would prevail in the minds of the designated executioners of SWA's army of angels. Or were they devils?

Everyone fondly remembered the days at the foot of that hill and sincerely wished that Sadhá had survived the shot and subsequent fall.

And everyone felt a need and urge to take the issue of secularism into their multitude. Each one wanted to do it in his way.

———◆◆◆———

Lacene wondered what the modus operandi would be for the actual execution of the project for the destruction of the religious sites. Would they start at sunrise in each of the locations as the sun travels to each longitude? It would mean that, as blasts started occurring from the east, others would be alerted? Or would they destroy all remaining sites at the same time so that none of them could possibly be saved? She had several questions, but she could not find answers in the diary.

She had only one clue, though, and George was the one who reminded her about it. She had told George after returning from the night at the hill that Sadhá and Thánu had made arrangements to send signals to the SWA executioner-angels on the morning of 9/11 through certain newspapers. They planned to look through the classified anniversary ad columns in the newspapers.

She did not sleep on the night of 9/10 and started looking through the columns in the online versions of popular newspapers. By midnight in Tel Aviv, it was already seven in the morning in Japan. If something had happened there, it should have happened by now – and in New Zealand. As she was poring over the pages, George called; there was excitement in his tone.

'La, did you see the anniversary for your favourite poet Bharathiar? There is an unusual photo of him – at least for me it's unusual. I have only seen his picture with that penetrating look, a dark thick mooch (moustache), turban, and round dot in his forehead. Look in the obituary columns of ToI (Times of India) and TH (The Hindu).'

Lacene scrambled for those pages and noticed the same anniversary message in those papers with the poet's picture in it with the words,

> 'Mahakavi Bharathi – 12/11/1882-9/11/1921 –
> May his dreams come true.'

Lacene could recollect that picture; it was a slice from a photo that could probably be the only picture the poet had taken with his wife.

For a change, Bharathiar was sporting a vertical line on his forehead in that picture – a rare picture and a rare symbol too, for Lacene.

'I know what is running in your mind, La. The explanations you gave me for the different marks on the foreheads adorned by most Hindus.

'But do you get the message, La? As much fury as he showed to all of us that last day, he shows he has a humorous side too! Bharathiar is sporting a námam!'

Lacene could hear George laughing on the other end, unusually loudly and uncontrollably! 'Vertical line says "stand and live", horizontal line says "fall and die", Ha ha!' Lacene took a few seconds to understand.

Then she smiled with relief.

Mahakavi Bharathi 12/11/1882-9/11/1921. May his dreams come true.

At the Situation Room in the White House, a concerned team of high-ranking National Security Council staff were watching the different stories flash across the screen, just as the President entered the room. He joined them for a Strategy review on the 'Religious War' raging in most parts of the world, presumed to be the after effect of the 'SWA' organisation's acts of destruction around the world.

Videos of the chaotic scenes from different parts of the globe were on display, with a panel on the left providing information about each location and the events taking place.

Edfu, Egypt:

The military opened fire on unarmed Christians and ran armoured vehicles over them, killing dozens in Edfu when the Christians were protesting following the destruction of a church by a Muslim mob.

Almost forty religious buildings, most of them Christian churches, had been destroyed by mob violence in Egypt in the past three months.

Baghdad, Iraq:

More than 1,000 people were killed in January in Iraq. Members of Asaib Ahl al-Haq, a Shiite group responsible for thousands of attacks on U.S. forces during the Iraq war, admit they have ramped up targeted killings.

Scores of bodies have been dumped in Iraq's canals and palm groves in recent months, reminding terrified residents of the worst days of the country's sectarian conflict and fuelling fears that the stage is being set for another civil war.

In the latest sign of the escalating attacks, the heads of three
Sunnis were found Sunday in a market in northern Salaheddin
province, while six Shiites were shot dead in the province in
response to a cascade of bomb attacks on their neighbourhoods.

Earlier only Sunny sect militants indulged in such ethnic attacks.
There was no second hand to do the clapping; now that the Shias
also have started to retaliate, civil war is not very far.

A few incidents of total destruction of the other sect's religious
sites have triggered the escalation of violent attacks by rival
factions.

Bangui, Central African Republic:

Human Rights workers say at least ten people were killed in
Bangui over the weekend.

A government minister in the Central African Republic has
warned that there is a risk of genocide as communities fight each
other on religious and ethnic lines. All communities have been
affected by the violence and now many Muslims are fleeing the
country, afraid for their lives. One imam in the capital Bangui
shared his fears with the news reporters.

'This spate of violence against Muslims started in December.
They killed us with machetes and firearms. Muslims have taken
refuge in one neighbourhood, called Kilometre 5.

'The anti-balaka vigilantes have been targeting us. They've
burned most of the mosques in the capital, only a handful of
mosques remain untouched in our neighbourhood.

'Mobs are targeting Muslim civilians in Bangui. I don't want to leave Bangui. I want to be the last Central African Muslim to leave the country or at least the last Muslim to be buried here. This country is the last resting place of both my father and mother.

'We Muslims of the Central African Republic cannot leave our country. If they want to kill us in Kilometre 5, so be it. We have no weapons but are ready to accept our fate because we believe in God, and we are confident that God will protect us.'

The trigger for this state of affairs in CAR is stated to be the destruction by an unknown mob of two churches and one cathedral in the region a month ago.

Peshawar, Pakistan:

The Taliban attack on the Peshawar church killing scores of people.

The terrorist attack on one of the oldest churches in the country, Peshawar's All Saints Church, was a shocker. It is now a familiar pattern. Pakistanis condemn acts of terrorism but do not demand action against terrorist groups. The terrorists are emboldened with each attack, as they sense acceptance of their ideologies after every such act.

More than 120 years old, the All Saints Church symbolises the history of Christian presence in Pakistan. Christians have lived in Pakistan long before it an independent nation. The attack on this ancient church clearly signals the 'religious-cleansing' desire of jihadi groups in Pakistan.

Mindanao, Philippines:

Frequent armed clashes between government forces and armed opposition groups occur primarily on the southern island of Mindanao. Recent months have seen escalation in the armed violent conflicts following the burning of two churches and one mosque in the island.

Quetta, Pakistan:

Suicide bomb attacks in city of Quetta killed more than 100 people when two bombs exploded within ten minutes.

A security check post was targeted in the first blast in the morning, killing twelve and injuring twenty-five. The building, owned by a preaching organization, collapsed to the second blast, killing 100 and wounding many. Many of the dead and wounded were from the Shia sect of Islam whom Sunni extremists regard as heretics. Shia community members continue to be slaughtered in cold blood while authorities only show indifference and a callous attitude.

An unknown group, United Baluch Army claimed responsibility. In 2012, a total of 2,050 people were killed and 3,822 injured in Pakistan in attacks by Islamic militants and violent sectarian groups.

Rakhine, Myanmar:

A quarter of the eight million Muslims of Myanmar live in Rakhine, bordering Bangladesh.

The Rohingya were officially declared foreigners in their native land and were restricted from owning land, travelling outside their villages, receiving an education, and even having children. Buddhist mobs, often aided by the security forces, have attacked and torched villages, schools, workplaces, and mosques. Hundreds of Rohingya have been killed and some 140,000 left homeless.

The most shocking development was that the leader of the democracy movement, the Nobel laureate Aung San Suu Kyi, was willing to condemn violence in general but refrained from condemning Buddhists attacks on Muslims. Many members of her National League for Democracy are openly involved in extremist anti-Rohingya organizations.

Colombo, Sri Lanka:

A Buddhist mob attacked a mosque in Sri Lanka's capital and at least twelve people were injured, the latest in a series of attacks on the minority Muslim community by members of the Buddhist majority.

A group known as Bodu Bala Sena or the 'Buddhist power force', has been in the forefront of campaigns against Muslims.

After Buddhist hardliners forced a nearby mosque to close, this damaged mosque was only built a month ago.

The US embassy in Colombo said the incident was particularly troubling in light of a number of recent attacks against the Muslim community in Sri Lanka.

'Targeting any place of worship should never be permitted, and we urge calm from all sides. We call for prosecution of perpetrators in this attack and an end to religious-based violence,' the embassy said in a statement.

N. M. Ameen, president of Sri Lanka Muslim Council, said more than twenty mosques had been attacked since last year.

In a separate incident, a hand grenade was thrown at a Buddhist temple in the Jaffna peninsula, on the northern tip of the island. There were no injuries, police said.

Jaffna is largely made of ethnic minority Tamil people, most of whom are Hindu and Christian.

The role of religion in most other global conflicts is increasingly becoming apparent.

Ambon and Poso, Indonesia:

Since 2000, the Jema'ah Islamiah group has been behind most of the mass civilian bombings in Indonesia.

The jihadis were locally trained in Mindanao in the southern Philippines. Ambon and Poso, where sectarian violence between Muslims and Christians was rife, was their target. The 2002 Bali bombings were their handiwork.

The Myanmar mission in Jakarta was attacked to revenge the persecution of Muslim Rohingyas in Myanmar.

Minor groups like the Front Pembela Islam and Hisbah group in the city of Solo are religious groups known for intimidating and attacking Shia and Ahmadiya Muslims, and Christians who are considered to be enemies of Islam.

———— •⋅◆⋅• ————

'Do we have clear evidence of Collusion between the "SWA" group and perpetrators of these acts?' the President's query, though appeared to be at the NSA Chief, was thrown at the entire team in the room.

His own son and daughter being active members of the group, the NSA chief's answer was guarded. 'Mr President, we do have evidence that about 12 percent of the incidents of attacks on religious sites around the globe have taken place at sites marked in the group's list. The remaining such attacks on other sites and the enormous events involving violent attacks due to religious reasons on people and property may not be linked to that group. So far no such incident has been reported in the USA. The six sites in our country mentioned in the list are safe and are being constantly monitored for any untoward happenings. Again, we could not establish solid evidence as to whether the incitement for such attacks sprung from that group. All traceable members of the group – more than a third are from the United States - seem to be peace-loving people.'

The call that the President had asked for with the Secretary General of the United Nations came through at that moment. He preferred to take the call in the same room. After exchanging pleasantries and following protocol, the talk touched on the burning issue of increasing incidents around the globe of violent attacks on religious grounds.

The President nodded his head as he spoke and said, 'Yes, the UN should convene an emergency meeting of heads of States. The United States will support any move that may help abate the frenzy of hatred that seems to permeate our society at large.'

The UN Secretary General had suggested something, it appeared.

'Of course, the United states of America will encourage its citizens who are willing to play the role of peace ambassadors and facilitate their participation in UN missions across the globe to promote religious harmony and secular policies.

'Please do whatever you may deem appropriate. We are with you on that score. Thank you.'

The President placed the phone quietly on his table and looked at his team. Understanding what his look meant, they all returned to him an approving and supportive look. Their look gave the president the assurance that the entire nation was behind him on that mission.

———◆•◆•◆———

Epilogue

George

Why is sleep evading me? I'm tossing in my bed! If Lacene is around, perhaps I may not get this nightmare. She's still in Tel Aviv and will be home after a week. Emy is happy sleeping in her bed unaware of all that runs through my head. Why is the scene on K2 running again and again in my mind?

Lacene's narration of Sadhá's adventurous rescue feat while the avalanche carried me away on my descent from Camp 3 to Camp 2 is ringing in my ears. I try to figure out how exactly Sadhá could have made it. The scene runs; I edit it; it reruns. Over and over again.

> *Sadhá had remained at Camp 3 when Mark and his team climbed to the summit of K2. He anticipated problems between Camp 3 and Camp 2 at that time of the day. It was past 7 p.m., and he expected that the team would stay put at Camp 3 on their return from the peak. But when he noticed that they were venturing on a descent to Camp 2, he decided to keep tracking them at close quarters. He had already ensured that the best of ropes left by previous climbers were in good shape, fastened tightly at different parking points.*

> *Just as he expected, a sudden wave of wind brought in an avalanche from the north-east and swept through the slope just below Camp 3.*

While three among the four fell down and were rolling with a firm grip on their ropes, only one of them was swept off his feet. He was flung into the air and was travelling along with the avalanche, airborne.

Sadhá, also caught in the avalanche and trying to stabilise himself by sliding as flat as possible along the ground, threw the sling with a noose as far as he could in the direction of the person on air, hoping that it would catch him somewhere on his arm or leg. He preferred a leg to an arm as chances of coming off after noosing around was less on the leg. And to his immense gratification, the noose went past the right leg of that man and fell on to his shoes, his foot slipping into the noose like a running zebra's head into the chaser's trap!

Tightening itself on his ankle, the sling held the man hanging upside down, with his head barely hitting the ridge of the mountain. After a few swings, he fell onto the ground just inches before the kilometre-deep crevasse on the other side of the edge, the backpack saving his spine from serious injury.

Holding the rope firmly and edging his way down towards that man, Sadhá kept shaking the rope to check if the man was responding.

The avalanche had passed by; the man was lying there motionless. Sadhá resuscitated him by pumping down on his heart and lungs; after thirty seconds, the man responded. Then Sadhá dragged him along with him sliding gently using the gradience and passing through firm and safer grounds. The sharp edge of the ridge of the mountain, to the other side of which was a steep fall, played hide and seek in that darkness; he had to place each step very cautiously on to the eastern side of the ridge. He managed to reach a location where he knew there was a safe hideout, a petit cave, a snow den.

After about four hours of lying there, and seeing the face using his headlamp, Sadhá decided to send the diary to Lacene. He had a few other persons in mind to bestow the responsibility of writing his memoirs, of whom Lacene was one. But he made up his mind then and there that it should be Lacene.

He did not intend to put the lists in George's bag; they were inside the book, and he slid the book into his bag, wanting to take out the lists after reaching the base camp. And he forgot to do that on reaching the base camp. Perhaps he was in a hurry to reach the 'hill'.

While rushing towards the 'hill' some hours later he realised his mistake. But it was too late to turn back. He was to be at the hills to receive the clerics as agreed with Thánu within the next forty hours.

So he sent message to Thánu through Siddhu who came with the clerics to the hill, asking him to somehow get that list from Lacene and George and forward that to the UN and Indian authorities. He could not reproduce that list from his memory and give to Siddhu.

Sadhá's feat has been haunting me from then on. Not only during nights when I go to sleep, but during the day, at work, while driving, while chatting with friends at the club, everywhere. Every moment.

This old man had travelled about 200 km in just two days without any airborne or land-driven vehicle! Partly skiing, partly rowing downstream, and partly running! Can a person really cover that distance after climbing K2 twice within three days and that too after saving another climber from a deadly avalanche?

Is it because I know I am not going to get answers for these questions that they are haunting me? I toss in my bed. I can hear my prayer to Mother Sleep.

'Dear mother of fresh thoughts and joyous health, embrace me now.'

The palm that saved Lacene is pulling on my ankle with a rope now, while I'm hanging upside down with the slopes of K2 in the background.

Morgan

Why does the scene of that priest falling off the cliff replay in my mind time and again? I was right in shooting him with my airgun. Sadhá had a proven track record of colluding with sworn enemies of the State. He had abetted in the planning and execution of several attacks on the properties or soil of the United States of America and its allies. He was one of the very few terrorists who evaded identification by intelligence agencies and had skilfully dodged all drone attacks on militant hideouts.

I should not feel guilty about attempting on his life. Even my seniors in the NSA had made it clear that they would defend my action with the Indian Government at all costs. With the unclear nationality of Sadhà, the Indian authorities didn't charge me of any wrong doing.

On the contrary, some Indian officials applauded me for having gone to great lengths in the elimination of a terrorist even under very trying circumstances, as deftly argued by our embassy officials.

Why then the replay?

No. I shouldn't think about that anymore, I should get on with my life. Here is Newark station. Irene and Uma must be waiting for me. I must manage my comfiture with a readiness to answer any difficult questions from them. Especially about Uma's grandfather. But why is Irene alone? And, why is she sporting a dot on her forehead like Uma, and Lacene?

'Hi, Dad,' she waves at me with the same joy with which she sent me off ten days ago. When I hug her, she is quite warm and affectionate. I don't see any grudge in her actions. Should I ask her about Uma? No, let me stop with niceties. What surprise does she say she has for me?

I build some courage to ask her about the dot on her forehead.

'Dad, that denotes the origin of us all - the red hot dot that existed before the big bang; that caused the birth of our universe!'

'And, what about this "dowgas" or "wasdog"? I ask her as she drives towards home. 'What does that mean? Is it "saw God"?'

'Almost, Dad, "Swa God" – God that came about on its own.'

'How did you become part of it, Irene?'

With no shock at my knowledge about her involvement, Irene answers proudly, 'Uma introduced me to it, and I was impressed with their vision for the future – a whole new generation without religious prejudice! What a wonderful idea! No hatred, no animosity, and no indifference! Only love for humanity and love for all creatures that thrive on this earth – and perhaps, even beyond! How wonderful!'

I cannot hold my anxiety. 'So, you know of this Secular World Angels?'

'What do you mean, Dad? We are among the high-flying Angels of SWA!' And as the car drives through the gate of our house, she continues, 'Look! What an angel we have brought for you!'

Indeed they have. What a pleasant surprise!

Greeting me at our doorsteps is Florence with a flower bouquet. Beside her are Uma and my mother-in-law with a garland of flowers!

'You must bear with us, Morgan,' she says. 'We could not refuse when Irene said she did not want her children to be reared by nannies other than her own mom and granny! So, here we are!'

I see a 'devil-transformed-into-an-angel' in her now!

I really do not know which of those four angels I should lift above my head to express my enormous joy.

After hugging and passionately kissing Flo, I end up lifting Uma!

'Can't say it any better, ladies! I'm so happy!'

As I lift her, I notice how much Uma resembles Sadhá, bringing the image of Sadhá standing on top of the hill when I shot at him.

My cheeks are getting wet with my tears!

Tears of joy.

Of gratitude.

And, of guilt.

About the Illustrator

With multiple Master's degrees in Arts and ongoing research for his Doctorate, illustrator Gopal Jayaraman is a well-established artist, having won several accolades, honours and awards for his outstanding contribution. He often displays his work to the public internationally. Also hailing from Pondicherry, he teaches Art at a college in Botswana. Some of his work includes restoring historical paintings and other significant artefacts in India. His talent speaks for itself through his illustrations in this novel.

Author's Footnote

1. On 12 April 2011, at the 46th meeting of the United Nations Human Rights Council (UNHRC), a Resolution - A/HRC/RES/16/18 – was adopted without a vote, containing most of the points highlighted in the demands by the SWA group, although not necessarily because of such a demand by any group.

2. All the news items – at the end of each chapter in this book and in the last chapter supposedly read by the US officials at the White House Situations room – are all true incidents as reported by the news media over the past three years.

Printed in the United States
By Bookmasters